C000255380

THE MONUMENT MURDERS

DORSET CRIME BOOK 4

RACHEL MCLEAN

Ackroyd Publishing

ackroyd-publishing.com

THE MONUMENT MURDERS

CHAPTER ONE

Shane Gisborne's mum had told him that coming down here before the castle opened was trespassing. But Shane didn't care, he'd done it often enough.

There was a spot down by the Globe he liked. Tucked in behind it, looking out to sea but nestled in the shelter of the massive concrete sphere. It was a good spot to squirrel yourself away and hide. To smoke weed. On Saturday he'd brought Lorelei, who he very much hoped was going to be his new girlfriend.

Today, he wasn't with Lorelei. Today, Mum had talked him into bringing Flossie.

Flossie was Mum's favourite child. A six-year-old Shitzu with short brown hair and a permanently dumb expression. She barely needed walking; just getting out of the house made her little legs move more than Shane's did during a whole day at school.

He hissed at her as she dragged on the lead, not wanting to go any further. She stood in the middle of the path leading past Durlston Castle and towards the cliffs.

"Oi. Bloody dog. Come over here. Mum says you've got to do a shit."

He wanted to keep close to the hedge so no one would see him. One of the nosey parkers working at the castle would probably stick their head out of a window, tell him to eff off.

This was public land, wasn't it? It belonged to the town. Besides, he wouldn't be long. Bring the dog down to the seafront, let her do her business on the grass. Mum had shoved a poo bag into his pocket, not that he'd use it. Eurgh.

Flossie yanked at the lead and he muttered at her.

"Stupid dog."

She bared her teeth and growled at him.

"It's not my fault. Take it up with Mum."

The dog growled again, then turned towards the cliffs. She began to move, making for the edge of the path. *At last.*

He allowed her to pull him down towards the seafront. He glanced at his watch. Seven thirty. He had to get home and grab his rucksack soon, or he'd miss the bus. Hopefully Lorelei would be waiting at the bus stop.

The dog stopped. Shane carried on walking, his mind in the clouds. They were grey today, festering over the sea. He almost tripped over the dog, catching himself just as he reached her.

"What are you doing, Floss? Do a shit and then we can get back."

The dog looked up at him. She looked away again, towards the Globe. She made a whiny, whimpery sound. It reminded him of the time she'd encountered his mate Egg, the guy from his Maths class who wasn't really a mate, but who you kept on the right side of if you knew what you were doing. Egg had kicked poor Flossie when she'd got under his feet. She'd made that same noise then.

Shane knelt down and ruffled the fur between her ears. "What's up, Floss? He's not here, promise. I'm not letting him come round again."

The dog started growling, a low rumble from the back of her throat. If Shane hadn't been crouched on the floor right next to her, he wouldn't have heard it. He tightened his grip on her fur.

"Floss, you're scaring me. Stop it."

He stood up and shook himself out, then gave the lead a yank.

"Come on, Floss. Have a shit and we'll go home."

He started to walk, but the dog didn't move. The lead went taut and he pulled on it. "Flossie, *come on*. I've got to get to school."

Shane was in year 11, GCSEs next summer. His mum kept nagging him to do more work, but he wasn't keen. Besides, it wasn't as if there were many jobs in Swanage. He could have the best exam results in the school. It wouldn't help.

He yanked the lead again. "Come on. Flossie, *now*."

She looked up at him, and then towards the Globe, her eyes wide.

He hissed through his teeth. Bringing the dog out before school was bad enough, being hauled out of bed and forced to come out in the cold. But this was something else. What the hell was she playing at?

He trudged back to the dog and crouched on the tarmac in front of her.

"Flossie, what are you being so weird for?"

She looked past him, towards the sea. She barked, just once. He clapped his hand over his ear.

"That was loud, Floss. Stop it!"

She barked again, three times. Shane stood and turned, following her gaze.

She wasn't looking out to sea. She was looking at the Globe.

"What's up, Flossie? What's wrong with it?"

He'd brought her down here plenty of times before. She'd tried to take a leak at the base of the thing, but he'd stopped her. He didn't want to sit down there with Lorelei if it smelt of dog piss.

"What is it, Floss?" he asked, squinting towards the Globe.

It was gloomy this morning and he couldn't see much more than shadows around the concrete sphere. He approached it. The lead tightened again.

"Oh, for God's sake, Flossie!"

He let go of the lead. It wasn't as if she was going anywhere.

The dog let out a bark, then turned and ran back up the hill.

"Floss!"

He clapped his hand to his forehead and watched as she sped away from him. He'd never catch her, even with those stubby legs of hers. He could only hope she'd head home and that Mum would have already left for work.

"Flossie! Wait in the front garden."

He looked back at the Globe. Something had caught his eye.

"Is that a...?" Shane advanced towards the Globe, his footsteps slow.

No.

He was imagining things. Shouldn't have smoked that hash last night.

He took a few more steps towards it.

This was no hallucination.

He could see a foot.

He edged around the structure, trying to find a better view without getting too close. There was a person up there, spreadeagled over the top of the Globe.

As he rounded it, the wind at his back, he saw blood pooling on the ground.

Shane swallowed, but kept going. Creeping around the Globe, staring up at the form that had been dumped over it. He blinked, his eyes stinging, his breath shallow.

He shuffled into the space between the Globe and the cliff behind, where the inscriptions were. The ones Lorelei thought were cool.

He stopped. He felt the skin on the back of his neck prickle, the hairs standing on end.

He retched.

He turned away from the Globe and vomited into the spot where he'd sat on Saturday, his breakfast spattering the ground.

CHAPTER TWO

ELSA WAS SITTING at the kitchen island while Lesley packed the last of her things into her work bag.

"See you later." Lesley put a hand on her girlfriend's shoulder and kissed the back of her neck. Elsa shivered and turned to her, smiling. Lesley leaned in for a kiss then pulled away.

"I'm going to be late."

Elsa raised an eyebrow. "See you later."

Lesley grunted. She threw open the door and pulled it behind her, not waiting to check if it had closed. She hurried down the stairs from Elsa's flat, emerging onto the street.

The flat was three streets back from the seafront in Bournemouth, and Lesley could hear seagulls shrieking out to sea. Not just out to sea, the damn things were everywhere. She looked across the road to see one tugging at something behind her car.

"Oi!" she hissed. "Leave it!"

She approached the car, her footsteps brisk. As she approached, a woman stepped out from behind it.

Lesley stopped walking and placed her hands on her hips. "What are you doing here?"

"What do you think?"

"I don't want to talk to you," Lesley said.

"I think you might when I tell you what I know."

Lesley's jaw clenched.

Sadie Dawes was a local BBC journalist. She was better at her job than the average local reporter: tenacious, scrappy. The last time Lesley had seen her, she'd been on Brownsea Island, having helped a murderer get access to a boat. She'd stood there filming that same man as he attacked his wife, and she'd only stopped filming when Lesley's colleague Tina had grabbed her phone.

Sadie might be a good journalist, but as far as Dorset Police were concerned, she was a pain in the arse.

"Your court case is ongoing," Lesley told the woman. "You shouldn't be talking to me."

"This isn't about what happened on Brownsea." Sadie's hand was on the roof of Lesley's car.

"Get away from my car," Lesley told her. "I've got to get to work."

Sadie took her hand off the roof. She rounded the bonnet and approached Lesley as she got in. Lesley put her hands on the wheel, trying to ignore the younger woman. Sadie bent down to peer in through the window. Lesley started the ignition. Smiling, Sadie reached out and put a hand on the bonnet.

Lesley turned to her and opened the window. "You're going to get yourself killed."

"Like DCI Mackie, you mean?" Sadie asked.

Lesley felt her chest tighten. "What about him?"

"He got himself killed."

DCI Mackie had been Lesley's predecessor in Dorset's Major Crime Investigations Team.

Lesley took a breath. "He committed suicide."

"You really think so?"

Lesley leaned back. She stared at the journalist.

As far as the world was concerned, Mackie had been suffering from depression following his retirement. When things had got too much, he'd thrown himself off a cliff near Swanage. But she knew different.

The question was, did Sadie know different too?

"I've got no idea what you're talking about. I wasn't even here."

"I think you do. We should meet."

Sadie reached in her inside pocket and pulled out a business card. She tossed it through the car window. It flew across Lesley's lap and landed in the space between the seats.

Lesley resisted the urge to bend down and pick it up. She didn't want Sadie knowing she was interested.

"Leave me alone," she snapped.

She pressed the button to close the window and put her foot on the accelerator.

CHAPTER THREE

DETECTIVE CONSTABLE MIKE LEGG was the only person already in when Lesley arrived. She breezed through the office, wondering where DS Frampton could be. This was the fourth day Dennis hadn't been here. It wasn't like him to take time off sick.

"Morning, Mike," she said.

"Morning," he muttered.

"Is that the best you've got?"

Mike pushed his chair back and looked up at her. "Sorry, boss," he said. "Just finishing off the paperwork for the Colton case."

She nodded. "Glad to get that one done and dusted."

He grunted. "What d'you need me to do when I finish this?"

She shrugged. "Give me a couple of minutes at my desk and I'll let you know if anything's come in."

"Right, boss." He returned to his work.

Lesley walked to her glass-walled office. As she pushed the door open, she felt air on the back of her neck, the outer door to the office opening. She turned to see PC Tina Abbott enter.

"Morning, boss," Tina said. "Nice day, isn't it?"

Lesley looked out of the window. Their office was at the front of the Dorset Police Headquarters in Winfrith. The front wall was made entirely of glass, which meant they couldn't escape the weather. When Lesley had arrived, back at the height of summer, that had been a blessing. Now, in October, it was less so.

Lesley peered at the clouds. "Not sure what your idea of nice weather is."

Tina shrugged. "It's not raining, at least."

Lesley laughed. "Thankful for small mercies, I guess."

The phone rang on Tina's desk. As she listened to whoever was on the other end, the PC's expression changed from interest, to surprise, to resignation. Lesley folded her arms and let the door to her inner office close behind her. She had the feeling that whatever it was, she'd need to get involved.

"Well?" she asked as Tina put the phone down.

"You've heard of the Swanage Globe, boss?" Tina asked.

Lesley shook her head. "What is it, a theatre?"

Mike snorted. "This isn't London."

Tina gave him a frown.

"Sorry, boss." He looked up at Tina. "What's happened?"

"A dog walker found a body."

Lesley felt her shoulders slump. It had been two months since their last murder case. She was just beginning to get used to a quieter life in Dorset's Major Crime Investigations Team. Not that she'd been sitting on her backside doing nothing; she was working on pinning something – anything – onto the local organised crime boss. The quiet meant she could slowly build a case. It was the kind of police work she enjoyed, the kind she'd never had much time for in her last job in Birmingham.

Now it seemed she was about to be torn away from it.

"Who?" she asked Tina.

"Who what, boss?"

"Who's the body?"

Tina shrugged. "No identification yet. The dog walker was Shane Gisborne, sixteen years old, out walking his mum's dog."

Lesley didn't need to know that. But then, 'finding' a body was a good way to cover up a murder. Even for a sixteen-year-old.

"He puked up right next to the scene," Tina added.

Lesley grimaced. Maybe not a suspect, then.

"OK," she sighed. "Tell me what this Swanage Globe is and how I get there."

"It's right on the seafront," Mike said. "South of the town, up past Peveril Point."

"None of this means anything to me." Lesley had rarely ventured as far as Swanage. The closest she'd got had been the cliffs to the north of the town. Where DCI Mackie had died.

"Mike, why don't you come with me?" she suggested.

"No problem, boss." He stood and grabbed his jacket from the back of his chair.

"I'll see what background I can get while you're en route," said Tina. "I'll call it through."

"Thanks," replied Lesley. "Let's go."

CHAPTER FOUR

OCTOBER MIGHT HAVE MEANT gloomy weather, but at least it also meant light traffic. Lesley sat in the passenger seat of Mike's Golf, drumming on the door handle beside her. They sailed through Corfe Castle, and she couldn't help remembering the traffic jams she'd sat in here through the summer.

Tina's optimism about the weather had been misplaced and it was starting to drizzle. Lesley could only hope that Gail and her forensics team would already be at the scene and had protected the body from the elements.

"So," she said to Mike. "Tell me about this Swanage Globe."

His gaze flicked to his rear-view mirror and then back to the road ahead. "It's a big concrete globe next to Durlston Castle."

"Swanage has got a castle?"

"Well, it's not really a castle," he replied. "Nothing as grand as that. It's more of a country pile built by some Victorian guy. But with a dirty great globe out the back. The walls around it are inscribed with information about the planets and the natural sciences."

"Thinktank for the nineteenth century," she murmured.

"What's a thinktank?"

"Science museum in Birmingham. Half the exhibits are broken and as far as I can tell the best bit is a kids' playground."

"This is just a globe and a wall."

"Something gives me the feeling you were dragged there as a kid."

He smiled. "My dad was into that kind of thing."

Lesley realised she didn't know much about Mike's family. Dennis had his infamous wife Pam, Johnny had his wife and a baby on the way, but Mike... All Lesley knew was he was single. She wasn't about to pry.

"So why would somebody dump a body there?" she asked.

"Something symbolic, maybe? Something to do with the scientific nature of the place?"

"Hmm."

Lesley gazed out of the window. The rain was thickening, the sky darkening. She pulled her jacket tighter around her shoulders. Lesley had transitioned from the skirt suits that she'd been accustomed to wearing in the West Midlands, to trouser suits. Still businesslike, but a little more practical and easier to wear boots with instead of her old heels. She'd learned the hard way that killers around here liked to dump their victims in muddy fields.

"Mike," she said as they approached the outskirts of Swanage. "Can I ask you about something?"

"'Course, boss." His voice was edged with unease. "What is it?"

"Sadie Dawes," she said. "Have you had any dealings with her before?"

"Only on the Brownsea Island case. And I didn't deal with her direct." He slowed behind a bus as they approached the town centre and the beach. "Why? Has she been causing trouble?"

"She might be," Lesley replied.

She hadn't spoken about DCI Mackie's death with her team. Especially not with Dennis. Dennis and Mackie had been close, the former DCI a kind of mentor to Dennis. She wasn't sure what kind of relationship Mike had had with him, but she still wasn't ready to discuss the case.

"Nothing I can't handle," she told him. "And what about Dennis?"

"What about him?" Mike's voice tensed further.

"Have you spoken to him since he went off sick?"

Mike indicated to turn right up a steep hill. "I didn't want to intrude. He'll be back soon. You know the sarge."

"I do," Lesley replied.

Since she'd arrived five months ago, Dennis hadn't had a day off sick. He'd only taken two days' holiday, and that was after he'd been injured when they were apprehending Harry Nevin's murderer. He ought to have taken sick leave, but he'd refused.

So what was going on now?

There'd been no sign of illness before he'd gone off last week, and he hadn't spoken to her. All she'd had was a message from the front desk, saying Dennis's wife had called in on his behalf.

She needed to speak to him, to investigate. But she also needed to follow up on what Sadie Dawes was up to, and it was looking like she had a murder to deal with.

Lesley dragged her hand through her hair as Mike pulled into a car park. This was going to be a busy day.

CHAPTER FIVE

Sherry Watson was pissed off.

She was convinced her husband was lying to her, but she couldn't prove it.

She sat on the phone, listening to the on-hold music at his architect's firm. His PA, Daria, had told her to wait. She'd couldn't have been waiting more than a couple of minutes, but it felt like an hour.

What wasn't Daria telling her, and why had Paul left the house so early this morning?

The on-hold music clicked off and Daria came back on the line.

"I'm sorry, Mrs Watson, I didn't mean to keep you waiting."

Don't call me Mrs Watson. "That's OK," Sherry lied. "So can you get a message to Paul, or not?"

"I'm sorry, but he's in a meeting."

"Tell him to call me when he's finished, will you?"

"I'm not sure when he'll be back in Dorset," Daria

replied. "The meeting's here, in London. At least, that's what it says in his diary."

Daria had worked for Paul when he and Sherry lived in London. She still did, but he hadn't made her move here. It was far from ideal, as far as Sherry could tell.

Sherry sat down at the kitchen table. "He's in London?"

Paul hadn't got home till she was asleep last night, and he'd left the house before she woke that morning. He sometimes went for a run before work, but he hadn't said anything about going to London.

They'd lived in London until three months earlier, a flat in Putney overlooking the river. His firm still had a branch there, managed by his old partner. Sherry knew he needed to go there from time to time. But until now, he'd always let her know in advance.

"It's OK, Daria," she sighed. "I'll call his mobile."

"OK. Thanks, Mrs Watson."

Sherry grunted and hung up. Daria was the only person who called her that. At work, and with her friends, she was Sherry. Or Ms Kane.

She called Paul's mobile. Voicemail.

"Paul, it's me. Are you in London? Call me, will you? Amelia's off school and I've got a house viewing this afternoon. I need you back for three."

In London, she and Paul had covered childcare equally. But in the last three months he'd been increasingly absent. She didn't like it.

She heard noises from upstairs. Amelia was watching TV up there, when she was supposed to be sleeping. Sherry was pretty sure the girl was faking it, but she'd lost the will to argue.

She pulled in a breath and slung her phone onto the sofa. She made for the stairs.

Paul, where are you?

CHAPTER SIX

By the time Lesley had got out of the car, Mike had disappeared around a hedge. There was no sign of a castle. Or of a globe, for that matter.

"Mike," she called. "Wait!"

He was keen, all of a sudden. This was a bit different from attending a crime scene with Mike's old colleague, DC Chiles.

But then, the less said about Johnny Chiles, the better.

Mike re-emerged from around the hedge. "Sorry, boss. I thought you were behind me."

Lesley gave him a look. "I've never been here before. So where's this castle, then?"

"Down here," he said. "The Globe's beyond it."

They approached a square, unattractive building that looked nothing like a castle as far as Lesley could see. This was no Corfe.

There was an entrance ahead of them, signs in the windows indicating this was the tourist entrance. Mike ignored it and walked around the side of the building, heading down the hill.

Lesley followed him along a steep pathway towards the sea. Low cloud engulfed the cliffs, meaning Lesley could only just make out the water. She could hear the waves, though, and above them, voices up ahead.

Lesley continued, and the landscape ahead opened up. There was a grassy bank and then an almost sheer drop. They rounded a bend, and finally Lesley could see what everybody had been talking about. A concrete globe, nestled into the hillside. A path swept down on each side, the two meeting in front of the Globe and leading down towards the cliffs.

Two white-suited CSIs worked between the Globe and the hill behind it: one tall and thin, the other short and stout.

She followed the path down and stopped beside the Globe. She felt something soft underfoot and looked down.

"Jesus!" she cried. "Why didn't somebody warn me about this?"

Mike was behind her. "Sorry, boss," he said. "Didn't see it."

Gail rounded the concrete Globe, grimacing. "Morning, Lesley. You found our pile of puke, then?"

Lesley screwed up her nose. "Why hasn't somebody put a cordon around this?"

"We only just got here. You're five minutes behind us."

Lesley looked down at her shoe. "Are you going to need this as evidence?"

Gail laughed. "No. The vomit belongs to Shane Gisborne, the kid who found the body."

Lesley looked around. "Is that him over there?"

A young man sat on a bench with his back to them, a uniformed constable beside him.

"That's the one," Gail said. "We managed to persuade him to stay until you arrived. His mum's on her way."

Lesley looked at Mike. "Find out if he's old enough to talk to us without his mum present, and if he is, get a statement off him."

She knew from experience that once the parents arrived, kids suddenly clammed up.

"You want to see the body, then?" Gail asked.

"No, I just thought I'd come down for a stroll," Lesley replied.

Gail raised an eyebrow. "Touché. Come on then."

She led Lesley around to the back of the Globe where it was partially sheltered by the hillside behind. Above Lesley's head was a pair of feet. One was enclosed in a shoe, the other naked.

"What do we know so far?" she asked, craning her neck to get a better look.

She rounded the Globe, her eyes on the body. It was spreadeagled over the top of the structure, the feet facing towards the castle. It had been placed symmetrically; the head was pointing straight out to sea. Lesley wondered whether that was deliberate. She continued around the Globe, occasionally glancing down to check for vomit.

Lesley reached the front of the Globe, where it faced out to sea. The head was less obvious, but now she knew what she was looking for, she couldn't miss it. It seemed to be a man: short dark hair, mid-brown skin. Blood pooled around the shoulders and dripped onto the ground after trailing along the surface of the Globe.

She followed the body's gaze out to sea. The clouds were

lifting and the occasional patch of sunshine glimmered off the waves. She shivered.

She turned to Gail. "How long before you can get him down?"

"We need to do a thorough examination of the Globe itself first. Take samples from around the body, see if there's evidence of a struggle. Anything left behind by a possible attacker."

"Any chance it could be a suicide?"

Gail shook her head. "We're sending a drone up to take a look at him from above. But from what I've been able to make out from up on the clifftop, his throat was slit. I guess someone might do that to themselves. But it's unlikely."

"Haul yourself onto the top of that thing, position yourself just so, then cut your throat."

"And stay perfectly positioned," Gail added. "While you did all that."

"Hmm." Lesley started walking away from the Globe down the hill. She turned and looked back up at it. The body was barely visible from this angle.

"You get a better view up there." Gail turned and pointed towards the castle.

Lesley followed her gaze. Had the body been placed like this deliberately, so that the inhabitants of the castle would see it?

She frowned. "Does anyone live up there?"

"It's a visitor attraction. No one's lived there for almost a century. The council's owned it since 2003, they turned it into a tourist spot."

"So our body could be an employee."

"Anyone can access this site, as you've seen. He could be anyone."

"He?"

"From the size of the body, I'm confident it's a man. We'll know more after we send the drone up."

Gail's colleague stood to one side, frowning at a remote control in his hands. The drone was on the grass next to him, buzzing.

"Let me know when you've got it working," Lesley told her. "I want to see the state of him."

"Course." Gail turned to her colleague.

Lesley sighed. She wanted a better view. And she needed to find out if the location was relevant.

Mike had left the witness and was climbing the steps towards her. Lesley nodded at him.

"What did he say?"

"His dog – well, his mum's dog – spotted it. Smelled it, probably. Dragged him over. He says he walked round the back, realised what it was, then saw the blood."

"And puked on the ground."

"You can't blame him, boss. He's sixteen."

"No. Where does he live?"

Mike checked his notes. "Towards Swanage."

"OK. Let him get back home. Let's see if we can get a better angle."

She started climbing the hill towards the castle, not caring that her boots were going to get muddy.

CHAPTER SEVEN

Sometimes being resourceful was a real bonus, even if you were just a junior reporter for the local BBC.

Sadie Dawes, of course, had ambitions beyond the local news. She had her eyes on London and Broadcasting House.

Maybe this story would help her get there.

Today, her resourcefulness had got her access to another boat. She was out to sea north of Swanage. The guy who owned the boat, Dave, had insisted on coming with her. It was October, he'd told her, no time for a 'young girl' to be out here on her own. Sadie had gritted her teeth and resisted the urge to tell him just what she thought of that. She was thirty-two years old, for God's sake. She knew how to pilot a boat, she'd taken one to Brownsea Island when she'd been investigating the murders there. It had almost got her the scoop of the century, until that bloody constable had nicked her phone and wiped the video.

They stuck close to the cliffs as they made their way north out of Swanage. Dave insisted she didn't want to go far out to sea at this time of year. But the water looked pretty still today. It had been misty when Sadie had left home this morning, but now the sun was starting to come out. Sure it was a low sun, but it made Sadie feel optimistic.

A few miles north of the town, the boat slowed.

"So where is it you want to go, then?" Dave asked.

"Just up there." She pointed ahead.

There was a section of the cliff where the rocks had tumbled down. Sadie didn't know if the slide had been caused by DCI Mackie throwing himself off, or if it was more recent. But she was confident this was the spot. She'd been up to the top, worked it out from what the police had told them when he'd died. Before they'd gone quiet on the subject.

It had been almost a year since Mackie had died. Sadie didn't believe he'd killed himself. Sure, there'd been a suicide note, she'd reported it on the evening news. But Sadie had done some digging, and she'd discovered that the man had shown no signs of depression.

So what were the police covering up? Was there a murder case here that no one was talking about? Were the local police investigating it, but not telling anybody?

Sadie had tried knocking on Mackie's widow's door, but she'd refused to talk. Sensible woman. Sadie didn't like sensible women.

Dave put the boat into reverse, causing it to stop. He turned it towards the cliffs.

"I'm not going any closer, love. It's not safe."

Love. Sadie gave him the brightest smile she could muster, then grabbed her rucksack from the bottom of the boat. She took out her binoculars and scanned the cliffs. One of her mates from the Bournemouth Echo had taken photos not long after the 'suicide'. They hadn't run in the paper or on the local news, they hadn't even made their way onto social media. It was a non-story, her boss had said.

If this was a murder, it certainly wasn't a non-story.

"Can we moor up?" she said. "I want to get onto the bottom of the cliffs."

"No chance. Not safe."

"I'll pay you extra."

He threw her a frown. "Your money ain't worth my life, miss. How long you planning to keep me out here for? There's a storm brewing over Bournemouth."

Sadie looked past him towards the mainland. She couldn't see any sign of a storm, but she knew that men like Dave could feel the weather in their bones.

"Not long," she told him.

She put down the binoculars and grabbed the SLR that she'd also brought with her. She fired off a series of photos. Should she record video?

Not yet. If she found more evidence, she'd come back and film a piece to camera, even if she had to do it on her phone. She'd need more evidence first. Maybe that new DCI would provide it, if she could talk the woman into speaking with her.

"OK," she said, placing the camera back in her bag and zipping it up. She didn't want it getting wet, it had cost her a fortune.

"Good." Dave gunned the engine and they headed back towards Swanage.

CHAPTER EIGHT

Lesley climbed the grassy bank towards the castle, Mike at her heels. At the top, she turned to look down. The clouds had lifted and the scene was laid out below her.

Gail's colleague Gavin, the one so tall it made Lesley do a double take every time she saw him, was operating a drone, hovering it above the body. Gail peered into a computer screen: video from the drone.

Lesley wanted to see this.

She hurried back down the bank, just stopping herself from slipping at the bottom.

"What have we got?" she asked.

Gail glanced up, then returned her gaze to the screen. "He's on his back," she said. "Spreadeagled. His throat has been cut."

Lesley leaned over to get a better look. The man was Black, in his late thirties or possibly early forties. Blood pooled around his neck and chest. It had congealed around his neck and soaked through his clothes. He wore a dark jacket of some kind, even darker where the blood had seeped in. She could just about make out the flesh under his collar, which was dark red.

"That's not fresh."

"No," Gail replied.

The drone moved, giving them a view from the side. Some blood had dripped onto the Globe, but not as much as was in his clothes.

"So how did they get him up here?" Lesley asked.

Gail shrugged. "It's about three metres high," she said. "It wouldn't have been easy."

"They'd need a winch or something." Lesley looked around. There was no sign of any equipment that might have been used to haul a body up there.

"We've been looking for anything that could have been used to get him up there," Gail said. "Once we've got his body down, we'll have a look at him and his clothing. That'll give us more of an idea."

Lesley nodded. "We need to wait for Whittaker."

Henry Whittaker, the pathologist, was obstreperous and arrogant. But he knew his job.

"There's no way he'll examine the body up there," Gail said. "We might as well get him down."

"No," Lesley replied. "I want him to at least look at him from up the hill."

Gail looked up. "Since when were you into making Henry Whittaker's job easier?"

"I just want to do this thoroughly."

"Fair enough." Gail would know she was right. The crime scene manager had a reputation for thoroughness herself. One she deserved. "You're the SIO." She paused. "I assume you are?"

Lesley gave her friend a smile. "Who else?"

The drone buzzed as it landed on the grass a distance away.

Gavin approached. "Get anything useful?"

"We got all the angles we needed. We'll examine it in more detail later when we get back to the office."

"Did you see that object under his jacket?" Gavin asked.

Gail nodded.

"What object?" Lesley asked.

Gail tracked back in the video from the drone. She zoomed in on the man's chest and pointed to the screen.

"Piece of paper, I reckon. Sticking up out of his jacket."

Lesley frowned. "What the hell is it?" She could say things like that, now, with Dennis away. She knew she'd have to rein it back in when he got back.

"I reckon that's a note," said Gavin.

"Let's not assume."

"The killer leaving us a message, maybe?" suggested Mike. Lesley hadn't realised he was standing behind her.

"That would certainly be convenient," she said.

"Yeah," said Gail. "*My name is Fred Bloggs and I live at...*" She smiled at Lesley. "You could wrap the case up, go back to your knitting."

"I don't knit."

"Figure of speech." Gail stood up and stretched her back. "What *do* you do in your spare time, anyway?"

Lesley sniffed. Spare time wasn't something she'd made much of over the years.

"So we have a killer with a sense of the theatrical," she said. "Leaving a body spreadeagled over a local landmark, dripping with blood and – possibly – leaving a note."

"Maybe reads his Agatha Christie," Gail suggested.

"You think the killer's a man?"

"You'd have to be pretty strong to get a body up there," Gavin said.

"Excuse me!"

Lesley turned to see a woman at the top of the hill. She wore a tweed suit and had her hair tied up in a bun. She looked like she'd walked straight out of the 1950s.

Lesley put her hand over her eyes and looked at the woman. "This is a crime scene. Please don't come any closer."

"I'm the manager here," the woman replied. "What's going on?"

Lesley looked at Gail. *Shit.* "Didn't you speak to her?" she hissed.

"No sign of anyone when we got here."

Lesley put a hand on Gail's shoulder. Gail gave her a nod and then closed the laptop screen.

"We need to cordon off this pathway," Gail muttered.

"Pronto," Lesley added.

Lesley hauled herself up the hill and held up her ID for the woman.

"I'm DCI Clarke. I don't imagine you need me to tell you, but a body was discovered here this morning."

"I can see that." The woman glanced down towards the Globe and swallowed. "Who is he?"

"We haven't got that information yet. I don't suppose you recognise him?"

The woman grimaced. "Not from here. Sorry."

"Your name is?"

"Michaela Frodsham. I work for the trust that manages the castle. We oversee the Globe, the land around here too."

"I'm afraid there'll be no visitors here today. We don't want anyone past the castle."

"Coastal path runs past there." Michaela pointed.

"Then we'll close that off too."

"You can't do that, it's a right of—"

"It's a crime scene."

The woman stepped forward. Lesley put a hand out to stop her.

"Is it one of our staff?"

"We're working on an ID." Lesley knew that from this angle, it would be near impossible for the woman to recognise the dead man. "When we've brought him down, we'll be able to get closer to that."

"But—"

Lesley glanced at Mike, who stood behind the woman, up the hill. "Can we go inside, Ms Frodsham?" she asked.

"Miss."

"We need to know if anyone from the castle might have seen anything."

The woman stared past Lesley at the body. The sooner they got it down, Lesley thought, the better.

Where *was* Whittaker?

"Miss Frodsham?" Mike prompted.

The woman turned to look at him, frowning. "Yes. Of course. Follow me."

CHAPTER NINE

MICHAELA FRODSHAM's office was exactly what Lesley had expected. It wasn't a small space, but it gave the impression of being cramped thanks to the overwhelming clutter and chintz. Threadbare floral armchairs sat in two corners, both piled high with files and books. The carpet was worn so thin she could see the floorboards beneath the desk, and the desk itself had barely a millimetre of free space. Photographs of a haughty-looking white cat adorned the desk and a trophy from a cat show sat at the centre of a bank of shelves. Pride of place, Lesley thought.

"You're into the cat fancy," Mike said as he moved a pile of files aside and took the seat Michaela had indicated.

The woman smiled. "Mr Darcy is my pride and joy."

"Mr Darcy?" Even Lesley knew enough about literature to know that he was a character from a Jane Austen novel. Although only because she'd watched it on TV.

Michaela gestured towards the photos. "He's a three-year-old Persian. Caspian Denali Montague is the name he goes by for the fancy."

Mike nodded. "Mine's a moggy called Tigger."

The woman sniffed. "Oh." Her smile dropped.

Lesley suppressed a laugh. *Nice try, Mike.* She perched on the edge of a chair, a file digging into her backside. "What hours is the castle open?"

"The Globe is accessible twenty-four hours a day. The coastal path is a public right of way, you know."

Yes, I know. Lesley was taking more of a dislike to this woman with each passing second.

"Do you have CCTV up here? Anything pointing towards the Globe?"

"Of course. You'll be wanting copies of the files." Michaela sat at her desk and moved a pile of files to reveal an ancient-looking laptop.

"Send them to us, if you can." Lesley held out her business card. "Email address is on here."

"Certainly. I do hope you won't be inconveniencing us for too long. The path is popular, even at this time of year, and the school holidays are coming up—"

"We'll keep the site closed for as long as we need to," Lesley said.

"But we'll let you know when we're done," added Mike.

Michaela gave Mike a smile which morphed into a sneer. Lesley couldn't help snorting. *Probably thinking about his cat.*

"I hope you don't expect us to clean up." The woman looked at Lesley, putting a hand to her neck. "The Globe..."

They were the police; they had every right to leave the crime scene a mess if they wanted to. But Lesley knew Gail better than that.

"I'm sure the worst of it will be cleaned up for you."

"I don't mean to sound heartless. But it's a world-famous landmark."

Lesley raised an eyebrow. If it was world-famous, she'd have heard of it before someone decided to leave a body on top of it.

"We've created a cordon at the top of the path. Once the pathologist has been, we'll move him and then you'll be able to have your site back."

Movement caught her eye and she looked up. Gail was standing on the other side of the office door, waving through the glass.

Michaela Frodsham turned to follow Lesley's gaze. "Oh. Does this mean they're finished?"

"I doubt it." Lesley stood up and squeezed past Mike. She put a hand on his arm to indicate for him to stay put.

Outside the room, she closed the door behind her and moved out of sight. Gail glanced past her and followed.

"Everything OK?" Gail asked.

"Fine. What's up?"

"Only you look like someone's taken away your favourite toy."

"I'm fine. Have you found something?"

Gail held up an evidence bag. "Driving licence."

"Whose?" For a moment, Lesley held out a wild hope it would be the killer's.

"Paul Watson. Photo matches the victim."

Lesley peered at the licence in the bag. Paul Watson, 43 years old. His face was expressionless in the photo. He had short hair and mid-brown skin.

"Address is in Swanage," she said.

"Less than a mile away."

Lesley held up her phone and snapped a photo. "Thanks."

Her next stop would be that address.

CHAPTER TEN

SHERRY WATSON PUT her hand on Amelia's forehead.

Maybe she'd misjudged her daughter. The girl's forehead felt hot and clammy. She was sobbing, and she'd said she was in pain.

It looked like a bug of some sort, not an attempt to bunk off school.

Sherry had been so worried about her house viewing this afternoon, and about Paul disappearing to London, that she hadn't stopped to consider that perhaps her daughter wasn't faking it this time.

"I'm sorry, love." She kissed her daughter on the top of the head. Amelia shuddered.

"You lie down. I'll leave the TV on."

She stood up, moving slowly so as not to disturb the bed.

"I'll get you a drink. Hot Ribena, yeah?"

Amelia nodded, her eyes half closed. She'd probably be asleep by the time Sherry got back.

She left her daughter's room and eased the door closed.

As she crept down the stairs, she spotted a shadow in the doorway: somebody beyond the glass.

Just the postman. They were still getting plenty of mail redirected from their old address.

As she passed the front door there was a rap on the knocker.

Sherry jumped. The neighbours here weren't friendly, these houses being large and set back from the road. The house opposite was rarely occupied, probably a holiday home. She wasn't used to social calls.

She turned back towards the door and pulled it open, expecting it to be a salesman. She pasted on her *not today, please* face and opened her mouth.

The woman in front of her was blonde, with short hair and a well-fitted trouser suit. Her expression was stern. She didn't look like she wanted Sherry to buy something.

"Sherry Watson?" she asked.

Sherry drew back. "That's me."

The woman fished in her inside pocket. ID, Sherry thought. So she *was* a salesperson.

But when the ID came out, it wasn't for some door-to-door company. It was Dorset Police.

Sherry felt her stomach clench.

"What's wrong?"

She looked past the woman to see a man standing behind her. He was mixed race, wearing a grubby blue suit. He had the look of someone about to impart bad news.

Sherry's breath caught in her throat.

"Is it Paul?" she asked. "What's happened?"

The woman returned her ID to her pocket. "My name is DCI Clarke, you can call me Lesley. Can we come in please?"

Call me Lesley. That could only mean bad news. Police who were about to ask difficult questions or who suspected you of something never told you to call them by their first names.

Sherry pulled back from the front door and flicked her gaze up the stairs. Hopefully Amelia would be asleep, or at least engrossed in the TV.

She swallowed. "Come into the kitchen."

Turning her back on the two police officers, Sherry walked through to the kitchen at the back of the house. It was still not quite finished, a few units missing.

She gestured towards the table in the corner. "Take a seat."

Whatever this was, all her instincts screamed at her to delay it.

The woman was right behind her. Lesley something. A DCI, was that what she'd said? A DCI, that could only be bad.

Sherry put her hand on the back of a chair.

"I think you should sit down," the woman said.

Sherry nodded and did as she was told. The two officers sat opposite her. Sherry put her hands on the table, realising they were shaking.

"Tell me," she said. "Get it over with. Is it Paul?"

The woman leaned in. "I'm sorry to tell you this, Mrs Watson, but I'm afraid we found your husband at Durlston Head this morning."

Sherry narrowed her eyes. "Durlston Head?"

He was supposed to be in London, wasn't he? She'd been expecting a road accident or something on the trains.

"Durlston Head?" she repeated.

"I'm sorry to tell you your husband is dead."

Sherry fell back into the chair. From the moment she'd opened the front door, she'd known this was what they were going to say. But still...

"How?" she whispered.

The second officer, the man whose name she hadn't been given, shuffled in his chair. "Shall I make us all a cup of tea?"

Sherry chewed her finger. Her body felt hollow.

He looked at his colleague who gave him a nod. He made his way to the kettle, filling it noisily.

Sherry stared into the female detective's eyes. "How?" she repeated. "What happened?"

The detective cocked her head, her eyes roaming Sherry's face. She was trying to work out whether Sherry knew more than she was letting on. Sherry stared back at her, her stomach churning.

"I'm afraid your husband was murdered," the detective said.

CHAPTER ELEVEN

LESLEY STOOD in the driveway of the Watson house, watching as Mike closed the door behind him. They'd left Sherry Watson in the kitchen, PC Hughes having arrived for his stint as Family Liaison Officer. Fifteen minutes of questions had been all the woman could take before her mind had gone numb. They could always come back.

"What do you think?" she asked Mike.

He looked at her as if surprised she wanted his opinion. "She seemed pretty shocked."

Lesley looked past him at the front door. It was made of heavy wood with a stained-glass window in the middle. The house was solid, built of red brick. Broad, and deep, too. Tasteful, inside. She wondered how much it was worth.

"She certainly seemed to be," she said. "But there was something she wasn't letting on."

"How d'you mean, boss?"

"When we asked where her husband was supposed to be this morning, her eyes kept shifting between you and me. There was something she wasn't telling us."

"She said he was supposed to be at work."

"But she didn't say where at work. I don't reckon she thought that was where he was."

"Why would she lie about that?"

"Beats me," Lesley replied. "But we need to find out everything we can about Paul Watson. Find out if there's someone he might have been going to meet this morning, and if his wife knew about it. Get background."

"Fair enough," Mike said. "Should I call Tina?"

"You do that."

He walked towards the car, pulling his phone from his pocket. Lesley hung back, her eyes roaming the house.

A small girl was watching from an upstairs window. Lesley gave her a smile. The child stared back.

An adult appeared behind the girl: Sherry Watson. Poor kid. She was about to learn that her dad was dead.

Lesley turned away, giving the pair some privacy, and drew her phone out of her pocket. There was someone else she needed to chase down.

"Swanage 5432, can I help you?"

It had been years since Lesley had heard somebody answer the phone like that.

"I'm calling for Dennis," she said. "Dennis Frampton."

"He's not well," came the response. "Can I ask who's calling?"

"It's DCI Clarke."

"Oh."

"Is that Pam?" Lesley asked.

"It is," came the reply. "I'm his wife."

I know, thought Lesley. Dennis talked about his wife often enough.

"I need to speak to him," she said. "Check he's OK."

"He'll be back as soon as he can."

Lesley gritted her teeth. "I'm very sorry, Mrs Frampton, but I really do need to speak to your husband."

"He's asleep. I don't want to wake him."

"How is he?"

"He'll be back at work as soon as he can. You can rely on that."

That wasn't what Lesley had asked. What was going on?

"I'd like to come and visit," she said. "Just a welfare call."

"Oh, I think that's overkill," the woman replied. "I don't imagine that will help him. He'll be back as soon as he can."

The line went dead.

Lesley held her phone out in front of her, her mouth open. Dennis would never talk to her like that.

But his wife, it seemed, had no problem being rude.

CHAPTER TWELVE

"EVERYTHING OK?" asked Mike as Lesley got in the car.

"Fine."

"I spoke to Tina," he said. "She's on the case. And Gail just called. Whittaker's turned up."

"So he's graced us with his presence, has he? Let's get back there."

Five minutes later, they were back at the crime scene. The drone was on the ground, Gail and Gavin huddled over her laptop. Lesley wanted to see what else they had, but first she needed to speak to Whittaker. He stood halfway up the hill, looking at the body and making notes. Lesley stood next to him.

"Morning, Henry."

"DCI Clarke. So you're the SIO on this one, are you?"

She shrugged. "Who else were you expecting?"

He grunted.

"So," she asked. "Murder or suicide?"

A muscle in his forehead twitched. "How the bloody hell should I know? I haven't even got close yet."

"Will you be able to?"

Whittaker was in his sixties; she didn't imagine him climbing up the Globe to get a closer look. Gail's team had brought in tall step ladders, but she couldn't picture Whittaker up them either.

"I'll manage it," he told her. "Don't you worry about that."

"So you've got no hypothesis about the cause of death?"

He turned to her, that muscle twitching again. He'd lost more weight.

"Are you OK?" she asked.

His face darkened. "Of course I'm OK. Not too pleased to be brought all the way out here, but other than that, absolutely fine."

He turned away from her to look at the body. He held himself stiffly.

Lesley sighed. Whittaker's health was none of her business, and he wasn't about to confide in her even if it was.

"OK," she said. "Let's get on with it, shall we? The longer we leave him up there, the more chance of rain."

He nodded, not looking at her, and shuffled down the hill.

Lesley skidded after him. The grass was damp and the procession of people up and down had left muddy tracks.

Whittaker stopped at the edge of the grassy bank. Below him was a cutting, the path surrounding the Globe itself and the wall behind it, with its scientific notations and lists of planets. Below him, Gail was crouched on the ground, scraping up the vomit that Shane Gisborne had left. Lesley wrinkled her nose.

"I thought that wasn't evidence," she called down.

Gail looked up. "Just cleaning up."

"Surely that's not your job?"

"Who else?" Gail asked. "I'd rather work a clean crime scene than one where we could be sliding around in puke."

Whittaker coughed.

"Morning, Doctor," Gail said. "D'you need to use our ladders?"

"I do," he replied. "Can you bring them over here?"

Gail gestured for Gavin to move the ladder closer. He set it up in the space between the bank and the Globe, so that it bridged the gap. Whittaker would be able to step across and examine the body. Lesley was surprised he was contemplating it.

"Have you got a harness or anything?" she asked Gail.

"What for?" Gail asked.

Lesley nodded towards the pathologist. "We don't want him falling onto the body while he's examining it."

Whittaker turned to Lesley. "I think you should just let me get on with my job."

Lesley stared back at him. If the man wanted to put himself at risk, that was his problem. But if it contaminated the crime scene...

"You'll be careful?" she said.

"Of course I'll be bloody careful, woman. How many bodies do you think I've examined during the course of my career?"

"A lot," she replied.

"One hundred and twenty-eight, to be precise."

"That *is* a lot," Gail called up from below. "I don't think I've seen that many."

"You're not as experienced as me," Whittaker said.

"True." Gail went back to cleaning up the vomit.

Lesley called down to Gavin. "Hold the ladder in place, will you? Mike, you too."

Mike was already on the ground, standing on the other side of the ladder from Gavin. He stepped forward and grabbed it in both hands. Gavin took the other side.

Whittaker gave the two men a disdainful look and then stepped out onto the ladder. Lesley held her breath. Whittaker landed forcefully and climbed up two steps. He leaned over the top of the ladder, peering down at the body.

He wrinkled his nose as he leaned in closer. Lesley winced.

If he fell forwards...

Whittaker coughed and straightened up. He shuffled around on the ladder, and looked back at her. She stared into his face, not wanting to look at his feet and consider the possibility that he might slip.

"Any joy?" she asked.

"There's something under his shirt."

"What kind of something?" She knew it was the paper, the note, whatever it was, she might have told him about it before he'd gone up. But it played to Whittaker's ego to have him thinking he'd found something nobody else had noticed, and anything that made the man easier to work with was worth it.

"Looks like a piece of paper. His shirt is soaked in blood, but there's something beneath it which isn't."

"OK," she said. "Can you reach it?"

He shook his head. "It's too far. You're right, health and safety." He sneered.

Lesley had seen enough coppers get injured to know how important it was to be careful. Hell, she'd been injured herself. She put a hand to the back of her neck.

"We've got photos from that drone," she told him. "How close in did you get?" she asked Gail.

"Pretty close," replied the crime scene manager. "But no idea what that paper is without getting access to it."

"Only one way to find out, and that's to get him down," said Whittaker. "Which I'd rather we did sooner than later."

He looked out to sea. The clouds were darkening in the north.

"Suits me," said Lesley. "So how are we going to get him down?"

"There's a crane on its way," Gail told her.

"How will that get down here?"

"You'd be surprised," Gail replied. "This isn't my first rodeo, you know."

"Fair enough," said Lesley. They'd just have to wait, and hope the weather didn't change.

CHAPTER THIRTEEN

LESLEY STOOD DOWNHILL from the Globe, watching as a crane lifted Paul Watson's body. She held her breath as he swung through the air.

"Jesus Christ," she muttered.

"It'll be fine, boss," Mike said. "There was another body we had to do the same thing with over in Lulworth."

"When was that?"

He screwed up his face, thinking. "Two and a half, three years ago? Woman was halfway down the cliff, only way to get her off was a crane from above."

That would have been even more unsafe. Lesley wished the fact gave her confidence, but until Paul Watson was safely in the morgue, she knew she wouldn't relax.

She watched as his body was lowered onto the plastic sheeting Gail had prepared. She and Gavin guided the body into place as it came down. As the CSIs unhooked it from the crane, Lesley felt the tension drop from her shoulders.

"Thank fuck for that."

"Don't let the sarge hear you talking like that," Mike said.

Lesley smiled. "He'd get his swear jar out."

"It's still in his filing cabinet, boss."

"He doesn't use it when I'm around?"

"It seems you've changed him."

Lesley doubted it. Dennis Frampton was like these clifftops. Unchanging, solid, reliable. A pain in the arse at times, but she knew she could depend on him.

Except when he suddenly went off sick with no apparent reason and wouldn't speak to her.

"OK," she said. "Forget about Dennis, let's take a look at this body."

Whittaker was crouched beside it when they arrived, Gail standing over him.

"He's been dead at least eighteen hours," he said. "Probably longer."

Lesley looked at her watch. "It's eleven o'clock now, so that means he was left here yesterday."

"What time does it get dark this time of year?" Mike asked.

"You should know that, Mike," Lesley told him.

"Sorry, boss." He thought for a moment. "Six pm. Give or take."

"Very good," said Gail.

"OK," said Lesley. "So that means it was light when he was left here." It would have been quiet, at this time of year. But dragging a body onto the Globe in daylight wouldn't be easy to conceal.

She approached Paul Watson's body. The man wore a navy bomber jacket and a pair of dark grey trousers. The jacket was crusted with blood around the collar and cuffs, and there was staining near his ankles. His throat had been slit, deeply. The note that Whittaker and Gail had seen was poking out from the top of his jacket.

"Let me take a look at that," Lesley said.

Whittaker raised a hand. "Let me do my job first."

Lesley sheeshed out a breath. "Give me a bloody cause of death then."

"I'd thought that was rather obvious, wouldn't you?"

"You can't make assumptions." She pointed at Paul's neck. "That might have been done post-mortem."

"Not with the amount of blood lost," he told her. "That neck wound killed him."

She frowned. "How much blood was on the Globe?"

"Not as much as you'd expect," replied Gail.

"He was killed somewhere else," the pathologist added.

"Not near here," Lesley said. There was no blood anywhere but immediately below the Globe. Certainly not in the kind of quantities produced by a fatal neck wound.

"They might have cleaned up," Whittaker suggested.

"No," said Gail. "We'd have found evidence of the spot where they did it. He wasn't bleeding when he was brought here."

"Which means we're looking for a second crime scene," said Lesley.

"At least," replied Gail.

"And that he could have been brought up here after dark last night, when he'd already been dead for hours."

"So how did he get up onto the Globe?" Mike asked.

Whittaker pointed to the man's arm. "You can't see much because of the bomber jacket, but there's chafing on his wrist. A small amount of blood on the cuffs of his trousers. I imagine his ankles have the same chafing. I'd hazard a guess they used ropes, hauled him up."

"More than one killer?" Lesley asked.

"Possibly," Whittaker replied. "That's for you to work out."

"It could have been one," Gail said. "Somebody already dead wouldn't put up a fight. If you position yourself correctly, you could drag him over the top of that globe."

"Are there injuries on his back consistent with being dragged over the concrete?" Lesley asked.

"Give me a moment." Whittaker turned the body over.

Sure enough, the bomber jacket was ripped in places. There were scuff marks on the back of the victim's trousers. On the exposed foot, the skin was torn around the ankle.

"That's consistent with him being dragged on his back," Whittaker said. "I think you can safely say he was hauled up there using ropes or similar."

"How long after he died?" Lesley said.

"Before rigor mortis set in," the pathologist replied. "It would have been too difficult afterwards."

"OK," Lesley said. "So he was killed, brought down here, and then dragged up there within six or eight hours of death?"

"Possibly longer," the pathologist said. "Depends on the ambient temperature."

"But he's been here overnight?"

"Once I get him to the morgue, I can give you a more accurate time of death. But rigor is only just easing. For now, I think you're safe assuming that somebody brought him down here last night. And that they killed him earlier yesterday."

"Dragging him up onto the Globe would have reopened some of his wounds and explained the blood on the concrete," added Mike.

"Well done, Detective," Whittaker said. "You'll be after my job next."

Lesley gave him a sarcastic look. "He won't. But thanks for your help. Let me know when you'll be doing the post-mortem."

"Of course."

Lesley felt a drop land on her face. She looked up; it was starting to rain. "The note. It can't get wet."

"We'll get it bagged," said Gail.

"I want to take a look at it first."

Gail shook her head. "Bag first, then we can look at it."

She had a point. Lesley watched as Gail used a pair of tweezers to extract the note from inside the man's jacket and slid it into an evidence bag.

She handed the bag over to Lesley and watched as she read it.

"It's written in blood," Lesley said. She was aware of Mike next to her, leaning in to see.

"So we have a killer with a sense of the macabre," said Gail.

Mike's breath was on Lesley's neck. She raised a hand and he moved back. She turned the note in her hand.

"What does it say?" asked Gail.

Lesley looked at her. "Two words. *Go home.*"

CHAPTER FOURTEEN

LESLEY AND MIKE sat in Mike's car, staring out at the weather. Heavy drops of rain fell onto the windscreen. Down at the crime scene, Gail had erected a tent over the body. Whittaker was giving it his final examination, while Gail and Gavin searched the rest of the site for clues before they were wiped out by the weather.

"It's always the same," Lesley sighed.

"What is, boss?" Mike asked.

"The bloody weather here. It makes it so hard for us to do our job."

He shrugged. "Just how it is. Part of living in a rural area."

She nodded. "Get Tina on speakerphone, will you? I want to see what she's got on Paul Watson."

"Boss." Mike dialled.

"PC Abbott, Major Crime Investigations Team."

"Tina, it's Lesley."

"Boss. I'm glad you called."

Lesley smiled. "Why's that?"

"I've got more info on your victim."

"Go on then."

"He's an architect. Was. He was overseeing the new apartments at Peveril Point. Controversial one. And he lives nearby with his wife Sherry."

"We know that," said Lesley. "We've already been to see her."

"How is she?" Tina asked.

"Shocked, but hiding something."

"Poor woman." Tina hesitated. "Having your husband die like that..."

Lesley grunted. "What else have you got?"

"They moved down here three months ago. His firm have been expanding from their London office, opened up a new office in Swanage."

"In Swanage?" Lesley said. "Not Poole or Bournemouth?"

"As far as I can tell, their only client is the Horizon development. It's less than a mile away from where he lives, half a mile even."

"So you think he came down here just to work on that?" Lesley said. "Bit drastic to move house for one project."

"It's a big one," Tina said. "It's pissed a lot of people off around here. Oh, sorry, boss."

Lesley smiled. "I'm not Dennis. So where was he working before?"

"London. His firm's still got an office up there. It's run by his partner, Bella Phipps."

"What have you got on the firm?"

"Not much, I'll carry on looking," Tina replied. "But I can tell you about the objections to the development. There's been a lot."

"OK."

"There's a man called Laurence Smith, he's been spear-heading it. Getting himself onto the local news. He's trying to stop them, says it's a blot on the landscape."

Bloody nimbys, Lesley thought.

"To be fair," Tina continued, "it is in a beauty spot."

"Well, I guess that's why people want to buy flats there," Lesley said. "Tell me more about this Laurence Smith."

"He's a small-time politician, local councillor. Small-minded, in my opinion. Sorry, boss, I know you don't want my opinion."

"That's fine," Lesley said. "Background is good. So where does he live?"

"I've just texted his address to Mike."

Mike's phone pinged. He flicked it on and nodded at Lesley.

"OK," said Lesley. "Looks like that's where we're going next."

CHAPTER FIFTEEN

LAURENCE SMITH's house was in a cul-de-sac a couple of streets away from Paul Watson's. It was a similar size, but that was where the similarity ended. Paul Watson might not have designed his own house, but it had the stamp of an architect all over it: streamlined, modern and tasteful.

Laurence Smith's house wasn't streamlined or tasteful. It was one of those houses that was trying to look like a Grecian temple, but spectacularly failing.

Its front was pink-rendered, adorned with an imitation portico. At least twenty garden gnomes sat among the shrubs in the front garden. And on the roof of a red-brick garage so out of place it might have been dropped down next to the house by a spaceship, were three stone pigeons.

Lesley stared at them for a moment, wondering if they might just be live pigeons with very dull feathers. But no, they were made of stone.

"Why would you put stone pigeons on your roof?" she asked Mike.

He followed her gaze. "Surely they're real pigeons, boss?"

"I've been watching them for the last minute, they haven't moved a muscle." She cocked her head. "Should I try throwing a pebble at them, see if they budge?"

Mike glanced at the front windows of the house. They had heavy net curtains, sparkling white and made of an elaborate lace that probably came from some sort of historical catalogue. Or maybe just the Kays catalogue.

"One of those curtains just twitched," Mike said. "We're being watched."

"So we are," Lesley replied.

"I guess we'd better not chuck anything at that pigeon then."

Lesley looked back at the pigeons. They were fake, alright.

She shook herself out and walked towards the front door. The doorbell was in the shape of a lion's head, the kind of thing that would have been used as a knocker in a Dickens book. But here instead of a knocker, there was a button where the lion's nose should be. Lesley felt somehow dirty as she pushed it.

"Dear God," she said. "This place is hideous."

Mike laughed under his breath.

The door opened immediately. Whoever had twitched that curtain was ready for them.

Lesley pushed her shoulders back and tried to hide her reaction to the house. A woman stood in front of them. She wore an apron with frilly edges and a blouse with so many nips and tucks that Lesley wondered just how long it would take to iron the thing.

Lesley held up her badge. "Mrs Smith?"

The woman shook her head, a grave expression on her face. "Oh, no, my dear. I'm just the cleaning lady."

Lesley felt Mike shift next to her. Who said *cleaning lady* these days?

"Is Mr Smith in?" she asked. "We're from Dorset Police."

The woman's eyebrows rose. They'd been plucked so thin they were barely there. But there was enough of them left for them to register surprise. Lesley felt Mike stifle a snort. She elbowed him in the ribs and he straightened his back.

The woman gave Mike a disdainful look. "He's in the conservatory, I'll go and get him."

"That's OK," Lesley said. "We'll come through."

The woman stared back at Lesley and then shrugged, deciding it wasn't worth arguing with two police officers.

"Follow me, then," she said.

As they passed through the hall, the woman removed her apron and tucked it into the pocket of her skirt. Her skirt was heavy and full, made of a dark purple fabric that clashed with the nipped and tucked blouse. She led them through a plain living room into a conservatory with a wide view of the sea.

An elderly man sat in a chair. His head leaned back and his eyes were closed. A thin line of drool ran from his open mouth to his chin.

The nameless cleaning lady coughed loudly. The man's eyes twitched a few times before he opened them. He stiffened. His eyes widened, and he stared at the cleaning lady, followed by Lesley and then Mike. His gaze stayed on Mike.

"Who are you? What are you doing here?"

He sat up and rubbed the drool from his chin. He

straightened the maroon cardigan he was wearing, not once taking his eyes off Mike.

"My name is DCI Clarke, I'm from Dorset's Major Crime Investigations Team. Am I right in thinking you're Laurence Smith?"

"I am," he replied, his eyes still on Mike.

Lesley glanced at the DC. Was it because he was a man and Smith was expecting him to be the senior officer and not her? Or was it something else?

"Er, excuse me," she said. "Like I said, my name is DCI Clarke, this is DC Legg. We want to ask you some questions about the Horizon development."

The man leaned back in his chair. He snorted and turned his head away from them, looking out at the view.

Lesley had to admit it was one hell of a view. The house looked out over the cliffs between Durlston Head and Swanage. It was nestled into the hillside and had an uninterrupted view of the sea. Lesley could see as far as the Isle of Wight. Expensive, she thought.

"I hear you're spearheading a protest against it," she said.

The man turned back to her. "You could put it like that."

"And how would *you* put it?"

"Defending this town." He looked at Mike again. "Do you have a warrant?" he asked.

"No," Lesley replied. "We're just looking for information at the moment."

Smith placed his hands on the arms of his chair and pushed himself up. He was tall, if skinny. The impression they'd got when they'd come across him, sleeping in his chair, drooling like some doddering old geriatric, had been misleading. There was a glint in the man's eye. Lesley could imagine he would be formidable if you went up against him.

"Defending the town against who?" she asked.

"Against *whom*." He tutted.

Lesley's jaw clenched. "Who are you defending the town from?"

"Outsiders," he told her. His gaze flicked to Mike again. "People who aren't welcome."

Lesley looked down to see that Mike's fist was clenched at his side. She could only imagine how it would feel for him, standing here under this man's gaze.

"Why do you feel the need to defend the town against outsiders?" she asked.

Smith took a step towards her. "I would have said that was fairly obvious, wouldn't you?"

"Did you know Paul Watson?" she asked him.

"*Did* I know Paul Watson, or *do* I know Paul Watson?"

Lesley blinked back at the man. She drew in a breath. "You'll read about it soon enough, I imagine. We found Paul Watson's body at the Globe. We suspect murder."

"And you think *I* did it?"

"I'm aware the two of you came into contact during your protest."

He laughed. "Not exactly."

"Like I said, did you know him?"

"No," came the reply. "All of my dealings with his firm were by letter. I'm very careful to keep these things in writing. You won't find me banging on people's doors, yelling at them all hours of the day. You won't find me going into people's offices and telling them what I think of them."

"So..." Lesley began, wondering what he was referring to.

Smith gestured towards Mike. "Does your monkey speak?"

Mike gasped. Lesley clenched a fist.

"Are you the only person involved in this 'protest'?" Mike asked. His voice was harsh.

Smith smiled. "So you do speak." He turned to Lesley. "Of course not, half the town is with me."

"Can you give us any of the names?" Lesley asked. "People working with you."

She wondered if one or more of them had gone 'knocking on Paul's door' or 'bursting into his office'.

"Of course not," Smith replied. "These things are confidential."

"I'm a police officer investigating a suspected murder," she told him. "It's in your interest to help us."

"Suspected murder or *actual* murder?" he asked. "How long ago did you find him?"

"This morning. What were your movements yesterday, Mr Smith?"

"That's easy. I had a council meeting in the morning, then I worked in my study here all afternoon. Taking calls from constituents."

"Were you alone in the house?"

"Yes." His gaze didn't waver. "And in the evening, I had dinner with my neighbours." He smiled. "Happy?"

Lesley caught movement out of the corner of her eye. Mike's fist had come up to his chest.

Leave it, she thought. *Don't let him win.* Besides, if Mike did thump the witness, she'd have to discipline him.

"Now," Smith said. "Do you have a concrete reason to be questioning me? Do you have a warrant? Or are you just trying to bother an upstanding citizen protecting the needs of his town?"

"We'll be back," Lesley said. She gestured to Mike and turned.

The 'cleaning lady' hovered in the doorway. Lesley brushed past her, spotting the woman move to one side as Mike passed.

The two of them left the house, Mike's footsteps heavy. Lesley let herself breathe as they reached the driveway.

CHAPTER SIXTEEN

LESLEY THREW herself into her chair.

Mike and Tina shuffled into the office and Tina closed the door. The two constables took the two chairs opposite Lesley's desk.

The office felt empty. No Johnny – he'd been at the Met for six weeks now – and no Dennis. Lesley needed to follow up on Dennis.

But first, Paul Watson.

She shrugged off her jacket and pushed it over the chair behind her, inside out.

"I feel unclean after that," she said.

Mike shuddered.

Lesley eyed him. "Sorry you had to go through that."

He frowned. "Why are you apologising to me, boss?"

"Well, he was clearly a racist. The way he looked at you..."

Mike sat up in his chair. "Just because I'm mixed race doesn't mean you need to treat me with kid gloves."

She gritted her teeth. "Sorry, Mike. You're right."

She'd worked with plenty of ethnic minority coppers in Birmingham. Why had she suddenly got jumpy with Mike?

"Anyway," she said. "He's got an alibi."

"Not the best," said Mike. "Taking calls. Alone, in his house."

"We need to check his phone records."

"Anyone can make a phone call. Doesn't matter where they were at the time."

Lesley eyed him. "You think he did it?"

"I don't think anybody did it yet. We need more from pathology and forensics. We need to find witnesses, too."

Tina raised her hand.

Lesley looked at her. "This isn't school, Tina."

"Sorry, Ma'am. I mean, boss. I've been talking to my colleagues in Uniform, they're knocking on doors. But I wouldn't hold out much hope."

"No?"

"There's houses running up towards the castle, but none of them have much of a view of the place. And it's not an area with a lot of people walking around at night. Too far out of town, too steep a hill. I'd be surprised if we find any witnesses at all."

"You never know," Lesley said. "There might have been somebody on the coastal path. What was the weather like last night?"

"It was raining," replied Tina. "Heavy."

Lesley rolled her eyes. Down here, she noticed the rain more than she had in Birmingham. She'd traded her skirt suits for heavy waterproofs and practical boots. It made her feel frumpy, but it got the job done.

"OK," she said. "So we've got this note. *Go home.* Our friend Mr Smith seems to be the sort of individual who might think like that. He certainly has strong views on *outsiders*."

Mike shook his head. "Just because he looked at me funny, doesn't make him a racist."

"No?"

"Er..." interrupted Tina.

"What is it?" Lesley snapped.

Tina lifted up her phone. "I found this article in the *Echo*. I think the boss is right, Mike."

Lesley grabbed the phone from the PC and scanned the article.

The newspaper had run a piece on Syrian refugees being moved into Bournemouth. Smith had given some quotes.

"'They'll degrade the character of the town'," she read. "Nice man."

Mike crossed his legs. "I don't have a problem with people like him."

"How so?" Lesley asked.

"He's open about his views. It's the ones who pretend to be friendly, you have to watch out for. That's half this county."

Lesley grunted.

"OK," she said. "So this *go home* note..."

She placed her phone on the table. She'd taken a photo of it.

Tina leaned over. "Written in blood?"

"Our killer likes to be dramatic," Lesley told her. "A note written in blood, a body spreadeagled over a local landmark. They certainly wanted to send *somebody* a message."

"Paul Watson's architectural firm?" Mike suggested.

"Could have been them, could have been anybody," Lesley replied. "We have to work on the basis that this is racially motivated. Check the local hate groups. And I want extra officers with his wife and kids. Not just the FLO."

"Hate groups?" Tina asked.

"Surely you have those down here?"

Tina shrugged.

"Well, find out," Lesley said. "Speak to your colleagues in Uniform. Mike, talk to local CID and check HOLMES, look for racially motivated incidents. Our killer might have started off with petty crimes. Punch-ups, maybe a bit of graffiti, shoving shit through somebody's letterbox. This kind of offender often has a pattern of escalation."

Mike wrinkled his nose. "Boss."

"OK," she said. "Until we've got forensics, that's all we've got to go on."

"What about the post-mortem?" Mike asked. "You want me to go along?"

"I think that would be an excellent idea." Lesley had never known Mike to attend a post-mortem. "You've been to them before?"

"Of course."

"Gruesome ones?"

"Nothing like this."

"It'll be good experience for you. Report back afterwards."

"No problem, boss."

Tina had Lesley's phone up to her face. She squinted at it, turning it to the side. "What's this?"

"What?" Lesley asked.

Tina put the phone back on the desk. "If you zoom in, there's a symbol there." She pointed. "Bottom left-hand corner. Upside down."

Lesley pulled the phone closer. She hadn't seen any symbol.

"Where?"

"It's faint, maybe a watermark. Not in blood." Tina shrugged. "Could be nothing."

"But it could tell us where he bought the paper."

Tina nodded. "I'll look into it."

"You do that." Lesley held up her hand and counted out their leads on her fingers.

"First, we've got local hate groups. Tina, you look into that. Second, that symbol. Find out what it is, try to identify where the paper was bought. Third, racially motivated crimes. Mike, you're on that. Number four, the post-mortem. Mike again. Then we've got forensics. How long till Gail reports in?"

Mike and Tina exchanged glances.

"Sorry, haven't heard anything," Mike said.

Lesley nodded. She was missing Dennis. They couldn't handle a murder case with just the three of them.

"What will you be doing, boss?" Mike asked.

Lesley gave him a look. "Cheeky."

"Sorry." He lowered his eyes.

She smiled. "It's a good question, Mike. I wouldn't leave all the investigating to you two, would I? Sitting here on my arse all day filling out paperwork isn't really my thing."

He shrugged. "Some DCIs prefer to."

She jabbed a finger into the desk. "I think you know me well enough by now to know I'm not one of those DCIs. This is a small team and I don't want to overwhelm you. I'll be looking further into Paul Watson. I want to know more about his firm, his family, his acquaintances. This might not be racially motivated at all."

She leaned back. "Come on then, you've got work to do."

Mike and Tina rose from their chairs. "Sorry, boss," Tina said.

"What for?" Lesley asked.

"Sorry. I didn't mean to..."

Lesley splayed her fingers out on the table. "If you say sorry one more time, I'll have no choice but to get Dennis's swear jar out."

Mike laughed. "That'd be a good use for it."

Lesley needed to speak to the DS. But Mike didn't have to know that.

"How much do you know about Dennis's home life, Mike?"

"Er... Well, his wife. She's..."

"Go on."

"You don't want to mess with her, that's all I'm saying."

"Don't be ridiculous." Lesley had no doubt Pam Frampton was just a woman with the ability to speak her mind. Women like that weren't scary, they were strong.

Mike put his hands in his pockets. "You'll find out," he said.

CHAPTER SEVENTEEN

As Lesley hurried down the stairs, she heard her name being called. She turned to see Superintendent Carpenter at the top, hands in his pockets.

"DCI Clarke, a word please."

She resisted checking her watch and took a breath before stepping upwards.

"Anything wrong, sir?"

"No. I just think we need to discuss your current case."

Lesley frowned. What she needed was to get on with solving the case. But she knew better than to refuse.

In Carpenter's office, he closed the door and took the chair behind his desk. He leaned back and twisted his lips, looking at her.

"I was on my way out to follow up a lead, sir. I—"

"I won't keep you."

Good, she thought. *In that case, get on with it.*

"Sir."

"I've heard a rumour that the crime might be racially motivated."

Lesley scratched her chin. How had he got this, so quickly?

"There was a note left on the body, sir. *Go home.* It might have nothing to do with the victim's ethnicity, but—"

"I think you should take it seriously. Racial crime is less common here than in your old patch, I imagine. We need to tread carefully."

"Of course, sir." Lesley swallowed her irritation at the assumption.

"Which is why I think we should involve a psychologist."

"A psychologist?"

He nodded and opened a drawer in his desk. Lesley watched as he pulled out a file and placed it in front of her.

"Doctor Petra McBride," he said. "She resists being referred to as a profiler, but that's what she is, essentially. She'll help you understand the killer's mindset. Their motive."

"With respect, sir, I think the evidence will—"

"And what evidence do you have, right now?"

"There's the note, sir, and we've been speaking to a local group that's been protesting about the development Paul Watson was working on."

"I'm aware of that. Laurence Smith, local councillor. He's formally complained about your behaviour towards him, and that of DC Legg."

"Mr Smith called DC Legg a monkey."

Carpenter raised an eyebrow. "I'm not saying he's a nice man. But he's influential. Stick to the proper procedure, yes? Nothing personal."

"I hope you know me well enough now to know I would never—"

"Of course." Carpenter rubbed his forehead. "So do you have anything else? Forensics? Anything concrete?"

"Not right now. But it is early days."

"All the more reason to take advantage of any assistance we can get."

Lesley had a feeling that however much she objected, she was going to have to accept this psychologist's help. She opened the file to see a photograph of a round-faced woman with dark hair piled on top of her head. Doctor Petra McBride, criminal psychologist, Dundee University.

She looked up.

"I know her, sir. We hired her for a homophobic hate crime case in the West Midlands."

"Well, that's all settled then." Carpenter leaned back, smiling. "She'll be flying into Bournemouth Airport. Make sure you send someone to welcome her."

CHAPTER EIGHTEEN

At first, Sherry had hated having a police officer in her house.

She'd been surprised to be assigned a male family liaison officer, but then she told herself not to be sexist. She was well aware that he was here to watch her as much as to look after her.

But she'd grown used to his presence. Having him here meant she didn't have to answer the door. It meant she could shut herself away in the back room and try to process her grief. She'd even got him to phone the office and cancel that viewing this afternoon.

But she'd made damn sure he was well out of earshot when she'd spoken to the girls.

When Pippa had come home from school, she'd taken her into Amelia's bedroom, and told her to sit at the end of her sister's bed. The two of them had stared at her, eyes wide. They knew she was about to give them news. They knew it wouldn't be good.

They'd cried, of course. Amelia more than Pippa. But

Pippa's features had collapsed as the words had sunk in. Her reaction wasn't as vocal, but it was deep.

Sherry had folded the two of them in her arms, bending over the bed to hang on to them. Focusing on them had helped her get through the day so far. But she couldn't lean on them. She was the parent.

Now the girls were together in Pippa's bedroom, watching TV. She'd been putting her head round the door every fifteen minutes or so, registering their glazed expressions. Pippa had told her to leave them alone. She hated being shut out. But she knew they'd draw together. Her girls had always been close.

For the tenth time, she pushed the door open again.

"Hey, you two. How are you feeling?"

Amelia had brought a teddy bear from her room. She was sucking her thumb. Sherry felt her stomach hollow out at the sight.

"We're OK, Mum," Pippa said, her face darkening, but still staring at the TV. "We need some time." She turned to Sherry. "I'll come down when she's asleep."

Sherry nodded. Pippa was old for her thirteen years, but it wasn't her job to look after her sister.

"I'll sit with you."

"No."

"Amelia? Do you want me to sit with you?"

Amelia turned and looked up at her sister. They were on the bed, huddled together. She looked at Sherry and shook her head.

"You know where I am if you need me."

Sherry retreated and crept down the stairs, listening out for DC Hughes. Two other officers had arrived and stationed themselves at the front door. For her safety, they'd said. It only intensified the sensation of being under surveillance.

In the kitchen, DC Hughes placed a mug of tea on the table for her. She smiled her thanks and sat down, gazing at it. It would be too sweet, like the last cup he'd made.

Paul had had a sweet tooth. When they'd eaten out, he'd always ordered dessert. If he could, he'd have ordered three desserts instead of a starter and main course.

She chewed on a fingernail and spat it out. It fell to the floor, unseen.

The place needed cleaning, all these people in and out. Police officers taking Paul's computer away, going through his filing cabinets. Would they find anything that hinted at someone who'd wanted to kill him?

She wiped away a tear. Who could have wanted to kill Paul? He was an architect, for God's sake. OK, so those *keep Swanage for locals* nimbys hated him. But it wasn't personal, it was just the development. And it wasn't his development. It wasn't Paul who'd decided to put it there.

How could he possibly be blamed?

Sherry swallowed. She wrapped her fingers around the cup, knowing it wouldn't give her any warmth.

Was there something more sinister about his death? She'd seen people look at her funny in the local shops. Everyone she'd met so far had been white. And there'd been the sideways glances when she and Paul went for a walk along the beach.

She'd tried to talk Paul into moving to Poole or Bournemouth, but he preferred to be close to the development. He wanted to be on the doorstep. And they could afford a nicer house here.

She took out her phone.

Daria at the office had told her Paul was in London. She should let them know what had happened. Had the police done it already? She didn't know.

She checked the clock on the wall as the phone rang. Half past five. They would still be there.

"Watson and Phipps, can I help you?" Not Daria's voice.

"Hi, Celestine, it's Sherry." Celestine worked for Paul's partner, Bella. "Where's Daria?"

"She's on her break. Can I help you?"

Sherry gritted her teeth. So the office didn't know.

"I've got some bad news, I'm afraid. Is Bella there?"

"She's taken a couple of days off."

Bella Phipps was a workaholic who never went on holiday. She and Paul were equal partners in the firm, but everybody knew it was Bella who won the big contracts. She was the one whose face was regularly plastered all over the architectural magazines.

"Is she at home?" Sherry asked.

"I believe she's gone to Paris."

Believe. Bella would have made damn sure Celestine knew where she was.

"OK." Sherry sighed.

Would she call Bella's mobile? Did she want to talk to the woman while she was on holiday?

Did she want to talk to her, anyway?

"Celestine," she said. "I need to let you know…"

"What's happened?"

"It's Paul," Sherry said, her throat tight. "He's… He's been…" She coughed.

"What is it?" Celestine's voice was quiet. "Is Paul OK?"

Sherry took a breath. "He's been murdered." She slammed the phone onto the table, unable to say more.

CHAPTER NINETEEN

DENNIS LIVED in a compact semi-detached house on the road between Wareham and Poole. Lesley pulled up outside, eyeing the two cars in the drive. There was Dennis's Astra, and next to it a red Fiat 500, presumably belonging to his wife.

She strode to the front door and put up her hand to knock. Before her knuckles could make contact, the door opened.

A thin, smartly dressed woman smiled at her. She wore a well-fitting red dress and a delicate silver chain around her neck. She looked younger than Dennis, by as much as ten years.

This wasn't what Lesley had been expecting. She'd imagined someone larger. Older. Frumpier.

"You must be Pam," she said.

"And you're DCI Clarke."

"How did you guess?"

"He's described you to me." The woman cocked her head. "He likes you."

Lesley smiled to herself.

"Come in," said Pam. "I'll call him down."

"You told me he was sleeping."

"That was almost two hours ago. I'm surprised he hasn't telephoned you."

Pam turned into the house. Lesley followed, puzzled. If Dennis was awake, and his wife wasn't being cagey about the fact that she'd tried to get hold of him, why hadn't he called her mobile?

Pam ushered Lesley through to a narrow living room. It had been tidied to within an inch of its life. A green sofa squatted in front of Lesley, and two comfortable looking armchairs flanked it. A CRT TV set that looked like it had seen its heyday decades ago sat in the corner.

Lesley took the chair in the window, anxious not to be blinded by the low sun. The chair was soft, if a little scratchy.

Pam nodded and left the room. "Dennis!" she called from the hall. "DCI Clarke's here to see you."

Lesley heard Dennis's muffled voice from upstairs, then footsteps.

Dennis smoothed back his hair as he entered the room. He wore a pair of trousers that were identical to the ones he wore at work, and a brown cardigan. Lesley had been half-expecting to see him in striped pyjamas.

"Dennis," she said. "How are you?"

"On the mend, thank you, boss." He glanced at his wife. "A cup of tea please, love?"

Pam gave him a surprised look and left the room. Dennis closed the door after her.

"You didn't have to make a personal visit." He took the chair opposite her.

"I was worried," she told him. "You never take time off sick. And you look fine. What's wrong?"

"Some sort of bug," he said. "Had me vomiting on Sunday night, but you don't want to know that."

"You think you'll be back in tomorrow?"

He frowned. "As long as I'm not contagious."

"You think you might be?"

He shrugged. "Pam took me to the doctor this morning. They took a throat swab, thought it might be tonsillitis."

"You don't sound like you've got tonsillitis." Lesley's ex-husband Terry had had it ten years earlier and barely been able to speak.

"I thought that too," Dennis replied. "But the doctor was insistent."

He looked down at his hands, clasped in his lap. Was he being entirely honest with her?

Lesley leaned forwards.

"Dennis," she said. "If there was a problem, you'd let me know, wouldn't you?"

He looked up. "There's no problem, boss. Just a bug. Probably not tonsillitis, but I'll tell you in the morning."

"So you think you'll be back in? We've got a murder enquiry to deal with. Mike's—"

The door opened. Using just her left hand, Pam pulled out two tables from a nest that sat beside the sofa, holding a tea tray deftly in her right. She placed one table in front of Dennis and the other in front of Lesley, her movements precise.

Dennis rose from his chair, gesturing that he'd help. Pam pushed him back into it.

Once cups of tea had been placed in front of each of

them, Pam sat in the centre of the sofa, right in the middle of Lesley and Dennis.

"It's so nice to meet you, DCI Clarke. Dennis has told me all about you."

Lesley picked up her tea. The cup was china, but modern and angular. "Did he tell you what I made him do with the swear jar?"

Pam coughed. "I know things have improved between you since then."

"I think they have." Lesley cocked her head. "Wouldn't you agree, Dennis?"

"Yes, boss."

Dennis clearly hated having her and Pam in the same room. But Lesley didn't believe the tonsillitis story. She took a gulp of the tea and then placed the cup back on the saucer.

She stood up. "I need you back, Dennis. I can't do this with just Mike and Tina."

"Mike will be fine," Dennis said. "He's a hard worker."

"Tina too."

"Of course."

Pam stood up, putting a hand out for Lesley to shake. Lesley looked down then took it. The woman's handshake was firm.

"It was lovely to meet you," Pam said.

"Likewise."

Dennis stayed in his chair, looking out of the window.

Lesley walked past him to the door. "I'll see you in the office bright and early. Unless you find out you *do* have tonsillitis, and even then, only if the doctor says it's infectious."

"Of course." He straightened in his chair, still looking out of the window.

"Good."

Lesley let Pam lead her to the front door.

"Thank you for coming. It's kind of you."

Pam's gaze was sharp. She knew Lesley wasn't here out of kindness. She opened the front door, closing it quickly once Lesley was outside.

She looked back at the front window. A hand grabbed the curtains and closed them.

Lesley sniffed. *What's going on, Dennis?*

CHAPTER TWENTY

LESLEY HAD EXPECTED Paul Watson's office to be a sleek, glass-fronted affair with a view to rival the spot in which his life had ended. But their victim had worked out of a drab-looking office above a shop on Swanage High Street.

The street was quiet, only a couple of shops still open. A fine drizzle hung in the air and the few people who were out and about were hurrying. Lesley checked her watch – five forty-five – and pulled up the collar of her coat.

She approached the uniformed constable outside the brightly lit door to the office, holding up her ID. She'd been here four months, but not everyone knew her.

"Afternoon, Constable. Many people up there?"

"Just the CSI guys, Ma'am."

Lesley gestured for him to move aside. She climbed the narrow stairs and pushed open the door at the top. It had faded paint and creaking hinges.

Inside, two men in white suits were opening drawers and rifling around the back of cabinets.

"Afternoon, folks," Lesley said. "Who's in charge here?"

One of the techs pushed down his hood and approached her.

"Brett Gough, Ma'am," he said. "I work with Gail."

"We've met," she told him.

He nodded.

"Found anything useful?" she asked.

"Nothing yet. I think the files and equipment from his office at the house will give us more. This place feels like it never really got used."

"No?"

"Those filing cabinets in the corner, there's about four files in them. They're from a project that isn't even in Dorset."

"So there's nothing here on the Horizon development?"

"Nothing, Ma'am."

"You don't have to *Ma'am* me," she told him. "You're a civilian."

"Habit. Mackie liked it." He blushed. "We'll be finished within half an hour, I don't expect to find anything useful."

"What did you get from the house?"

"It's all being catalogued offsite," he said. "We didn't want to disturb his wife any more than we had to."

Lesley nodded. "Let me know if anything jumps out at you, yes?"

She surveyed the space. There was a desk in the centre of the room: cheap and worn. The kind of thing found in the offices of third-rate businesses since time immemorial. Behind it was a chair that didn't look the slightest bit comfortable. It was a far cry from the Watson home; Paul's office there had boasted a designer chair and a glass-topped desk.

"I'm not surprised he never worked here," she said.

"Not much more than a place to receive post, I reckon," replied Brett.

The room smelt musty and damp. It held nothing of its former occupant.

"Was he the only person who worked here?" she asked.

"Just one desk," Brett said. "His PA in London says it was just him down here."

"PA?"

Brett shrugged. "Tina spoke to her. I don't know any more."

Lesley turned and hurried back down the stairs, squeezing past the uniformed constable as she left. She'd ask Tina more about the London outfit when she got back to the office. But Paul Watson hadn't just worked at a desk.

She jumped into her car and drove to Peveril Point, the site of the development Paul had been working on. She wanted to see what all the controversy was about.

She parked by a tall wire fence. There was no police presence here, no human presence at all, in fact. No sign of the contractor.

She pulled at the fence, but it was padlocked shut. She wasn't about to start climbing over it. She'd find out who the main contractor was and get a key. Either that or she'd come back in the morning.

But she wasn't leaving without a quick look around.

She walked along beside the fence. It led towards the clifftop and ended at a sheer drop, a hedge keeping her from falling. These flats would certainly have a view.

Why was Laurence Smith so opposed to it? The next building round the headland was another apartment complex, and there were two behind it. The town made its money from tourism. Holidaymakers brought money in, flats like these brought holidaymakers in. Surely that could only be a good thing?

She turned back towards her car. Two men stood next to it, alternately looking up and down the road and eyeing her car.

She watched them for a moment. One of them tried the handle of her car. Lesley grabbed her phone, fired off a couple of photos, then stepped out of the shadow of the hedge.

She walked towards the car.

"Oi!" she called. "What are you doing?"

The men exchanged glances. As Lesley approached, they turned and ran.

Lesley ran after them. "Police. Stop!"

The men went through a gap at the side of the road, slipping between two houses. Lesley turned to follow them.

She stopped. The space they'd gone through was narrow and dark. No one knew she was here.

Did she have reason to think they might be violent?

Stop it, woman, she told herself. *This is Swanage, for God's sake.*

She ran between the houses. At the back, she emerged into a scruffy patch of land. She scanned the space; nothing. Then she caught movement on the far side.

She ran across the grass. It was damp; her trousers would be ruined. At the far side was a fence.

Where had they gone?

She tugged at the fence then blew out a breath. All they'd been doing was trying her door handle. She was overreacting.

But then they'd run...

She shook herself out. She was tired. She should come back in the morning.

But before she did, she would run the photo on her phone past her team.

CHAPTER TWENTY-ONE

Tina tapped her fingers on the desk as she waited for the phone to be answered. She didn't know if the CSI team were back in their office yet, or still onsite. There were only a few of them, and in the days after a major crime, they tended to be difficult to get hold of.

At last, the phone was picked up.

"CSI, Sunil speaking."

Tina smiled. Sunil Chaudhary was just the guy she needed.

"Hi, Sunil. It's Tina Abbott from the Major Crimes team."

"Hey, Tina. How's things?"

"Busy," she replied.

"I can imagine. You're wanting to know more about this note left on your Swanage Globe victim, right?"

She leaned back in her chair. The office was quiet, echoey even. Very different from when there were five of them in there. She wondered when the sarge would be back.

"Have you seen it?" she asked Sunil.

"I've got a photo of it right here on my screen."

Sunil was an expert in digital forensics. But given the size of Gail's team, he covered pretty much everything.

"I wanted to know about that symbol on the bottom left-hand corner," Tina said.

"You didn't recognise it?"

"Should I have?"

"It's an acorn in a ring," he said. "I've managed to enhance it. You haven't seen it on the news?"

Tina frowned. "The news? When?" Had there been another murder, with one of these left behind?

"Local elections."

Local elections? "I don't vote."

Sunil sucked in a breath. "What do you mean, you don't vote?"

"The same idiots always get in. I make more of a difference as a copper than I do as a voter."

There was silence at the other end of the line.

"You still there, Sunil?"

"Voting is important, Tina," Sunil said. "You should do it. There are people in parts of the world who would die for the right to vote. Who *do* die for the right to vote."

Tina rolled her eyes. "I believe you. But can you just tell me what that symbol is?"

"Sorry, mate. It's the Dorset Residents Group."

"The who?"

"They stood in the county elections. Making out like they're the underdog, sticking it to the man. Nasty bunch. Dog whistle racists, nimbys. Act like they're the party for the unemployed and the workers, but of course they're run by a local millionaire."

"Who?" Tina had a feeling she was going to know the answer.

"You really should know this stuff," Sunil told her. "If you're in the Major Crimes team, you need to know what's going on."

"Sunil," Tina said, trying to sound more patient than she felt. "Just tell me who."

"Laurence Smith," Sunil replied. "Lives in Swanage, retired, politically active."

"I know the man," Tina said. "The DCI has already been to see him."

"Sounds like she might need to see him again."

CHAPTER TWENTY-TWO

Lesley knocked on the door of Paul and Sherry Watson's house. This place couldn't have been more different from his scruffy office down the hill.

PC Hughes answered the door. "Evening, Ma'am."

"Is she in?"

"She's in the kitchen."

Lesley passed through the hall, still light and airy after dark, and into the kitchen. Sherry was at the broad kitchen table, a pot of tea and a clean cup in front of her. Lesley could hear a TV from somewhere in the house. Other than that, silence.

Sherry didn't notice Lesley until the DCI was almost by her side. She looked up and wiped her eyes.

"Detective." She rubbed her nose with the back of her hand. "What is it? Have you arrested someone?"

"Not yet, Mrs Watson. D'you mind if I sit down?"

Sherry nodded and Lesley took the chair opposite her. She clasped her hands on the table, looking into the woman's eyes. Sherry stared out of the darkened window, her gaze distant, her eyes wet.

"I need to know more about the Horizon development," Lesley said.

Sherry shook her head.

Lesley leaned forward. "I heard there were protests. Local people who didn't like the idea of such a large development being built."

Sherry turned to face Lesley. "It was nothing. People get funny about building work, I see it all the time in my job."

"What is your job?" Lesley realised she didn't know.

"Estate agent. I'm the one who's going to be selling those apartments once they're built."

"So they won't be let out by the company that built them?"

Sherry shook her head. "The development company plans to sell them. Thirteen in all. One-bedroomed on the ground floor, ranging up to the penthouse at the top. The views are to die for."

The woman screwed up her face. She fell back in her chair.

Lesley gave her a sympathetic smile. "Are your children here?"

Sherry didn't look up. "They're upstairs watching TV. I've told them about Paul, if that's what you're wondering."

"Have you got someone who can be with you?" Lesley asked. "Not just DC Hughes. Any friends or family?"

"We've only been here three months, we haven't really made any friends. The neighbours." Sherry sniffed. "Well, the neighbours are hardly here. I didn't realise until I came here just how many houses would be used as holiday homes."

She raised her face and looked at Lesley. "Sometimes I can see Laurence Smith's point."

Lesley pursed her lips. "Do you think Smith might have wanted Paul dead?"

Sherry's eyes widened. "You think it was him?"

"We don't have a suspect right now. But I'd like to know if the man had any direct contact with your husband."

Sherry shook her head. "Smith's a nasty piece of work. But he's not a killer. I mean, Doreen – she owns the house over the road – she says he's a pillar of the local community. I guess that means a different thing down here from in London, but even so."

"So you're not aware of him or anybody else having made threats against Paul?"

Sherry shook her head. "Paul kept himself to himself. He went to work, he came home, he went to meetings in London occasionally." Her jaw stiffened.

"Did Paul often go to London?"

Sherry reached out for the teapot. She poured tea into the mug in front of her and picked it up.

It would be cold, Lesley thought. And there was no milk. She stood up, looking for the fridge. "Can I get you something to drink that isn't tea?"

Sherry smiled, just faintly. "There's a bottle of wine in the fridge door. Is that... inappropriate?"

"There's no such thing as inappropriate. It's your house."

"Then I'll have a glass. You can have one too."

"I'll have a glass of water, if I may?"

As Lesley made for the fridge, PC Hughes appeared from nowhere. "I'll do it, Ma'am."

"You heard that?"

"Glass of wine and a water."

"Thanks." As FLO, part of PC Hughes's job was to listen to what was going on in the house, without making his presence too obvious. From the look of things, he was getting rather good at it.

Lesley returned to the table, where Sherry was chewing her nails.

"Did Paul often go to London?" Lesley asked.

Sherry looked back at her, her eyes hard. "You're right, it's not a good idea."

"Sorry?"

Sherry looked down. "The wine. You didn't..."

DC Hughes put two glasses on the table. "Here we go, ladies."

"Oh." Sherry touched the base of her glass with her fingertip. Her eyes filled with tears. "Thank you."

"Pleasure." PC Hughes retreated.

Lesley drank from her glass. She hadn't eaten or drunk since dinner last night. There was a KitKat in her pocket, but now wasn't the time. "Sherry, did Paul often go to London?"

"As often as he needed to. For meetings, that's all. The firm had two offices. Still does." She closed her eyes. "Shit, what are we going to do with the office?"

"We've been in there," Lesley said. "It doesn't look like your husband used it much."

"It was just a base. Gave him an official presence down here. But he worked from the house most of the time. If it wasn't Laurence Smith, who do you think it was?"

"We don't know yet," Lesley replied. "Did you and Paul have any problems with racism since moving down here?"

Sherry stared at her. "Racism?"

Lesley nodded.

"No. Nothing serious. Funny looks, people muttering in the supermarket. Nothing we couldn't handle."

"No threats?"

"You think this was a racist attack?" Sherry's hand went to her chest. "Oh."

Lesley put out a hand but Sherry shrank back. She looked towards the window. "You think..."

"It's a possibility," Lesley said. "Please let me know if you remember anything. If your daughters had any problems..."

"They'd have told us."

They might not, Lesley thought. "Which school are they at?"

"The Swanage School."

"Thanks." Lesley would get one of the team to contact the school and find out if there had been any racist incidents "Sherry, there is one final question I'm required to ask you."

"Yes?"

"Can you tell me where you were last night?"

Sherry stared at her. "You think *I* killed my husband?"

"We have to rule you out. Can you tell me where you were last night?"

"I was here. I had a Zoom call, a work thing. They can vouch for me, it'll be on my computer records."

"That's fine," Lesley replied. "We'd like to take your laptop and check that out, if that's OK?"

"Of course. Mark has told me to take the week off."

"Mark?"

"My boss. I work for Howards, estate agents in Wareham."

"Not in Swanage?"

"Wareham's easier for customers to get to. Even if most of the properties they're looking at are in Swanage."

"OK." Lesley made a mental note of the firm's name. "Thanks for your time, Sherry," she said, standing up. "If you think of anything, anything at all, I want you to tell us. Someone that Paul fell out with, someone that might have wanted to do him harm. You can speak to the constable here."

PC Hughes was near the fridge, flicking through his notepad. He looked up.

"I know," Sherry said. "I know what he's here for."

Lesley put her hand on the table. "He's here to take the burden off you, Sherry. He's here to help."

Sherry grunted.

Lesley looked at her. The woman might have been struggling with grief, but she wasn't stupid.

CHAPTER TWENTY-THREE

LESLEY'S PHONE rang as she was driving through Corfe Castle towards her house in Wareham. The castle was lit from below and looked imposing in the dark.

"DCI Clarke."

"Lesley, I gather we're to be working together again."

Lesley knew that accent.

"Doctor McBride."

"Ach, call me Petra. We can be pals, yes?"

Lesley left the castle behind and drove into the night. She was tired and her skin itched.

"Petra, I expect you've had a call from Superintendent Carpenter. I really don't think—"

"Anthony says you've gone and managed to get yourself a race hate crime. In sleepy Swanage, of all places. Nice one."

"We don't even know it's racially motivated. It could be one of a number of things."

"There was a note, yes? Go home."

"There was."

"Written in blood?"

Lesley sighed. "Yes."

Petra laughed. "Oh I do love me a criminal with a sense of the dramatic. Can't wait to get my teeth into this one."

"I'd have thought a profiler like you would—"

"Hey. Just cos we're pals doesnae mean you can go talking to me like I'm a yank. This isn't the FBI, you know?"

Lesley allowed herself a smile. She passed through Stoborough and towards Wareham. She liked this route in, approaching the town via the level ground south of the river.

"Look, hen," Petra said. "Your man Carpenter has hired me to help you out so you might as well accept my help. They've sent me a ticket, I'll be with you tomorrow."

"I'll send an officer to collect you from the station." Lesley would humour Carpenter on this one. Petra would no doubt turn out to be wrong, but if there was any chance she could help...

"No' the station, Lesley. The airport."

"Bournemouth airport?" The place was little more than an airfield.

"There's a flight from Edinburgh. I'll be on it. Looking forward to getting some sunshine."

"It's October."

A laugh. "Have you been to Dundee at this time of year? I'm so blue you could make me the mascot for Glasgow Rangers. See you tomorrow."

Petra hung up. Lesley turned into her road, resigned.

CHAPTER TWENTY-FOUR

LESLEY TOSSED her keys onto the shelf in the hall of her cottage. She hadn't been here for a few days, having spent the last few nights at Elsa's flat in Bournemouth.

The place needed a good clean, but she didn't feel sufficiently attached to it to be bothered. Truth was, she needed to face up the fact that she might as well move in with Elsa. But not while her divorce from Terry was still going through.

She walked through to the kitchen and opened cupboards. A tin of baked beans sat on a high shelf. There would be next to nothing in the fridge. A bottle of gin, some butter, a carton of milk that had long since gone off.

She'd get a takeaway. Elsa was working tonight, helping her brother in the pub that he managed in Wareham. Lesley would pop in, maybe get something to eat there.

"Hey, gorgeous."

Lesley turned to see Elsa walking through from the living room.

"I wasn't expecting to see you here."

Elsa smiled. "I thought I'd come and see my favourite detective before I started work."

"You never rest," Lesley said. "You've just come from work, haven't you?" Elsa was a partner at Nevin, Cross and Short, criminal lawyers in Bournemouth.

Elsa shrugged. "No rest for the wicked."

"How are things at the office?"

"Still sorting out the ins and outs of Harry's estate. His wife gets most of it, but he's got some complicated instructions about splitting things between his daughters. And he left Aurelia a painting."

Aurelia was the third partner in the law firm. "Valuable?" Lesley asked.

"No idea."

"Nothing for you?"

"I'm the newest partner. Not a sausage, sorry."

Lesley sighed. Harry Nevin had been dead for months, and he was a lawyer. "Surely a solicitor should know better than to leave a complicated will."

"He wasn't a probate lawyer," Elsa reminded her. "We don't all cover everything."

Lesley nodded. Elsa leaned in to kiss her neck.

Lesley felt a shiver run across her skin. "Do you really have to work?"

Elsa laughed into Lesley's neck. "I can come back here afterwards if you want?"

Lesley smiled. "That would be nice. We spend a lot of time at your flat."

Elsa pulled away. "I still think you should move in. I know this place is handy for your work, but..." she gestured around the room. "It's not exactly you."

Elsa was right. The cottage had been rented for Lesley by

Dorset Police before she'd arrived. Some people might have called it cosy and atmospheric. Lesley thought of it as pokey and damp.

"So are you going to come to the pub for a bit?" Elsa asked. "Cindy's cooking tonight, stroganoff."

Lesley raised an eyebrow. Beef stroganoff was about as exotic as it got in the Duke of Wellington.

Her phone buzzed in her bag. "Hang on a moment." She read the message and set the phone face down on the kitchen table.

"Everything alright?" Elsa asked.

"It's fine," Lesley sighed. "Just a new case."

"A new one?"

"A murder."

"Ouch. Who?"

"Paul Watson, an architect. Don't suppose you've heard of him?"

"Never." Elsa picked up her jacket from the back of a chair. "I need to get to the pub. I'll see you there later, yeah?"

Lesley looked at her girlfriend. "I'm tired. I think I'll just have a lazy night at home."

"You still want me to come over afterwards?"

"I might be in bed when you get here."

"That's fine." Elsa's eyes sparkled. "I'll see you there."

CHAPTER TWENTY-FIVE

Sherry leaned over Pippa's bed and kissed her daughter on the forehead.

"Night, love," she said. "If you need me, I'll be in my bedroom. You sure you don't want to sleep with me tonight?"

"I'm too old for that, Mum."

Sherry stroked her daughter's arm.

"Stop it, Mum. Don't paw me."

Sherry felt a lump form in her throat. She wanted to comfort her daughter, but the girl was at the age where she wanted to push her parents away.

Parent, she realised. Not *parents*. It would never be *parents* again.

How did you help a teenager deal with the death of her father? Sherry had no idea. She'd never known anybody die at Paul's age, especially not so violently.

When the girls went back to school, people would be talking about it. It would be in the news. How could she protect them from that?

"Go, Mum," her daughter said. "I want to sleep."

Sherry closed the door quietly as she left. As she was about to turn into Amelia's room, PC Hughes came up the stairs.

"Sorry to disturb you," he said, "but there's a phone call."

"On the landline?" No one used that.

He nodded. "Like I say, sorry to disturb you."

Sherry drew in a breath and followed him down the stairs. She went into Paul's office, where the phone was kept. They never used it and none of her friends had the number.

So who was calling?

She felt cold grip her. It would be a journalist.

"Did they say who it was?" she asked the constable.

"Colleague of your husband."

Sherry felt her vision cloud. It would be Bella, his business partner.

She walked to the desk. The phone was the only thing left on it, everything else seized by the police. She paused and briefly considered simply putting it back in its cradle.

She would have to speak to Bella eventually. The woman would turn up for the funeral. It would be humiliating, and the girls…

She picked up the phone. "Bella," she said, her voice hard.

"Sherry. I'm so sorry to hear about Paul."

"Celestine told you."

"Yes. I'm away right now. Paris. If I was in the country, I'd come straight to Swanage. If there's anything I can do…"

"I don't need your help. We're fine."

"But you're on your own down there. The office, do you need help with—?"

"Leave it, please. I want to be left alone with my girls."

"I understand. But please, if there's anything I can help with. If you need someone to talk to."

"Why would I talk to you?" Sherry clenched her fist around the phone wire.

"I worked with him," Bella replied. "I'll miss him too."

"I bet you bloody will."

"Sherry, are you OK? Please don't—"

"Don't call me again." Sherry put the phone down. She bent over. The phone was plugged in behind the desk.

She'd never given this number out, wasn't even sure what it was. Nobody she wanted to speak to would use it.

She pulled the phone line out of the wall and let it drop to the floor.

CHAPTER TWENTY-SIX

LESLEY ENTERED the King's Arms pub, glancing around the room to check that nobody she knew was here. She'd hurried past the Duke of Wellington on the opposite side of the road, not wanting Elsa to see her.

The pub was quiet. Two couples in one corner laughed over their drinks and a solitary man propped up the bar. No sign of the person Lesley had come to meet.

She walked up to the bar. "Gin and tonic, please."

The barman gave her a quiet smile. He turned his back to pour the drink and then placed it in front of her. "Anything else?"

"That'll be all, thanks."

"You're on your own?"

None of your business. She gave him the most pleasant smile she could muster. *Don't draw attention to yourself.*

"For now," she said. "Meeting a friend."

She took a seat in the window, as far from the two couples as she could get. The door to the street opened and a woman walked in.

Lesley stiffened.

The woman walked to the bar, ordered a glass of white wine, and turned to look around the pub. Seeing Lesley, she nodded and walked towards her table.

She pulled out the chair opposite Lesley and sat down.

"So," said Lesley. "Let's keep this brief, shall we?"

Sadie Dawes leaned back in her chair. "You don't want anybody knowing that we're here?"

"What do you think?"

"So you haven't told your colleagues that you're looking into DCI Mackie's death."

"Who's to say I'm looking into his death?"

"You wouldn't have agreed to meet me if you weren't."

Lesley wasn't about to confirm or deny what she might or might not be doing regarding her predecessor. What her team didn't know was that she'd asked Zoe Finch, a former colleague from the West Midlands, to help. There'd been a moment when she'd suspected Dennis had rumbled Zoe, but between them they'd managed to fob him off.

Lesley put down her glass. "What was it you wanted to talk to me about?"

"I went to the crime scene this morning."

"Crime scene?"

"Where Mackie was killed."

"Mackie committed suicide," Lesley reminded her.

"You really think that?"

"According to the coroner. I wasn't here at the time."

Sadie snorted. "I think you know more than you're letting on. For example, that you've got a Detective Inspector from the West Midlands looking into it."

Lesley clenched a fist under the table. "I don't know what you're talking about."

Sadie smiled into her glass. She took a long drink.

"Fine," she said. "I know you're not going to admit to anything. But don't you think it would be in everybody's interest if the truth was uncovered about Mackie's death? I mean, you're in charge of MCIT now. What if you're at risk?"

Lesley shook her head. "I'm new to the county. I don't have any history here. Why would the nature of DCI Mackie's death have any impact on me?"

"Maybe someone's got it in for the Major Crimes team. Maybe it's one of your own."

"Don't be ridiculous."

"What about organised crime?" Sadie suggested. "You've pissed plenty of them off over the years."

"*I've* done nothing of the sort," Lesley said.

"Your team has. Maybe you've got too close. Maybe Mackie got too close?"

Lesley glared at Sadie. She was fishing. She didn't know anything, despite all her bluster.

But what if she did? That comment about a Detective Inspector from the West Midlands...

Sadie hadn't mentioned Johnny, thank God. He'd been transferred to the Met after she'd discovered he was being blackmailed by Arthur Kelvin. Dennis had known, and taken a while to tell her.

It rankled with her.

Still, Sadie clearly didn't know about Johnny.

"So," said Sadie. "Are you going to share anything with me?"

"Why would I do that?"

"You're admitting you have got something to share?"

"You're just trying to put words in my mouth."

"Maybe. But I can tell when somebody's lying."

Lesley leaned back in her chair. She steepled her hands in front of her and tapped her chin with her forefinger.

"I suggest you leave it alone, Sadie," she said. "I'm sure you've got more important things to report on."

"But that's the problem."

Lesley said nothing.

"See, the more you tell me to leave it alone," Sadie continued, "the more I think there's something you're hiding."

Lesley downed the last of her drink. She'd drunk it too fast, it was going to her head.

She stood up. "You got yourself into enough trouble on Brownsea Island, Sadie. You seem to have a habit of being in the wrong place. You shouldn't even be talking to me. I'm going home."

"Wait."

But Lesley was halfway to the door. She walked steadily, careful not to betray her anger. The barman was watching her. Lesley knew Sadie would collar him afterwards, find out if he knew anything about her.

What Sadie didn't know was that she was in the wrong pub for that.

As Lesley put her hand on the door, she felt a hand on her back. Sadie was right behind her.

"Leave me alone," she said, without turning round. "I've got nothing to talk to you about."

"What about DC Chiles?" Sadie asked. "Why did he move to London so abruptly? His wife eight months pregnant, too."

Lesley was ready for this. She turned to face the woman.

"He'd been angling for a transfer to the Met for months. One came up, I recommended him."

"Hmm." Sadie's eyes flashed. "I'll find out the truth, you know."

"You already have the truth."

Lesley turned and left the pub, pushing the door shut in the journalist's face.

CHAPTER TWENTY-SEVEN

MIKE LOOKED up to see Tina coming into the office. He gave her a smile. "Morning, T."

"Morning, Mike."

She shrugged off her uniform jacket and draped it over the back of her chair, patting it down as she did so. Mike turned back to his computer as Tina fired up hers. While she waited for it to come to life, she leaned across the desks.

"I wanted to check with you, Mike."

He looked up from his screen. "Check what?"

"Are you OK with this case?"

He bristled. "Look, I know the sarge isn't here and I'm the only detective apart from the boss, but—"

"That's not what I meant. I heard that Laurence Smith was a bit of a dick to you yesterday."

"I think Laurence Smith is a dick to everyone."

"But you, more than the boss..."

Mike's skin tingled. "I can handle people like him. You think I haven't been doing that all my life?"

She leaned in. "I just thought that with this murder being

racially motivated and a potential suspect being like that with you..."

"What do you mean, 'like that'?"

She flushed. "I'm sorry, Mike. I don't know what the right thing is to say."

"He wasn't 'like that'. He's a racist, T. He called me a monkey."

Her eyes widened. "He didn't?"

"He did."

"I didn't hear about that."

No, Mike thought. The DCI had clearly kept that to herself, and he certainly had.

He waved a hand, gesturing for her to go back to her work.

"I'm fine, Tina. It's a case, I'm a detective. If I let every racist idiot get to me, I wouldn't have lasted five minutes as a copper. Surely you get the sexist dinosaurs?"

She laughed, her expression uneasy. "That's different."

"Maybe, maybe not," he said. "And I'm not so sure this crime is racially motivated anyway."

Tina looked back at him. "What, even after what you had to put up with yesterday?"

"What I had put up with was nothing compared to having your throat slit and being dragged onto Swanage Globe. That guy had moved here from London, he was building houses that grockles are going to buy. Has it occurred to you that *go home* might be nothing to do with the fact that he was Black?"

"But..."

"But nothing, T. It might just have been because he was an outsider."

CHAPTER TWENTY-EIGHT

LESLEY HAD PICKED up a note on her voicemail on her way into work. A summons to Superintendent Carpenter's office.

She knocked on the door, straightening her jacket. She felt underdressed, not wearing a skirt suit like those she'd put on every working morning for eighteen years in West Midlands CID. But people around here weren't as smartly dressed as in the West Midlands. There were certain practical requirements that came with being a copper in Dorset.

"Come in," came Carpenter's voice. Lesley entered.

"DCI Clarke," he said. "Take a seat."

He was behind his desk, gesturing for her to take one of the hard chairs opposite. Not the sofa today.

"So how's the Watson case coming along?" he asked.

"We're getting there," she replied. "We've got two possible angles."

"Which are?"

"Firstly, the potential racial motivation. Laurence Smith."

"I already spoke to you about him. Tread carefully there, won't you, Lesley?"

She stared back at the superintendent. "I'll tread as carefully as I need to, sir."

"Good. Is Dr McBride here yet?"

"She's on a flight from Edinburgh, arriving later today. PC Abbott will be collecting her."

"Get her up to speed as soon as she arrives. What's your other angle?"

The Horizon development at Peveril Point. People aren't happy about it, I gather."

"No," he said. "They seem to forget that without the tourist trade, none of them would have jobs. But I've heard there was a note?"

"Yes, sir," she said. "*Go home.*"

"Which ties in with the racism angle."

"Exactly."

"Post-mortem been done yet?"

"Later this morning. I'm sending Mike along."

"And how's he coping with it all? Racially motivated and all that."

"He's professional, sir," Lesley replied. "I imagine he's dealt with plenty of racists in his time on the force."

"Mmm," said Carpenter. "This isn't Birmingham, remember."

Lesley imagined that racism was just as common down here, maybe more so.

"Anyway." Carpenter picked up a mug of coffee and took a slurp. He hadn't offered her one.

"That other matter that we spoke about a while ago," he said. "The delicate one."

"DCI Mackie?"

He frowned. "You know what I'm talking about. Am I right in thinking that the press is sniffing around?"

"They have nothing *concrete*, sir."

He raised a finger. "Forgive me if I'm wrong, DCI Clarke, but there is nothing concrete for them to have here. DCI Mackie committed suicide."

"That's what the coroner said, sir."

Both of them knew that was in doubt. Carpenter had as much as admitted it to her months ago. He'd been silent on the subject ever since.

"If there's any news on that score," he said, "you'll tell me, won't you?"

"Of course, sir."

"Good. Now go back to your team, I imagine they need your guidance."

CHAPTER TWENTY-NINE

MIKE STOPPED to compose himself before entering the morgue. His pulse was still racing, his body thrumming.

Tina had meant well, but he was fed up with people assuming that any investigation with potential racial undertones would affect him more than anybody else on the team.

Why shouldn't they *all* be angry that some racist bastard wanted to kill a Black man and dump him on Swanage Globe? Why was he the only one who was supposed to feel revulsion by it?

He clenched his fists at his sides, opening and closing them a few times, and licked his lips. He knew that people looked at him funny, a mixed-race police detective. Maybe that was common where the DCI came from, but here...

He had mates who said he should transfer to a more cosmopolitan force. Maybe the Met, like Johnny. But Mike was Dorset born and bred. His family lived here, and what few mates he had. He didn't want to move. Why should he have to move just because people were small-minded and patronising?

He shook himself out. Tina wasn't small-minded. Patronising maybe, but she thought she was doing the right thing. He should have a word with her sometime. Take her for a drink, put her straight. He allowed himself a smile. Tina was cute, and she'd never mentioned a boyfriend. This might be an excuse to get to know her better.

The door in front of him opened and a white-suited technician came out. She gave him a funny look.

"Can I help you?"

Mike brought himself back to the present. "DC Legg. I'm here to observe a PM, Paul Watson."

The woman nodded. "He's already started, go on through."

Mike cleared his throat and pushed open the doors to the morgue. He'd done this a few times in uniform, and once in local CID. Unlike Johnny, he wasn't easily nauseated. He'd learned to see a body as a data source, not as a human being.

But people were assuming that he would be more concerned with Paul Watson's humanity than others were.

Stop it. Focus.

The pathologist was playing loud classical music. It thundered from a speaker on the other side of the room, distorting as it echoed around the tiled walls.

Mike grimaced and stepped forward.

"Dr Whittaker, I'm told you've started."

Whittaker looked up. He'd already opened up Paul Watson's body and was examining his guts.

Mike approached the table. He checked for signs of queasiness: none.

"So she sent you, this time?" Whittaker asked. "She doesn't like doing post-mortems herself, does she?"

"DCI Clarke is busy running the case."

"If you say so. I've already examined him externally. Now I'm looking for internal injuries."

"You expect to find them?"

"Not necessarily."

"What about his external injuries? Anything we didn't identify at the scene?"

Whittaker pointed at the man's neck.

"You've already seen the throat injury. If they'd gone much further, they'd have decapitated him."

Mike frowned. "Definitely the cause of death, then?"

"Without a doubt," said Whittaker. "There was significant bleeding. He lost about four pints. But he didn't lose them on the Globe, you know that already."

"We do," said Mike. "We've got Uniform on alert for where he was killed."

"Your killer will have struggled to cover it up. Nobody can clean up that amount of blood and not leave something behind."

Mike nodded. That was the CSI team's job.

"Anything else apart from the throat wound?" he asked.

"Good question." Whittaker lifted Paul Watson's right hand. There were burn marks on his wrist.

"Rope marks," he said. "Just as I expected. If you look closely, you can see an impression from the rope itself."

Mike leaned over. Sure enough, there was a distinct mark. "That might help us identify the brand of rope."

"So it might."

"You've taken photos?"

Whittaker smiled. "Of course I've taken damn photos. What do you think I am?"

"I'd be grateful if you could send them to Gail Handsford."

Whittaker raised an eyebrow. "Surely that's your job?"

Mike frowned.

Whittaker laughed. "Yes, of course I'll send them to the crime scene manager. There'll be a detailed report when I've finished. It'll go to your boss and to Gail. Happy?"

"Happy." Mike plunged his hands into his pockets.

"So," said Whittaker. "Both wrists have significant chafing from the ropes. There's some on his ankles, but not as severe. So I imagine they used the ropes on his ankles for guidance, but on his wrists for haulage. They somehow got him semi-upright next to the Globe, and then dragged him up."

"Any bruising consistent with finger-marks?" Mike asked.

"Nothing that I found. But then, he was wearing a heavy jacket. That sort of mark might not have left bruises, particularly as there wasn't a lot of blood left in his body." Whittaker looked at Mike. "His skin would have been darker. Now, after losing all that blood, he's the same colour as you. If you don't mind me saying."

Mike felt his jaw clench.

It's just a comparison, he told himself.

Whittaker was a medic. He looked at skin differently.

Don't kid yourself.

Whittaker bent over the body. "I haven't found anything internally yet, no sign of him having swallowed anything. There will be a toxicology report, we'll take samples, let you know if he was poisoned."

"Do you think he might have been?"

"No reason to think anything, son," said Whittaker. "But we have to be thorough."

Son. Mike's fists clenched inside his pockets.

He reminded himself that Whittaker was like this with everybody, even the DCI. The man was an equal opportunities patronising bastard, after all.

So why did Mike feel so uneasy standing next to him?

CHAPTER THIRTY

Tina knew she'd done something wrong, but she wasn't quite sure what. Mike had stormed out of the office, heading for the post-mortem like he had a swarm of bees under his hat. If he'd been wearing a hat.

She peered into her computer screen, their conversation revolving in her mind. She'd been worried about him, concerned that he might feel singled out because of his race and the nature of the case. But his reaction... it was like he was pissed off with her more than he was with the racists.

There wasn't time to worry about Mike's fragility. She was researching the Horizon development, the project Paul Watson had been overseeing. She had background on the protests: a bunch of newspaper clippings, quotes from Laurence Smith. She shuddered at the thought of him. The things he'd said to the press about Paul Watson had been just on the right side of publishable, but just on the wrong side of acceptable for anyone who knew what to look for.

The development firm was called Sunrise Holdings. It was a bland name, one that didn't seem to be associated with any other developments or businesses, either locally or elsewhere.

She opened up the firm's Companies House record. If Sunrise Holdings was legitimate, its records and its accounts would be accessible here, as well as the list of company directors. She didn't expect Paul Watson to be one of them. He was an architect, an external hire. But if she could find out who was in charge of the development, she might be able to get more information on the protest. She wanted to know if there were any other reasons for Laurence Smith not wanting Horizon built.

She clicked through to the list of directors. Her mouth fell open.

"Shit," she whispered.

She stared at the screen. "Not you again."

She grabbed her phone. The boss would want to know about this.

CHAPTER THIRTY-ONE

LESLEY'S PHONE rang as she pushed open the door to the team room. Tina was inside, alone in the open plan space. The PC was on the phone.

As Tina spotted Lesley, she put her phone down and Lesley's own phone stopped ringing.

"Was that you calling me?" Lesley asked.

"Yes, boss. I've just got some information about the Horizon development."

"Good," Lesley said. "Where's Mike?"

"At the post-mortem."

The door opened behind Lesley.

"Wrong," Mike said. "I'm back."

Tina shuffled between her feet, not meeting Mike's eye.

"Excellent," Lesley said, ignoring the awkwardness. "Into my office, everyone."

She strode into her office, aware of how inappropriate 'everyone' sounded when there were only three of them here. Dennis hadn't turned up, despite their conversation yesterday. He told her he'd be back, and it wasn't like him to lie.

She perched on the edge of her desk. The board was filling up. Tina had added crime scene photos, a photograph of Paul Watson, another of Laurence Smith, and some newspaper cuttings: protests about the development.

"Do we really think this is about the development?" Lesley asked.

"It could be," said Tina. "I've been doing some digging and—"

Lesley raised a finger to stop her. She walked over to the board.

"This Laurence Smith. I want to find out more about him. Organisations he's involved with, whether he's threatened anybody in the past, and I also want to know if he's connected to these two."

She held up her phone: the photo of the two men who'd been at the development yesterday.

"Who are they?" asked Mike.

"Two bozos who were watching me when I went to the Horizon development."

Tina nodded. "Send it to me, boss. I'll get a printout."

"Thanks." Lesley hit send and heard Tina's phone ping.

"Find out if they're connected to Smith," she said. "If they're part of the protest, or any of the groups he's involved in."

"Will do, boss."

"How did the post-mortem go?" Lesley asked.

"As expected," said Mike. "The throat injury was deeper than we thought, it's been confirmed as cause of death. There were rope marks on his wrists and ankles. Whittaker reckons he was dragged up by the wrists. It's difficult to tell how many people were involved, but I think it would be difficult to do on your own."

"Two or more of them," said Lesley, thinking of the two men from yesterday.

"What about background on the architectural firm?" she asked Tina. "What have you found out about Paul's move down here?"

"He moved three months ago," Tina said. "His firm is Watson and Phipps, the other partner is Bella Phipps. She works at the office in London, which is where Paul was based until he moved down here. He and his wife have still got a house there, in Putney."

"Alright for some," said Lesley.

"They've been trying to sell it for six months," Tina said. "Initial sale fell through and then they moved down here anyway."

"OK," said Lesley. "So he could be in debt, find out more about that. If any of the money he might have borrowed to move down here was from sources other than a bank or building society."

"Yes, boss," replied Tina. "And then there's a holding company for the development itself."

"Go on." Lesley eyed the board, her eye travelling over the crime scene photos. What they'd done to Paul was brutal. And that *go home* message, what did it mean?

"It's called Sunrise Holdings," said Tina. "I had a look on Companies House, got a list of the directors."

"And?" said Lesley. "You're telling me Paul was one of the directors?"

"No," said Tina. "It's somebody we've come across before."

Lesley turned to her. "Who?"

"Arthur Kelvin, boss."

CHAPTER THIRTY-TWO

LESLEY THUMPED THE DESK. "Bloody hell, that man gets everywhere. Do you not *have* any other serious criminals down here?"

Tina shrank back. "Sorry, boss."

"It's not your fault."

Lesley dragged a fist through her hair. "I'm going to have to knock on his door, aren't I? Shit."

Either that or she'd need to talk to his lawyer. Elsa Short, her girlfriend.

Why did Arthur Kelvin manage to get involved in everything Lesley did down here? OK, so Dorset didn't have a lot of organised crime, but surely there might be someone else behind the occasional murder?

She thumped her hand on the desk again, her palm open. It stung.

"Right," she said. "Who are the other directors?"

Tina gave her a list of names, none of which meant anything to her.

"You recognise any of those?" she asked the two constables.

"Sorry, boss," said Mike.

Tina shook her head.

Lesley caught movement outside her glass-walled office. She looked up. The outer door to the main office had opened. A man walked in.

She tensed. "Dennis!"

He looked through the glass, the colour draining from his face.

Lesley beckoned him in, the gesture exaggerated.

Dennis opened the door. He pulled his shoulders back and looked her in the eye.

"Boss," he said. "I'm back."

"Glad to hear it," she told him. Mike and Tina exchanged uneasy glances.

"I haven't got time to bring you up to speed fully," Lesley said. "So here's the quick version. We found a body at Swanage Globe, name's Paul Watson, architect, moved down from London three months ago. He was working on a development, which as it turns out, is partly owned by Arthur Kelvin."

Dennis pursed his lips. "What?"

"Yes," Lesley replied.

She gave him a meaningful look. Neither Mike nor Tina knew about Johnny's relationship with Kelvin, nor the fact that Dennis had covered it up.

They would deal with that later.

"A note was tucked into his jacket," she told Dennis. "It said *go home*. It could have been related to the fact that the victim was Black, it could have been because he was an outsider. There've been protests against the development. Spearheaded by a man called Laurence Smith."

"I know him," Dennis said.

"Personally?" Lesley asked. That was *all* she needed.

Dennis shook his head. "I met him once at a community event, police and local politicians."

"He's a councillor," said Tina. "Swanage Town Council."

Lesley nodded. "He's a petty racist with his own personal fiefdom, but does that mean he's a murderer? Or do we need to be looking at the organised crime angle?"

"It could be something completely different," said Mike.

"Like what?" Lesley turned to him.

"His wife, maybe? His firm in London? We need to find out if there were any problems there. And don't forget that he could have been in debt, two houses and all that."

Lesley grunted. "Fair enough." She looked at Dennis. He gave her a tentative smile.

"I want somebody to go knocking on Bella Phipps's door," she said. "Where in London is she?"

"Putney," replied Tina.

Lesley frowned. "Where is it Johnny's based these days?" she asked Dennis.

"Wandsworth," he replied.

"How far is that from Putney?"

"No distance," said Mike. "He probably covers Putney."

"Good," she said. "Dennis, get in touch with Johnny. Ask him to go and speak to her."

"That's a bit irregular, surely we should—"

"I know what we should be doing," said Lesley. It was normal to involve another force when interviewing a witness outside the county. It wasn't normal to pick an individual detective.

"Johnny owes me one," she continued, ignoring Dennis's cough. "Just call him. I'll make sure his commanding officer is in the loop."

"Of course." Dennis looked down at the carpet.

"Right," said Lesley. "So we've got Johnny talking to Bella Phipps. Then there's Kelvin. I'll decide whether we need to have a conversation with him."

She gave Dennis a pointed look.

"We've still got Laurence Smith," she continued. "And we've got those two bastards from yesterday."

Dennis paled. "Which... people?"

Lesley wasn't about to apologise for swearing in front of him, not when she still didn't know why he'd taken almost six days off sick.

"I went to the Horizon development last night, there were two men watching me. I want to know who they are, and if they've got any connection to Paul Watson."

"I can follow that one up," said Tina.

"Good. In that case, Mike, can you go and talk to Sherry again?"

"Paul Watson's wife?" Mike asked.

"I want to find out about their finances. See what she can tell you about those two houses, and whether there were any tensions within the firm, or elsewhere."

"Right, boss." Mike glanced at Dennis, who nodded.

Lesley realised her fist was still clenched on the desk. She lifted it and shook it out. The muscles would be sore.

"You also need to know we're going to have an extra member of the team for this one. Temporarily."

"A replacement for Johnny?" Dennis asked.

Lesley looked at him. It would almost be worth bringing in a criminal profiler, to see Dennis's reaction.

"A psychologist. The super hired her, and I've worked with her before. She'll help us ascertain if this is racially motivated, and if it fits with a pattern."

"A psychologist, boss?" Dennis asked.

"Like I say, Carpenter's idea." She checked her watch. "She'll be here in a couple of hours, Bournemouth Airport. Tina, can you pick her up?"

"Yes, boss."

"Good." Lesley surveyed her team. "OK, everybody. Get to work."

CHAPTER THIRTY-THREE

LESLEY DRUMMED her fingers on her desk as the phone rang out. When it was answered, she forced herself to relax.

"Hi, sweetie," said Elsa. "What's up?"

"It's a work question," Lesley replied.

"OK. No pleasantries then?"

"Sorry. How's your day going so far?"

"Fine. How about you?"

"It's certainly been eventful."

"Your murder case?"

"That's what I'm calling you about."

"You've arrested somebody and you're about to send a client my way?"

"Nothing as tidy as that, I'm afraid," Lesley said.

She moved her hand from the desk to her knee, fingernails digging into her skin. She hated mixing the personal with the professional. But she'd known this would be a risk when she'd started dating a criminal lawyer.

"Paul Watson was working on the Horizon development," she said. "Peveril Point."

"I know the one," replied Elsa. "Controversial, I don't know why. It's not as if plenty of developments haven't been thrown up in Swanage in the last few years."

Lesley stretched her hand out in front of her. "So this one's been more difficult than others?"

"It's the only one with a strategic campaign against it. Billboards on the roadside, letters to the local papers. I know they've been petitioning the MP, I gather he's trying to steer clear of it."

"It's spearheaded by the local councillor," Lesley said.

"Laurence Smith. Nasty piece of work."

"That's the impression I got."

"You want to know if I've had any dealings with him?" Elsa asked.

"It's not about him," Lesley said. "It's another of your clients."

"Go on."

"The Horizon development is owned by Sunrise Holdings."

"OK." Elsa sounded wary.

"One of the directors is Arthur Kelvin."

"I don't see how that's got anything to do with me," Elsa replied. "I'm not a corporate lawyer."

Lesley sighed. She craned her neck back and looked up at the ceiling.

"I don't suppose you know anything about this company?"

"No," Elsa said. "I couldn't tell you anything specific. Besides..."

"I know," Lesley sighed. "Lawyer client confidentiality."

"Exactly. So why did you call me?"

"I don't know."

Truth was, she did know. She didn't relish the thought of going knocking on Kelvin's door. This was a delaying tactic.

"Sorry to bother you, love," she said. "Forget I called."

"I'll try. See you later?"

"Yeah. Love you."

CHAPTER THIRTY-FOUR

TINA'S COMPUTER pinged as an email came in. She switched from the HOLMES system to email, nudging her tongue against her lips.

"Cool," she muttered.

It was the CCTV. Two files were attached, one from 8pm to 11pm on Tuesday night, and one from 11pm to 2am.

Why hadn't they sent more? The boss had asked for a twenty-four-hour window.

Still, she'd go through these, and then she'd chase them for the rest. If she was lucky, she'd find something here.

She opened up the first video, 8pm to 11pm. She toggled playback onto double speed and sat back.

Three hours at double speed. It would take her an hour and a half. She checked the clock: 4pm.

She shuffled in her chair, trying to get comfortable. Ten minutes later, she was restless. She paused the video, stood, and left her desk.

Five minutes later she returned from the kitchen, a coffee

in one hand and a Twix in the other. She unwrapped the Twix and sipped at the coffee as she started the video again.

She'd have to speed it up more than this. She put it on triple speed: now it would take an hour. Maybe if Mike came back, he could go through the second video. She didn't relish the thought of two hours trawling through this.

Tina stretched her arms above her head and watched the screen, blinking to stop her eyes from glazing over. The camera was positioned on the rear of Durlston Castle, facing towards the Globe. The Globe was in a dip and difficult to make out. She could just see the top of it in the dark.

Every now and then, a security light flicked on. Tina paused the video the first time, squinting to see if anyone walked past. But there was nothing; probably just an animal. She clicked back onto triple speed and swallowed the last of the Twix.

Half an hour later, there'd been no activity. It was coming up to 5pm. She wasn't getting through this as quickly as she'd expected to, what with pausing every time the security light came on.

But this was footage of the crime scene. If they had pictures from the right time window, she could crack the case.

Tina shrugged her shoulders; it was chilly. She grabbed her jacket from the back of her chair. The office was spooky without anybody in it. She tugged her jacket over her shoulders and leaned in to watch.

After forty-five minutes more, she'd reached 11pm and seen nothing. She closed the video and clicked onto the next one.

Maybe she shouldn't have sped it up so much?

She'd watch this one, and if there was nothing there,

she'd get one of her mates from Uniform to help, two of them watching at the same time. They could work at closer to normal speed.

The second video picked up where the last one ended. No movement, nothing changing at all. A couple of minutes in, the security light flicked on. She slowed the video down, then rewound it a few moments.

She'd seen movement.

A figure entered from the left of the screen.

Tina squinted. It was indistinct, too far away to make out. But just one figure.

The figure moved across the screen and disappeared off the right-hand side. Tina felt her shoulders slump. It was just a walker, taking a late-night stroll along the cliff path.

But she thought maybe she'd run the video at double speed instead of triple speed for the next few minutes, in case they came back.

Twenty minutes later they hadn't returned. She sped the video up again, yawning. Almost 6pm by the clock.

She stretched her hands out in front of her and clicked her fingers. What were the others doing? No one had called into the office since the briefing. When she'd joined the Major Crimes team, she'd been excited about investigating murders. It hadn't occurred to her that she'd spend most of her time at her desk, trawling through data, searching through HOLMES and watching CCTV footage.

The security light onscreen came on again. Tina slowed the video. Another figure appeared, this time from the bottom left of the image. The top of their head was below the camera, covered by a hood. Tina swallowed and leaned in further. Another figure appeared behind the first, also hooded.

Damn hoodies. Every investigator's nightmare.

The two hooded figures were in the middle of the screen now. They carried something between them.

A body?

They made their way down the steps towards the Globe, then turned to round the wall.

Tina held her breath.

She slowed the video to regular playback. She was right. The object they were carrying was a body.

She stared into the screen as they moved towards the Globe. They placed the body below it, tucked behind the overhang where Tina couldn't see it. All she could make out was the movement of their heads. Up and down, adjusting something. Working on something.

The security light went off. Tina clenched her fist in her lap, willing it to come back on. She couldn't even see movement in the darkness.

She checked the timestamp on the camera: 12:34am. The sky was inky black, cloudy with no moon.

"Come on," she muttered.

Tina urged a fox to come past, anything that would make that light come on.

"Come on."

The light flicked back on. One of the hoodies looked up and raised an arm, suddenly aware of it.

Tina smiled and zoomed in. The face was blurred and indistinct, but it was a human face. She could give it to Sunil.

She punched her knee, anticipation and relief lifting her chest.

The two hooded figures bent out of sight. Attaching ropes to Paul's arms and legs?

Sure enough, moments later his body reappeared. One of

the hoodies disappeared round the far side of the Globe, hauling something behind them. The ropes.

Paul's body jolted upwards, scraping on the surface of the Globe. He moved slowly, haltingly, stopping every now and then. Either his killers were tired, or he kept catching.

Tina gritted her teeth.

At last, Paul's body stopped moving. He was spreadeagled over the top of the Globe, exactly as they'd found him. Tina put a hand to her chest, her eyes prickling.

The hoodie that had gone around the back of the Globe reappeared. He grabbed his colleague and pulled him away. Tina watched them return up the hill and disappear out of shot.

She picked up her phone.

Voicemail. *Damn.*

"Boss," she breathed. "You're gonna want to see this."

CHAPTER THIRTY-FIVE

LESLEY'S PHONE buzzed as she arrived at the building site. Two alerts: a voicemail from Tina, and a text from Sadie. She opened the text.

I've got more information. We need to meet.

Lesley gritted her teeth and plunged her phone into her pocket. The journalist was bluffing. But she couldn't afford to let Sadie Dawes find out how DCI Mackie had died. Not before *she* did.

But there was a murder investigation to run. And she had to consider the politics.

Three months ago, Carpenter had seemed eager for her to investigate, so long as no one else in the team knew. But now it looked like he was retreating from that position.

Lesley sighed as she climbed out of the car. The gates to the building site were open this morning, and there was activity on site. Hundreds of grey concrete blocks sat in neat piles to one side and on the other was a skip. In between, a makeshift pathway.

She walked in, looking around, trying to spot who was in charge.

"Hey!" called a man in a hard hat and high-vis vest. "You can't come on site without safety gear."

She held her arms up in a shrug. "Well give me some safety gear, then."

He pointed at her.

"You stay right where you are, lady. I'll get you a hat and jacket. Who are you anyway?"

"I'm here to speak to whoever's in charge." She pulled her ID out of her pocket. "DCI Clarke, Dorset Police."

The man took a step back. "Right. I'll get Darren."

"You do that."

She stayed where she was, taking the opportunity to look around the site while she waited.

Ten or so men were at work. Moving bricks, operating machinery, taking sidelong glances at her when they thought she wasn't looking.

After a few moments a man appeared around the wall. He was short with a round face and a grubby yellow high-vis jacket. He wore a white hard hat and a disgruntled expression.

"If this is about that permit from last week," he said, "we've already sorted it with—"

She raised her hand. "I'm from the Major Crime Investigations team. This has nothing to do with any permit."

He stopped in his tracks. "Major Crimes?" He turned, scanning the site. "Has something happened here?"

Lesley stepped forward. The man was facing away from her.

"Oi! Suggsy!" he called to the man who'd told her to wear

safety gear. "Did something happen here last night that I don't know about?"

Suggsy shrugged.

Lesley took a few steps forward. "Are you in charge?"

He turned to her.

"Darren Mathieson's the name. So what's happened?"

"Do you know Paul Watson, the architect on this development?"

He paled. "Is that what this is about?"

"You weren't expecting a visit from us?"

He shrugged. "I don't see why we would. He's – was – hardly ever here. I've only seen him a couple of times."

"But you knew his name as soon as I mentioned it."

"Of course I did. He's the lead architect, I'm the lead contractor. I've exchanged emails with the guy non-stop for the last six months. Not sure who's going to sign off on the rest of the work, not that—"

"So you don't know him well?"

Mathieson shook his head. "Sorry detective, he's not my cup of tea."

"In what way isn't he your *cup of tea*?"

"Posh. London. Incomer. Normally we use Jephsons, in Poole. Good firm of architects. Local."

"So you've worked on other developments locally?"

"Of course I have."

"Is there somewhere we can talk?" she asked. "An office?"

"Follow me."

He led her to a portacabin on the opposite side of the development from the fence she'd walked along the night before.

As they walked, she scanned the faces of the men they passed. Maybe those two she'd seen last night would be here.

But there was no sign of them.

Mathieson held open the door to his cabin. "After you."

She passed through. The portacabin was small but warm, an electric heater blasting in the corner. Lesley took a seat next to a scratched desk. Mathieson sat opposite her and rocked in his chair. The chairs were flimsy and plastic, the room echoey. Still, she thought, it was better than being out there in the cold.

"So most of your contact with Paul Watson was by email?" she asked.

"Yep," he replied, still rocking. "Like I say, I met him twice. There was the initial scoping meeting and then there was a review with the building inspectors a couple of weeks ago."

"And those are the only times he's been on site?"

"The only times he's been on site when I've been here. This isn't the only site I run."

"So you work for Sunrise Holdings?"

"We're contractors. Swanage Building Services."

"And where do you sit in the pecking order?"

"I'm the manager of Swanage Building Services. My client is Sunrise Holdings, my contact is one of their directors."

"Which director?"

"Amanda Bennett," he said. "She lives in Poole."

He stared at her, his eyes hard.

"Is there anyone else who would have seen Paul here?" she asked. "Any of your team?"

He shook his head. "He didn't mix with us lot, too far

beneath him. You'll have to speak to the directors, they're the ones what engaged him."

"I will."

She already had a list of the directors. She'd start with Amanda Bennett. Maybe Kelvin being a director was just a coincidence.

She pulled out her phone and brought up the photo of the two men from the previous day.

"Do these two men work here?" she asked.

Mathieson leaned in, squinting. "Difficult to tell. It's a bit grainy, isn't it?"

"It was taken from a distance," she said. "They were here yesterday, early evening, hanging around. I just wondered if maybe they'd come off shift."

He shook his head. "Difficult to tell, sorry. They don't jump out at me, though. Why? They your suspects?"

"I just wanted to know if you recognised them." Lesley pocketed her phone. "Were you aware of any tensions, higher up in the organisation? Any problems between the architects and the holding company?"

"That's above my pay grade," he said. "Wouldn't have a clue. Like I say, you'll have to speak to the directors."

"Can you give me Amanda Bennett's address?"

He hesitated, then bent to search through a desk drawer. He brought out a pad of Post-it notes. He scribbled an address on one, tore it off and stuck it onto the desk in front of her.

"That's their office," he said. "Not that you'll find any of them there, they've all got other jobs. Silent partners, lazy bastards most of them. But try there, maybe you'll get one of the secretaries."

"Thanks." She pocketed the note and stood up. "If you do remember anything," she said, "you'll tell me, won't you?"

She placed her business card on the desk in the spot vacated by the Post-it note. Mathieson looked at it but didn't pick it up.

"Nothing to remember," he said. "Like I said, Paul Watson was hardly ever here. You're not gonna find anything here."

CHAPTER THIRTY-SIX

Sherry Watson was in the living room of her house when Mike arrived. PC Hughes ushered him in, offering him a coffee. Mike nodded. It always helped to have something to do with his hands.

Sherry sat on a wide leather sofa, staring out of the window. It was raining, the garden blurred by drops on the glass.

Mike perched on the edge of an armchair.

Every room in this house was tasteful and expensive. He wondered what the Horizon development would look like when it was finished. Whether Paul's vision for it would be realised, or somebody else would take over.

"Sorry to bother you again," he said. "We've got a few more things we need to ask you about."

She turned, her head jerking. She hadn't been aware of him entering.

"Who are you?" she croaked.

"DC Legg," he told her. "Mike."

She frowned. "Have I met you before?"

"I was with the DCI yesterday morning."

"Oh." She gazed at him, her eyes glazed. "Sorry, I don't remember you."

"It's OK." He smiled at her. "I don't expect you to."

She nodded. "So why is your boss not here?"

"She's busy chasing leads."

"I suppose that's a good thing. Anything concrete?"

"We've got a few leads we're working on. I'm hoping you can answer some questions that'll help us with some of them."

She shifted, turning her knees towards him. "OK."

Mike looked up as PC Hughes entered with two mugs of coffee. He placed one in front of Sherry, who nodded thanks. He placed the other in front of Mike, on a coaster sitting on the surface of a smooth walnut coffee table. Mike had no idea how much a coffee table like this would cost, but he imagined you wouldn't want to get coffee rings on it.

"Are you alone?" he asked Sherry. "I mean, apart from PC Hughes."

"Don't mind me," PC Hughes muttered as he left the room.

Mike glanced after him then looked back at Sherry.

She shook her head. "The girls are in their rooms. They don't want to talk to me."

"Sorry to hear that."

She frowned. "Kids. Let's not talk about that. What is it you need to know?"

Mike pulled his notepad from his inside pocket. He flipped it open.

"Am I right in thinking you still own a house in Putney?"

"We couldn't sell it. The market in London isn't as buoyant as it used to be."

"So you had to borrow to move here?"

"Paul did."

"Can I ask you where he borrowed the money from? I don't mean to be rude, but if your house in Putney is as nice as this..."

She smiled. "Nicer," she said. "Three times the value."

Mike swallowed. He had no idea how much that meant. Millions?

"You said that Paul borrowed the money."

She nodded.

"Where did he borrow it from? A mortgage?"

"He did it through the business. They often take out loans to fund developments. They invest in property, do it up, sell it on. It was easy enough to put this house through the same process."

Mike nodded.

"Was it normal for Paul to do that for his own personal property?"

She shrugged. "He told me it was all above board."

"You're an estate agent, yes?"

She nodded. "You think I should have doubted him."

"I imagine you know a fair bit about this kind of thing."

"I do the selling. I don't deal with conveyancing. Paul knew more about that than me, or at least..."

"At least what?"

Sherry looked out the window. "His partner, Bella Phipps, she's the one who usually deals with that kind of stuff."

"We'll be speaking to her," Mike said.

She turned to him. "You will?"

"We want to find out if there were any business contacts who might have wanted to hurt your husband."

Her face tightened.

"Of course, you speak to Bella. She won't tell you anything."

"No?"

Sherry shook her head.

"Did Paul and Bella get along?" Mike asked.

Sherry snorted. "They got along famously."

Mike noted down her words in his pad.

"I know this is delicate," he said. "But did your husband and Bella have a personal relationship?"

"I don't think that's any of your business, do you?" she replied. "You can talk to her, she'll tell you what you need to know."

"We will," he said.

She stood up. "I'm sorry I can't help you more."

Mike shoved his notepad back in his pocket. She was hiding something from him, but what?

"I need to spend time with my girls now," she said, one arm out to usher him from the room. "I'm sure you understand."

"Yes."

He followed her gesture and left the room.

CHAPTER THIRTY-SEVEN

LESLEY SLID BACK into her car, feeling dirty. There was something about Darren Mathieson that had made her flesh crawl. He was helpful enough, but a little aggressive, and she found it difficult to believe that he'd only had two face-to-face meetings with the architect who'd designed the building he was constructing.

She sighed. She'd have to speak to his employers and do some digging.

Her phone buzzed, another voicemail from Tina. Damn, she hadn't called the PC back.

She dialled the office.

"Major Crime Investigations Team, PC Abbott speaking."

"Tina. Sorry I didn't return your call, what's up?"

"It's the CCTV," Tina replied.

"From the crime scene?"

"We've got two men dragging Paul Watson up onto the Globe at 12:34am."

"Captured on camera?" Lesley felt her skin prickle.

"The whole thing. They come into shot, they're carrying him, they drag him onto the Globe."

"Using ropes?" Lesley asked.

"Looks like it, boss."

"Good. Can you see their faces?"

"The security light comes on from time to time. I couldn't make out their faces on my computer, but I'm sure if I give them to Sunil in the CSI team..."

"You do that," said Lesley. "Send it over there right now. Two men, you say?"

"Yes."

"You're sure they're men?"

"From the build of them and the size, I think so."

"OK," Lesley said. "Good work. Call me if you get anything from CSI, won't you?"

"Yes, boss."

Lesley hung up. She allowed herself a fist bump against the steering wheel. At last they were getting somewhere.

Maybe now they were making progress on this case she could spare a moment to focus on the other matter that had been intruding on her thoughts.

She dialled Zoe.

"Morning, Lesley," Zoe said.

Lesley smiled. At last Zoe had stopped calling her 'boss'. It had been months since Lesley had actually been her boss, but the habit had died hard.

"Morning, Zoe," she replied, "I've got an update for you."

"OK."

"That journalist I told you about, Sadie Dawes."

"I've been watching some of her clips on TV. She's a bit of a Rottweiler, isn't she?"

"You could say that." Lesley didn't mention that Zoe

herself sometimes displayed Rottweilerish tendencies. "She reckons she knows more about DCI Mackie's death than we do."

"How?"

"She's not saying, but it's got me worried. Can you spare any more time to dig into this?"

"I was going to call you about this," Zoe said. "I've got good news."

"You found something?"

"Sorry, no, but I've got some leave due. Frank's told me I have to take it."

DCI Frank Dawson was Lesley's replacement. He'd been a DI reporting to her, and in theory he was acting up temporarily. But the longer she stayed here, the harder she found it to imagine going back.

"When are you coming down?"

"Tomorrow," Zoe said.

Lesley put a hand on the steering wheel. "That's quick."

"We don't move slowly up here," Zoe laughed. "Am I going to have to get used to a different pace of life?"

"Don't be so sure. We had another murder the day before yesterday, and I'm already working on four leads. Including Arthur Kelvin."

"He gets everywhere, doesn't he?" Zoe said.

"He certainly does."

"I'll call you when I'm on my way down. Do you think there might be a link between your new case and Mackie's death?"

"There's no sign of that."

"With Arthur Kelvin involved in both..."

Zoe had a point. But surely the man couldn't be linked to every case she took on.

Kelvin was at the periphery of too many investigations. Was it a coincidence, or not?

CHAPTER THIRTY-EIGHT

SHERRY WALKED through to the dining room at the front of the house. The curtains were drawn, as were all the windows facing the street.

She tweaked the curtain to one side to watch the detective walk back to his car. He glanced back and she pulled away from the window.

Why was he asking about the loan for the house? It was just money. Paul borrowed money for houses all the time.

When he'd started the practice with Bella, most of their work had been flipping houses. They'd started by investing in something small, doing it up, making a little money, moving onto something bigger. And so it went. After a year, they had two properties going at the same time, and then more and more. They'd hired subcontractors, expanded the business, and then taken on some more prestigious projects, including the Horizon development.

It had been the biggest project Paul had worked on, something for which he hoped to receive awards. They were using cutting edge technology, cantilevering the building out over the cliffs so that the apartments would feel as if they were floating. And so the building could be tucked into the cliffside and invisible from the town.

She didn't see how the finances for their house could have any bearing on Paul's death. Surely it was something to do with the protests against the development. There were people here, people like that Laurence Smith, who hated Paul. He stood for something modern and progressive. And, of course, he was Black.

The detective's car pulled away from the drive and Sherry let the curtain drop.

He'd be phoning Bella, or one of his colleagues would have phoned her already.

What would she say? How much would she tell them? Sherry didn't want to drag up the past.

She thought she'd escaped Bella by moving down here. Paul was still working with her, but they no longer had social contact, and Paul only saw her for the occasional meeting. He always went to London; she was too grand to travel down here.

Sherry leaned against the table, clutching the edge of the wood. Her body felt heavy. She needed to get through to her daughters, to help them through this. They couldn't do this alone, and neither could she.

Taking a deep breath, she walked through to the hallway. She paused and then hauled herself up the stairs, determined not to let her daughters reject her this time.

CHAPTER THIRTY-NINE

DENNIS AND TINA were in the office when Lesley returned.

Tina looked up from her screen.

"Boss," she said. "Do you want to watch the CCTV?"

Lesley waved in dismissal.

"In a moment, I need to talk to DS Frampton first."

Dennis stiffened in his chair. It had been months since she'd referred to him by his title.

"You want me in your office, boss?" he asked.

"Please."

She strode through and waited for him to follow. He closed the door and leaned against it.

"Sit down," she said.

"I'd rather not."

She rounded the desk and sat in her own chair.

"I said sit down, Dennis. We're not doing this standing up."

He walked to the chair, his eyes not leaving her face.

"You're angry with me, boss?" he said.

Lesley looked up at the ceiling and drew in a shaky

breath. Yes, she was angry. She was confused, she was puzzled. But Dennis had just returned from sickness, and she had to do this properly.

She looked at him.

"This is your return to work interview, Dennis. There are some questions I need to go through with you."

He looked surprised.

"You're doing a formal return to work interview?"

"I am. Got a problem with it?"

"No, boss."

"Good. Hang on a minute."

She opened up her laptop and scrolled through to the section of the HR handbook that told her how to do this.

Lesley might have been happy sticking to procedure when investigating crimes, but she wasn't really known for it when dealing with her team. She tended to trust her instinct, and liked working with people in a way that suited them and her, rather than following a list of instructions from up above. But she had a feeling that if she didn't do this properly, it could come back to bite her.

"So," she began, looking at the document on screen. "The first thing I need to do is ask you how you are?"

"I'm fine, boss." He clasped his hands in his lap. "I wouldn't be back if I wasn't."

She turned to him. "What was the reason you gave for your sickness?"

"Flu," he replied. "It was flu, boss."

"You had the flu?"

"I did, boss. Made me feel really rough. I didn't want to come in and pass it to the rest of the team."

"How many times over the course of your career have you had the flu, Dennis?"

He pouted. "Three or four?"

"And did you always take time off?"

He opened his mouth to speak, and then paused.

"Once," he said.

"When was that?"

"1998, I was in CID. My sergeant told me I needed to take a day off because he was worried I'd collapse on the job."

"So you've had the flu a few times, but you've only taken one day off over the course of your career."

"There have been other times I've taken days off," he said.

"You fractured a bone three months ago," she told him. "While you were apprehending a suspect. You didn't take any sick leave then. I tried to talk you into it but you insisted you were going to be OK. But the flu means you have to take time off?"

"Like I said, boss, I didn't want to pass it on to the rest of the team."

She leaned across the desk. "Is there something you're not telling me, Dennis?"

His gaze went to the computer. "Is this one of the official questions?"

She raised her eyebrows.

"No, Dennis. It isn't, but this is you and me here. I know we got off to a bad start when I came down here, but I've grown to trust you. You're a good detective, a reliable second in command. It's not like you to go off sick with something like the flu."

He looked down at his hands, which were clasped tightly in his lap.

"Sorry, boss. Won't happen again."

"Did you get a doctor's note?" she asked him.

He looked up. "I was only off for five days, you don't need a doctor's note until a week."

"Really, Dennis?" she said. "You're going to throw regulations back at me?"

"I thought we were doing this by the book?" he replied, his jaw tight.

Lesley stared back at him.

"If you change your mind, Dennis, and you decide you want to tell me what's really going on, I want you to know that my door is always open."

"There's nothing going on."

She shrugged. "I won't give you a bollocking, and I won't tell the super. I just need you to be straight with me."

He looked back at her, his gaze level.

"I am being straight with you. I had the flu, I'm fine now, I'm back. I want to get to work."

"I'm sure you do. Laurence Smith," she said. "Keep an eye on him, will you? See what he's up to."

He nodded. "Of course. Am I dismissed?"

Lesley laughed, and forced herself to relax.

"You don't need to wait to be dismissed, Dennis. Let me know if he does anything suspicious."

CHAPTER FORTY

MIKE PARKED his car on Shore Road, looking over Swanage beach. He liked it here, especially out of season. The parking spaces were separated from the sand by just a narrow pavement and at this time of year, the sea felt that much closer.

He lowered his window and breathed in the sea air. His mates who told him he should move to a city force had no idea how beautiful Dorset could be. He got to spend his working life driving around the county that he'd loved since he was a child. How could he leave this place? He'd take as much insularity and small-mindedness as they could throw at him and still love it.

And DCI Clarke was an improvement on DCI Mackie. Mackie had played favourites, Dennis followed by Johnny. Mike had barely been acknowledged. Not that there had been anything he could do about it, or any point dwelling on it. That wouldn't have helped him do his job, and he knew how hard it was to prove that sort of thing.

He opened the car door and got out. About to walk away

from the car, he remembered he'd left the window open. He dived back in and hit the button to close it.

He strolled down to the sand. His shoes would get sandy, but he didn't care. Mike wore practical shoes; it was essential for a detective here.

The wind pummelled him as he walked along the beach, throwing his head back. The air was damp, rain threatening. Clouds were gathering out to sea and seagulls swooped further along the beach. Somebody had dumped some rubbish up there.

Mike smiled. Dumping rubbish wasn't something he approved of, but it kept the birds happy, and they were impressive to watch.

He grabbed his phone and dialled.

"Mike," came the reply. "How's things?"

Mike turned to face out to sea.

"Hi, Johnny," he said. "I'm standing on Swanage beach. There's a storm brewing out to sea and seagulls doing their thing a few paces away. Are you jealous?"

DC Chiles laughed. "I'm at the entrance to a tube station. There's a homeless guy pissing against the wall next to me and two kids giving my colleague some aggro."

"So it's a bit different in London?"

"It certainly is, mate," replied Johnny. "Exhilarating. I'm loving it."

Mike raised an eyebrow. "Really?"

"Who would have thought it? Johnny Chiles, happy in the Big Smoke."

Mike smiled. "I'm pleased for you. I couldn't do it myself, but I'm glad it's going well for you."

"This isn't a social call, is it?" asked Johnny.

"How did you guess?"

"It's five o'clock in the afternoon. And I've seen the news. You've got another murder case, haven't you? Swanage Globe."

Mike turned and continued walking along the beach. Streetlights were coming on along the promenade.

"You're still following the Dorset news? I don't imagine they report it in London."

"You not heard of the internet?" asked Johnny. "It's this wonderful new thing. You can use it to find out what's happening anywhere in the world."

"Yeah, yeah," replied Mike. "You're right, though. It is the Swanage Globe case I wanted to talk to you about."

"Fire away."

Mike reached the seagulls and they scattered. "We've got someone connected to the case, in London. An address in Putney."

"That's just around the corner from me," said Johnny. "You spoken to my bosses?"

"The DCI's doing it."

"You know this isn't the normal procedure?" Johnny said.

"The DCI wanted you."

Silence.

"Johnny?" Mike said. "There a problem?"

"I'll need to check," Johnny replied. "I can't go getting involved in your investigation unless my commanding officer knows about it."

"What's the name of your commanding officer?" Mike said.

"DI Jackson," replied Johnny.

"I'll tell the DCI, she'll give them a call."

"OK," Johnny said. "But I can't do anything till that's happened."

"Since when were you such a stickler for the rules?"

"You try working in the Met, mate. Rules are sacrosanct here. Politicians breathing down our neck. There are some bad apples, means the rest of us have to do our jobs and make sure we don't put a foot wrong."

Mike grimaced. "Like I said, I really don't envy you."

He turned back towards the car, walking along the beach.

"Her name's Bella Phipps," he said. "We need you to talk to her."

"What about?"

"She's the business partner of the victim, Paul Watson. There might be something dodgy going on with his finances. He's got a house in Putney, bought another one down here. His wife says he borrowed money through the business to pay for the second house as they couldn't sell the first one. I want to know where he borrowed the money and whether it was legit."

"You think he was embezzling?"

"You should see this house. It took a lot of money to pay for it."

"It would be five times the price here."

"Again," said Mike. "Not jealous. I'm standing on a beach, you've got some tosser pissing on the wall next to you."

Johnny laughed. "Send me an email, yeah? Make it official. Give me a list of questions, I'll tell you what I can get from your Bella Phipps."

CHAPTER FORTY-ONE

DENNIS YAWNED and checked his watch: 7:45am. He'd been up since six, Pam had been fussing about whether he was well enough to go into work. She worried, more than she needed to.

He'd insisted he was fine. And he was.

The house he was watching was dark, no sign of movement yet. Dennis considered knocking on the door. But surveillance would be more useful with this one.

He leaned back in the seat and stretched his arms above his head, his elbows grazing against the roof. He shuffled in his seat. This car was uncomfortable. Maybe he should think about replacing it.

A light came on in the house's hallway.

Dennis shuffled down, anxious not to be seen. He'd picked a spot away from street lamps and on the opposite side of the road. His car, nondescript and beige, looked just like any other vehicle parked along the road. Luckily, this was a road with plenty of cars parked along it.

The front door opened and a man emerged. He was tall,

elderly, with thinning blond-grey hair, wearing a traditionally cut blue suit. His face was briefly visible in the light of the porch. He turned, checked his front door was locked and walked to his car.

Dennis put his hand on his key, ready in the ignition.

Don't turn it just yet. Don't draw attention to yourself. He watched as Laurence Smith backed his car out of his drive and drove off.

The road was deserted. Dennis didn't need to follow particularly close; he would catch up soon enough.

After a suitable pause, he turned the key and began to follow.

Smith turned left at the end of the road, heading out of Swanage. So he wasn't going to a meeting at the town council, and he wasn't going to the Horizon development.

Dennis settled into the drive, following Smith as he drove along the A351 through Corfe Castle and out the other side. Whatever this trip was, it wasn't local.

They continued, passing Wareham on the bypass and going straight on towards Poole at the Saxon roundabout. Dennis tightened his grip on the steering wheel. He was still tired, recovering from his time off.

He yawned. Somewhere in the glove compartment was a packet of mints. That would wake him up.

He waited until they'd stopped at the roundabout with the A35, then leaned across to grab the packet. He shovelled a couple into his mouth.

Smith was two cars in front. He seemed to have no idea he was being followed. He turned right and Dennis followed, the traffic thickening as they approached Poole.

They continued for a few miles before Smith left the main road, making for Poole Harbour. Dennis kept glancing in his rear-view mirror, the act of following making him suddenly aware of the possibility that he might be followed too.

They reached the harbour and Smith continued along the shore towards Sandbanks. Why had he taken the land route all the way through Wareham, instead of driving to Studland and getting the ferry?

The ferry meant buying a ticket, which, now they'd stopped taking cash, required a credit card. If Smith went that way, there would be a record of his journey.

But surely Laurence Smith would use the Sandbanks Ferry regularly?

Dennis popped another mint into his mouth as Smith pulled his car over. He parked next to the water. Dennis drove past and found a space a few cars ahead.

He waited, resisting the temptation to get out.

He was confident that Smith wouldn't recognise him. They'd met, but that had been eight years ago. Dennis had been a lowly DC, Laurence Smith already a local bigwig.

He shuffled across to the passenger seat and turned to get a better view. Smith had left his car and was waiting for a gap in the traffic. He crossed then walked in Dennis's direction.

Dennis held his breath, waiting for Laurence to turn towards him. But Smith carried on walking. Past Dennis, past the turnoff to the beach, and towards the ferry.

Dennis would have to follow on foot. It was solid double-yellows along there.

He slid back into the driver's seat and got out. Smith had disappeared.

Dennis chewed his lip. He should have moved sooner.

It will be fine. There was hardly anybody around, Dennis would catch up.

He waited for two cars to pass then hurried across the road and turned along Banks Road, in the direction that Smith had gone. He passed the road to the beach and the car park and continued straight on to Banks Road.

No sign of Smith.

Dennis picked up pace, his heart racing. He was sweating.

He rounded the headland, checking side roads as he went. Eventually he found himself back at his car.

Smith's car was empty.

He must have gone into a house.

If so, why park all the way along here?

Dennis looked back towards the headland. He considered driving another circuit, but he might miss Smith returning to his car.

Annoyed with himself, he got into his car and waited.

If Smith had gone into a house along there, whose was it?

Arthur Kelvin had a house on Banks Road. Surely...

Dennis shook his head and settled in to wait.

CHAPTER FORTY-TWO

Amanda Bennett lived in a large, white-rendered house in Branksome Park, between Bournemouth and Poole. Lesley could tell as she climbed the steep driveway up to the front door that the back of this house would boast a spectacular view. She pulled on the lever for the doorbell and waited, ID ready in her hand.

A slim middle-aged woman with dark curly hair and a healthy-looking tan opened the door.

"Can I help you?"

Lesley held up her ID. "Amanda Bennett?"

"That's me. What's wrong?"

"Nothing's wrong," said Lesley. "I just need to ask you some questions about Sunrise Holdings."

The woman frowned. "Why?"

"You'll have heard about the death of Paul Watson in Swanage on Tuesday."

The woman's hand went to a silver chain around her neck. She tugged at it.

"Tragic business. His poor wife. He had two children, didn't he?"

Lesley nodded. "Two girls."

Bennett shook her head. "Doesn't bear thinking about."

"Do you mind if I come in?" Lesley asked.

"Of course. Come through to the lounge."

Lesley followed her into a room that stretched from the front to the back of the house. She'd been right, there was one hell of a view. The house was perched above the cliffs with views across to Boscombe Beach.

"Can I ask what your connection is to Sunrise Holdings?" Lesley asked.

"I'm a non-executive director." Bennett motioned for Lesley to sit down on a grey sofa.

"What does that involve?"

"Not much. I have a significant shareholding in the business. I'm involved in certain key decisions, but I don't have a day-to-day role."

"And who does?"

"Ah, well that's an interesting question," Amanda said. "We just sacked the Chief Executive."

"Why?"

"He was suspected of embezzling money."

"What's his name?" Lesley asked.

"Warwick Harris."

The name meant nothing to Lesley. "Can you give me his contact details, please?"

"Some of it is subject to a legal case. I can tell you what I'm permitted to."

"If he was suspected of embezzling, did you make a complaint to the police?"

Bennett hesitated. "It didn't need to go that far."

"But embezzlement is a crime."

"One moment, please."

The woman stood up and left the room. After a few moments she returned holding a slim handbag. She sat opposite Lesley and rummaged in it. Eventually she brought out a gold-trimmed address book. She placed the handbag on the sofa and leafed through the book.

"Here we are," she said.

She held out the address book.

"This is Warwick's mobile number. It's probably best if you speak to him. I'm not sure where he's living these days, however."

"Where *was* he living?" Lesley asked.

Bennett held out the address book again, pointing to another entry.

"Can I take this?"

"I'd rather you didn't."

Lesley took the book and snapped a couple of photos. "Thanks."

"My pleasure." Bennett put the book back in her handbag.

"I'd like to ask you about the other directors," Lesley said.

"Of course."

Bennett brushed her hands together, as if she was removing flour or dirt from them. "What is it you want to know?"

"Do you have much contact with them?"

"No, it's all done virtually. No physical meetings."

"And do you know who they are?"

"Of course I do."

"So you know Arthur Kelvin."

The woman's face fell. "He's new. I haven't met him, but his voice sounds..."

Lesley knew what Arthur Kelvin's voice sounded like. "When you say *new*," she asked, "when exactly did he become a director?"

Bennett scratched her chin. "Three months ago, I'd say. Yes, because it was July, just before I went on holiday. Francis Dashwood stood down and Mr Kelvin came on board."

"Were you given a reason why?"

"These things happen. Francis was retiring. Mr Kelvin acquired a significant shareholding, became a director. Non-executive, like me."

"And do you have dealings with Darren Mathieson?" Lesley asked.

"The builder?"

"That's the one."

"What kind of dealings?"

"On the Horizon development."

"Not on that, no."

"He tells me you're his contact in the business. You're the one who hired him."

Bennett frowned. "I wouldn't put it quite like that. I recommended him to the other directors, I talked to him about the project a few times back at the start. But we don't really talk about it these days."

Lesley nodded. Why had Mathieson claimed Amanda Bennett was his contact when it would be so easy to confirm that she wasn't?

"Why did you recommend him?" she asked.

"We'd lost our previous contractor, a firm call Adnams

based in London. The architect brought them along with him." A pause. "Poor Mr Watson."

"Why did you lose them?" Lesley asked.

"They went bankrupt."

Lesley raised an eyebrow. "When was this?"

"Two months ago," Bennett replied. "We had to find another contractor in a hurry. Fortunately, Darren had availability and I was able to put him in touch with the other directors."

"Had you had dealings with Darren Mathieson before?"

"Of course."

"What kind of dealings?" Lesley asked.

"He's my brother."

CHAPTER FORTY-THREE

LESLEY WAS LOOKING at the board, Petra McBride behind her desk, as the team filed into her office. There was a full turnout today: Dennis, Mike, Tina, and Gail too. Lesley gave Gail a smile as she entered.

Gail looked at the psychologist. "Who's...?"

"Everyone, meet Dr Petra McBride. She's a profiler—"

"Psychologist," Petra interrupted.

"— here to help us get into the mind of our killer."

"Don't mind me." Petra looked around the team, reserving her brightest smile for Tina. She shuffled in her chair, which made a squeaking sound. "Carry on like I'm not here."

Dennis gave Lesley a quizzical look. She ignored it.

"You've finished at the scene?" Lesley asked Gail.

"Wrapped it up this morning. Didn't get much, I'm afraid. Sorry."

Lesley wasn't surprised. Durlston Head had been exposed to the elements for too long. The Globe was made of rough concrete and so were the paths and walls surrounding it. Even a stupid killer wouldn't have left prints there, and she didn't believe they were dealing with a stupid killer.

"OK," she said. "Dennis, let's start with Laurence Smith. Any developments?"

Dennis pulled out his notepad.

"I followed him, boss. He drove all the way from his house in Swanage to Sandbanks. He took the land route."

"But that'll take at least half an hour longer," said Gail, who lived in Swanage herself.

Dennis nodded. "It did. I reckon he was doing it so that there wouldn't be a record of him paying for a ferry journey."

"So where did he go?" Lesley asked.

Dennis flushed. "I'm afraid I lost him, boss. But the spot where he disappeared wasn't far from Arthur Kelvin's house."

Lesley pursed her lips. "Arthur Kelvin, again. You're sure?"

"Not sure, no. It was in the general area, but there's plenty of houses and flats in Sandbanks. Could have been a coincidence."

"So did you see him coming out of a house or flat?" Lesley asked.

"I waited in my car. He reappeared about an hour later, got in his car, took the land route home again. From then up to when I left half an hour ago, he hasn't left the house."

"You were outside all afternoon?"

"I was."

"Hang on," said Petra. "Who's Arthur Kelvin?"

"Organised crime, or so we've been trying to prove," Lesley said. "Laurence Smith is—"

"I know about him." She returned Lesley's stare. "What

d'you think I did on the plane? Petty bigot. Not a killer, in my view."

Mike nodded. Tina frowned. Lesley wondered how Petra could jump to such quick conclusions despite having only been here five minutes.

"Right," said Lesley. "So Smith may or may not be meeting Arthur Kelvin, but we haven't got the time and manpower to pursue it seriously. He could have been going to any one of hundreds of houses."

"They're big houses, boss," said Mike. "There aren't hundreds of them."

"Dozens," she said. "Mike, did you speak to Sherry?"

"I did. She was hiding something."

Lesley felt her shoulders slump. "Still?"

"You thought she was, too?"

Lesley put a hand on the board, her fingernail resting on Paul Watson's photo. "There's something going on with Paul Watson's firm that Sherry's not telling us about."

"I reckon it's Bella Phipps," said Mike. "She got very agitated when I mentioned the woman. Maybe she was having an affair with Paul."

"You think so?"

"Can't be sure, but there was definitely a tone. Sherry claimed she wasn't friendly with Bella, but that Paul was."

"That could simply have been because they work togeth-er," said Dennis.

"Maybe," agreed Lesley, "but it might be something more. What made you think she was hiding something, Mike?"

"She was really defensive. Told me it was none of my business. Then she cut off the conversation and told me to leave. Said she needed to talk to her kids. She'd already said they weren't speaking to her. She definitely didn't want me pushing that subject."

"In that case," said Lesley, "we need to speak to Bella herself. Has anybody made contact with Johnny?"

"You're wasting your time," Petra said.

"I'm sorry?" Lesley asked. She was wishing she'd briefed Petra without the team here.

"If his ex-girlfriend killed him, it would have been a crime of passion. Which doesn't fit with the way he was dragged onto that sphere."

"Globe," Dennis said.

"Globe, schmobe. Whatever. This isn't an ex out for revenge."

"Still," said Lesley. "I want to know more about her history with Paul. Is Johnny on it?"

"I've had a chat with him," Mike confirmed.

"And I've spoken to his commanding officer," said Dennis. "He'll be visiting her in the morning."

"That's not soon enough," Lesley said. "What if Sherry warns her? Mike, can you give Johnny a call? See if he can hurry it up?"

"I don't think he will," said Mike. He twitched as Petra snorted.

"No?" asked Lesley.

"He's worried about going against protocol, says they're sticklers for that kind of thing in the Met."

Another snort from Petra.

Lesley smiled. "Good for them. Try anyway, yes?"

"Will do."

"Thanks. Tina, what have you got?"

"The CCTV from Durlston Head," Tina said. "Two

men, both wearing hoodies. They brought Paul in and dragged him up onto the top of the Globe using ropes."

"That fits with the post-mortem," Mike said.

"Have we been able to enhance the image?" Lesley asked.

Gail cleared her throat. "That's where I come in. We may not have any prints, DNA or useful blood spatter, but you'll be pleased to know we've been working on that video. Can I borrow your computer?"

Lesley gestured for Gail to go ahead. Gail rounded the desk and bent over the computer. After a few moments she turned it to face the rest of the team.

"Here you are."

The image on screen was a still from the video, magnified and enhanced. The face of one of the two men was visible. He had white skin, a glimpse of a blond fringe under the hood and a scar at the corner of his mouth.

"Do we know him?" Lesley asked.

"I recognise him," Tina said. "I arrested him eighteen months ago."

Lesley turned to the PC. "What's his name?"

"Harry Coutts. I'm pretty sure he's been arrested more than once."

"What did you arrest him for?" Lesley asked.

"He was at a demo in Bournemouth, WDL thing."

Lesley felt her skin tense. WDL, or the Wessex Defence League, were an organisation with groups across the south-west. They liked to stage marches in towns like Bournemouth, insisting that they were only exercising their right to peaceful protest. They were anti-immigration and known for racist attacks.

"Which would fit the *go home* note," she said, "and the

theory that this was a racially motivated attack. Petra, does this sound more like it?"

"It could do." Petra surveyed her fingernails, which were long and bright pink. "Might not, though."

Lesley frowned. "Where does he live?"

"I'll get his address from HOLMES," replied Tina.

"You do that. I'd like to have a word with that Harry Coutts."

Lesley's skin was tingling, despite her annoyance at the psychologist. At last they had a suspect. His membership of the WDL, previous arrests, the note, and Paul being Black... It all fit.

"So what about the other one?" she asked. "On the video. Have we been able to enhance his image, Gail?"

"Not yet, sorry. He's facing away from the camera most of the time. Sunil's still working on it."

"Was he arrested with anyone else, Tina?"

"Sorry, boss. There were half a dozen of them."

"OK," Lesley said. "Dennis, you get onto Uniform. I want a squad car outside Coutts's house, now. We'll follow."

"Boss." Dennis hurried out of the room.

CHAPTER FORTY-FOUR

Johnny was standing outside Bella Phipps's house when a text came through from Mike.

DCI wants u to see Bella Phipps ASAP. Can u get there 2nite?

Johnny smiled. He tapped out a response.

About to go in. Will let u know how I get on.

A thumbs up emoji came back.

Johnny pocketed his phone and walked to the front door. Bella lived in a narrow terraced house in Mortlake, about two miles from her firm's office. He'd already tried the office and she hadn't been there. Just a secretary insisting that he come back tomorrow.

But Johnny preferred not to wait; he had his own caseload to deal with. He wanted to get this done, report back to Mike, and put it behind him. Getting involved in Dorset's cases made him uneasy.

He rang the doorbell and waited. A short woman with cropped blonde hair and enough makeup to sink a ship opened the door.

"Bella Phipps?" he asked, holding up his ID.

"Yeah. What d'you want?"

"I'm DC Chiles. I've been sent to ask you some questions about Paul Watson."

Her face lost its tightness. "Paul."

She backed away from the door. "Come in, I'll get you a coffee."

Johnny followed her into a narrow kitchen. She clattered around, opening doors, pulling out mugs, rattling teaspoons. She was shaking.

Johnny didn't know much about the case, but he was intrigued by this woman's reaction. From her body language, he wondered if she was more than a business partner.

He leaned against the wall. "You worked with Paul?"

"I did," she replied, her back to him. She carried on banging around the kitchen.

"How long have the two of you worked together?"

She turned to him. "Twenty years. Twenty years next month." She turned away.

"So the two of you knew each other well."

The kettle flicked off. Bella poured water into two mugs and handed one to him. She leaned against the worktop opposite him, sipping her own.

"You think I was sleeping with him. I can tell it from your eyes. You think I killed him because I was jealous of his wife, or because we had an argument."

"I'm not part of the investigating team," he replied. "I don't think anything."

"So what are you doing here if you're not part of the investigating team?"

"It's customary when a witness lives in another part of

the country to ask an officer from another force to do the interview."

"That all sounds very official," she said. "So they got you to knock on my door?"

"They did."

"And you want to know if I was shagging Paul?"

Johnny felt his face twitch at the directness of her language. He held her gaze.

"So were you?"

"Not any more," she said.

"How recently?"

"Eighteen years," she replied. "Paul and I were an item when we first set up the business. We were engaged for a while, soon realised it was a bad idea. It was an amicable split. We carried on working together, became business partners. He's my best mate. Was. Has been for years."

"So if you split up from him eighteen years ago, when did he meet his wife?"

"About six months after we split," she said. "Blind date, internet thing. Back when meeting somebody on the internet was vaguely dodgy, but it worked out. They were married within six months, they had those kids."

"Do you see much of Paul and Sherry?" Johnny asked.

"Not Sherry," she said. "Paul, yeah. We don't work out of the same office any more, he moved to Swanage three months ago. But you know all that."

"Did the two of you meet regularly after his move?"

"He came up to London occasionally after the move. Maybe," she paused, frowning, "four times? Something like that, anyway. He was working a different project from me, the Horizon development. That's why he moved down there.

It's our biggest project, prestigious. Paul was hoping it would win us an award. The cantilevering over the cliff."

Johnny put down his mug. The coffee was good. "I don't need to know about the engineering, Ms Phipps. I just want to talk to you about Paul. Is there anyone he worked with, or that the two of you worked with, who might have wanted to hurt him?"

She paused to take a gulp from her drink.

"Not that I know of," she replied. "We're just architects. You don't make enemies in this line of business."

"You've never been sued by a client, anything like that?"

"Goodness, no. You think we'd be doing a project like the Horizon development if we had a history of being sued? No. Paul was fine, great guy, got along with everyone. Like I said, my best mate. I'll miss him."

"And do you know anything about Paul borrowing money to buy his house in Swanage?"

She nodded.

"He put it through the business, standard process. Before we started getting these big commissions, we were flippers."

"Flippers?"

"You buy a house, do it up, flip it. Make a profit, use that to buy another one. We started out with a pokey little flat in Golders Green. Sold that, made a few grand, bought something bigger. We carried on going until it reached the point where we could have more than one property going at the same time. That's when we had to start borrowing money to make it work."

"So you were used to borrowing money to buy properties?"

"Standard practice for flippers. Nothing dodgy about it."

"Even when you borrow money to buy a house that you're going to live in yourself?"

Bella put her mug on the counter.

"Look, Detective. Most people who do it tend to live in the house while they're doing it up. That's what you do at the beginning, even if you're planning on being more commercial after you've got established. So, yeah, it's completely normal to borrow money and live in the place."

"So Paul was planning on moving out of that house after he'd finished the job in Swanage?"

Bella shrugged. "I think that was the original plan, but he liked it down there. Sherry did, too. She liked being away from me."

"The two of you don't get on?"

"She found it difficult to believe that I didn't have designs on her husband."

Johnny smiled. His own home life was simple. His wife Alice, and the baby. OK, so he was permanently knackered and never got any sleep, but the thought of either of them contemplating an affair was absurd.

"Where were you on Tuesday night?" he asked her.

She spat out a laugh. "You're asking me for an alibi?"

"Where were you on Tuesday night?"

"Let me see," she said. "I went out for drinks with a couple of mates. Clara and Manjit. You can ask them if you want. Here." She pulled her phone out. "You want their numbers?"

"Please," he said.

She held out her phone. Johnny noted down the numbers of her friends.

"Thank you, Ms Phipps. You've been helpful."

CHAPTER FORTY-FIVE

LESLEY STARED AT PETRA. The team had left the office, chasing down Coutt's details.

"We need to talk."

"I'm only trying to help."

"You undermined me. I'm the SIO."

"I just want to stop you wasting your time and resources. This isn't a revenge killing. And I don't think it's racial, either."

"Why not?"

"Too obvious."

"Surely that's the whole point?"

Petra shook her head. "You need to look closer to home."

"His wife?"

A shrug. "That's normally the best place to start."

"The woman's distraught."

"They often are. Even when they're guilty."

Lesley gripped the edge of her desk. "Sherry is hiding something, but I don't think..."

Petra raised a thin eyebrow. "It's personal, or business.

You need to dig further into the victim's life. Know the victim, know the killer."

"So what do you think I should dig into?"

On the other side of the glass, Dennis waved. Lesley ignored him, her skin taut.

"So?" she asked Petra.

Petra turned to her. "I'm not sure yet."

Dennis was waving frantically now.

"I've got a concrete lead," Lesley said. "I have to go."

Petra smiled. "You do that."

"Are you going to do anything useful while I'm gone?"

"Of course I am. I'll talk to your lassie in the uniform, get into the case files."

"Good." Lesley ran out of the room, worried Dennis was about to burst a blood vessel.

CHAPTER FORTY-SIX

THE ADDRESS on the system for Harry Coutts was in Weymouth.

"You drive," Lesley told Dennis. She'd never been to that part of the county and had no idea of the quickest route. "How long will it take?"

"Half an hour if the traffic's good. An hour if it's not."

"Let's bloody well hope it's good."

"Boss. *Please*," he muttered.

"Let's just *hope* it's good," she said, giving him a pointed stare. Now wasn't the time to worry about the niceties of her language.

"Use my car." She tossed him the keys as they crossed the car park. She'd recently been given a Mondeo, significantly more powerful than his car.

"Right," he said, eyeing the car nervously.

"It's just a car," she told him. "You'll be fine."

"Boss." He took a breath and eased into the driver's seat. Lesley rounded the front of the car and jumped into the passenger seat. As she did so, she spotted Petra standing in the window of her office, looking down. The psychologist gave her a small wave.

"Christ."

"Boss..."

"Sorry, Dennis. But that woman, she's..."

"She might be useful."

"You think so?"

He shrugged.

"Just go," she said.

Dennis reversed carefully out of the space, checked his mirror, put the car into first and put his foot on the accelerator. The car lurched forwards.

"Goodness," he said. "I see what you mean."

She smiled. "We'll get there in half an hour, don't you worry."

"Let's hope so," he said, his eyes on the road.

Thirty-five minutes later, they pulled up outside a dilapidated-looking house that had been converted into flats. Two squad cars sat outside and a uniformed constable was stationed at the front door. Lesley jumped out of the car and approached him.

"You got him?" she asked.

He shook his head. "No one here, Ma'am. Sorry."

"Shit."

She rapped her forehead with the palm of her hand and turned back to Dennis. He was still getting out of the car.

"Nobody here," she said.

She turned back to the constable. "You stay here, keep an eye on the street. Watch if he comes back."

"With respect, Ma'am. If I'm standing outside, he won't come back."

"You're right. Where's the nearest CID branch?"

"Weymouth."

"Good," she said. "Get a couple of DCs from there, they can sit outside and check to see whether Coutts comes back."

"Boss," said Dennis. "Shouldn't we handle this?"

"I'm not waiting for Mike and Tina to get here," she told him. "We need somebody stationed out here right now. We can sort out what we're going to do long term once that's in place."

"Very well."

"Good."

She strode back to the car and threw herself into the passenger seat. Dennis bent over and knocked on the window. She fumbled for the button and opened the window.

"What is it?" she snapped. "There's nothing to see here."

"Shouldn't we go inside?" he suggested. "He might have left evidence."

"Of course." Where had her brain gone? She'd momentarily lost all sense of logic.

"Of course," she repeated, getting out of the car.

They walked back to the house.

"We OK to go inside?" Lesley asked the constable.

He handed her the login sheet and she signed her name, Dennis repeating her actions a moment later.

"OK," Lesley said as they entered. "I want at least one CSI in here checking for evidence of Paul Watson having been in the building. Blood, fibres, fluids, anything."

"Should we have a look around first?" Dennis suggested.

"Of course," she replied, her tone sarcastic. "But we also need the CSIs here. If we find something, they can do more with it. If we don't find anything, they might be able to unearth what we couldn't."

"I'll call Gail."

"Good."

Dennis hung back. Lesley walked up the stairs. Another constable stood at the top.

"Which door is it?" Lesley asked the woman.

"It's a bedsit through there," replied the PC, pointing.

"Thanks."

Lesley pushed open the flimsy door and walked into a narrow room. In one corner was a single bed, a threadbare duvet scrunched up against the wall. Beside it was a kitchenette and a small scratched table. No chair.

"This is where Coutts lives?" she asked. It was a dump.

Dennis was behind her. "This is the address we've got for him."

"No sign of anyone living here," she said.

"But the duvet?"

She walked over to the bed, snapping on a pair of gloves. She prodded the duvet.

"It's cold. Damp." She looked up to see a damp patch on the ceiling.

"And look at the kitchen."

Dennis followed her gaze.

In the sink was a pile of dirty dishes, mould spilling over the top of a mug.

"That's been there at least a week," Lesley said.

Dennis approached the kitchen. He picked up one of the mugs and sniffed.

"Sour milk," he confirmed.

"Open the fridge," she told him.

"You sure, boss?"

"It won't bite."

"It might do."

"Just open it, Dennis."

The fridge was under the counter. Dennis bent to open it and stepped backwards.

"Heavens," he said. "It stinks."

"Coutts may be registered at this address," Lesley said. "But he hasn't lived here for a while. Either he was expecting us to arrive at some point, or he's moved out anyway."

Dennis pushed the fridge door shut and straightened up. He waved a hand in front of his face, his nose wrinkled.

"He hasn't been here since before Paul Watson died."

"No," Lesley replied. "Which means we won't find any forensics."

"I'll call Gail," Dennis said. "Tell her we don't need her."

"It's OK," she told him. "I want her to go over the place, just in case."

"Fair enough. What now?"

Lesley gritted her teeth.

"Call the office. We're still looking for Coutts."

CHAPTER FORTY-SEVEN

Mike stood behind Tina as she picked up the call from the sarge. She was silent as she listened. He clutched the back of her chair, desperate to know what was going on. The two of them had been left here to check background on Harry Coutts and relay it to the DCI and the sarge.

Tina hung up. "He wasn't there."

"Coutts?"

"Nope. No sign of him having been in his flat for a while, apparently the fridge was rank."

Mike grimaced. "What now?"

"We get back on HOLMES," she said. "See if we can find any potential contacts. I bet you he's at his mum's."

"You think so?" Mike asked. "The guy's just murdered somebody and he's gone to his mum's house?"

"Well, where would you go if you'd just killed someone?"

"That's not an easy one to answer," Mike replied. "Seeing as I've never killed anyone."

She turned in her chair. "Put yourself in his head for a moment, imagine how you'd be thinking. You'd want to go somewhere safe, be with somebody who you were confident wouldn't dob you in."

"You reckon his mum will lie for him?"

"If anybody's going to, it would be his mum. Either that or a girlfriend."

"OK," Mike said. "Let's see what we've got on the database."

Tina nodded and turned back to her computer.

"There we are," she said after a minute or so. "His mum lives in Wareham."

"Right," Mike replied. "I'll let the sarge know."

His phone rang: Johnny. He looked at it and then at Tina.

"Can you call the sarge?" he asked her.

"Will do."

Mike answered the call. "Johnny, you got news for me?"

"I sent you another text last night. Didn't you get it?"

Mike frowned. "Sorry, mate."

A sigh at the other end of the line. "I went to see your Bella Phipps. Last night."

"And?"

"No love lost between her and Sherry Watson."

"No?"

"She was tetchy, angry about something. But she didn't give me anything concrete. She and Paul Watson used to be an item, eighteen years ago. They split up before he even met his wife."

"So you don't think they were having an affair?"

"It felt like she was telling the truth," Johnny replied. "She and Paul were close, best mates. But she didn't act like a woman who'd just lost the man she loved."

Mike nodded. Tina was on the phone to the sarge, relaying Harry Coutts's mum's address.

"Thanks, Johnny," he said. "Did you ask her about the loans? Anything dodgy in the business?"

"She said it was all above board," Johnny said. "Nothing unusual about borrowing money to buy a property. Apparently they did it all the time when they were starting out, it was just an extension of that for him to use it to buy his house."

"Surely it would have put him under pressure, being in hock for that much money?"

"Bella Phipps reckons that's the norm in their line of business. Flippers, she called them."

"Yeah," Mike said. "I've heard that term. Buy a house, do it up, sell it on."

"Bella thought that was what he was planning to do with the house in Swanage," Johnny added. "At first, anyway. After he'd finished working on your Horizon development. I remember that one, controversial, wasn't it?"

"Local nimbys trying to stop it."

"You think they might be behind this?"

"We've got a suspect," Mike told him.

"Yes?"

"Guy called Harry Coutts. Did you come across him at all when you were here?"

"Never heard of him, mate. Sorry."

"Worth a try. So did Bella give you anything else? Anyone Paul worked with that might have wanted to hurt him?"

"She couldn't think of anybody," Johnny said. "She said architects weren't the kind of people who had enemies."

"There's something else," Mike told him. "The Horizon

development is owned by a business called Sunrise Holdings."

"What about them?" Johnny said.

Mike pulled away from Tina's desk. "One of the directors is Arthur Kelvin."

There was silence at the other end of the line.

"Johnny, you still there?"

"Yes." Johnny's voice was quiet. "Sorry. Just went under a bridge for a moment. Arthur Kelvin, you say? You think he's mixed up in this?"

"He gets his fingers in everything," Mike said.

"I wouldn't know," replied Johnny. "I'm well out of it. D'you need me to go and see her again?"

"No, thanks. I'll let you know if it changes."

"Good." Johnny hung up.

Mike stared at his phone. It wasn't like Johnny to be so abrupt. But then, he was interrupting his work for the Met.

He looked at Tina. "What's happening?"

"They're on the way to Coutts's mum's house. I've told Uniform to send a squad car too."

"Where are they?" Mike said.

"Just leaving Weymouth."

"That's miles away. We're only five minutes from Wareham. Come on, you drive."

CHAPTER FORTY-EIGHT

LESLEY CLUTCHED her seatbelt as Dennis pulled up sharply outside Sheila Coutts's house. She'd been impressed by his driving; he was clearly enjoying her car.

Three squad cars were already outside. She approached the uniformed PC outside the door.

"Who's in there?"

"One of my colleagues, two of yours."

Lesley looked back at Dennis, who was checking the car was locked, then at the PC. "Two of mine?"

"PC Abbott," the PC said. "And one of your DCs."

Lesley hurried into the house, Dennis behind her.

"Did you hear that?" she muttered to him. "Tina and Mike are already here."

"They would have been closer."

"That's not the point." She'd given them specific instructions to stay in the office so they could relay information.

The first doorway opened and Tina emerged, leading a woman. The woman had messy grey hair and wore a pink fleece that had seen better days.

"Boss," Tina said. "He's in there."

"Harry Coutts?"

"Mike's arrested him."

"We told you to stay in the office."

Tina glanced at the woman. "We figured we could get here before you, boss. I knew it was urgent."

"Uniform were already on their way," Lesley told her. She clenched and unclenched her fist, softening. "But well done. You made the arrest. Who's this?"

"Sheila Coutts, his mum."

"You've arrested her?"

"No, boss. She had a funny turn, I'm taking her outside for some fresh air."

"I'm bloody fine," the woman snarled. "Put me down."

"You need fresh air, Mrs Coutts," Tina said.

Lesley stood back and let Tina lead her out.

"Don't let her go anywhere," she said. "I want to question her."

"Boss."

Lesley walked into the living room. The smell of cigarettes and damp mingled in the air. A young man sat on an ugly brown and yellow sofa, Mike beside him.

Mike stiffened as he saw Lesley. "Boss, Tina and I came on ahead. This is Harry Coutts."

Coutts gave Lesley a look of disdain and then looked back at his hands, which he was pulling at in his lap.

"You made the arrest?" Lesley asked.

"Yes, boss," Mike replied.

"OK, get him in a squad car. I want to know how it went down."

"Of course."

Mike nodded and nudged Coutts.

The young man stood up, kicked at the sofa and then grimaced at Lesley.

"Harry Coutts," she said, "I'm DCI Clarke. We'll be talking to each other shortly."

He grunted at her. Mike put a hand on his shoulder and ushered him out of the room. Coutts glared at Lesley as he passed, but didn't argue.

Lesley turned to Dennis. "Looks like they did our job for us."

"They showed initiative."

"They went against a direct order," she replied. "What if we'd needed them to attend another address? What if Coutts hadn't been here?"

"But he was," said Dennis.

Lesley tugged at her jacket. "Uniform got here first, would have kept Coutts and his mum here till we arrived."

"With respect, boss," Dennis said, "they were showing initiative. They wanted to make the arrest, and Coutts might have been expecting us. And with his history, both of them have a stake in this."

Lesley's chest was tight. "We've all got a stake in this, Dennis. This is not personal." She pulled in a thin breath. "OK, then. Let's get back to the office, we've got an interview to do."

CHAPTER FORTY-NINE

Mike and Tina were already in the team room when Lesley and Dennis arrived back at the office. Petra was also there, staring out of the window.

"Right," said Lesley, "I want to know exactly how that arrest happened."

"It's my fault boss," Mike said. "It wasn't Tina's decis—"

"That's not true, Mike," Tina interrupted.

"I'm a member of CID," Mike continued. "I should take the fall for this."

Tina looked at him. "Don't patronise me. I was just as much a part of it as you were. I drove, for God's sake."

"OK," said Lesley. "Let's all stop fretting about who was to blame and tell me what happened."

Tina turned to her. "We realised that Coutts's mum lived in Wareham, and that it would only be a five-minute drive for us. You were all the way over in Weymouth. We agreed it would be sensible for the two of us to go. Make sure we got there before he could do a runner."

"And what made you think he might do a runner?" Lesley asked.

"If someone saw you arrive at his place in Weymouth," Mike said. "One of his neighbours or a mate. They might have called him."

"It's a fair point," said Dennis.

"Hmm," said Lesley. "So tell me what happened when you got there."

Tina checked her notepad. "His mum answered the door. We told her who we were, she let us in. Coutts was asleep on the sofa."

Dennis smothered a laugh.

"He was asleep on the sofa?" Lesley asked.

Mike grinned. "Easiest catch I've ever made."

"So, who arrested him?"

"I did," said Mike.

"Then what?"

"His mum was in the room the whole time," Tina said. "She just sat there in an armchair watching us. I reckon she was too scared to do anything."

"Of you, or of her son?" Dennis asked.

Tina shrugged. "Not sure. Both, to some extent."

"She'd have seen her son being arrested before," Mike added. "It is a habit of his."

"I don't care how many times he's been arrested," said Lesley. "You do it properly, every single time. I'm not going to patronise you by checking you read him his rights correctly. Were Uniform there before you arrived, or did they arrive after?"

"Same time as us, boss," said Tina.

"Did anybody go around the back of the house?" Dennis asked. "There were two of them on that video."

"He was asleep, Sarge," said Mike. "It was easy."

"That's not what I mean." Dennis frowned. "If the other suspect was with him, he might have heard you and left by the back."

"PC McGuigan went round the back, Sarge," Tina said. "There was no way out without climbing over the fence and landing in the next garden."

"And you're sure no one did that?"

"Positive, Sarge."

"Let's hope you're right," Lesley told her. "Our next priority is to find out who his mate is. Dennis, I want you with me in the interview."

Petra took a step towards them. "Ask him why he did it."

Lesley rolled her eyes. "I'm sorry, I forgot all about motive. Thanks for reminding me."

"You think it's racially motivated. I'm not so sure. Ask him why he did it."

"We will." Lesley turned to Dennis. "Come on."

"Mike made the arrest, boss. Maybe he should—"

"I want you, Dennis."

"Yes. Not a problem."

"OK," Lesley said to the two constables. "I appreciate you showed initiative, but I had asked you to stay here. Next time, you run that sort of thing past me or the DS, OK?"

"Yes, boss," said Mike.

"Sorry, boss," said Tina.

"Don't apologise," Lesley said. "It irritates me."

Tina nodded.

"And Johnny called," said Mike.

"He's seen Bella Phipps?" Lesley asked.

"Yeah."

"Anything I need to be aware of?"

"Not really."

"Not really, or not at all?"

"Nothing, boss."

She sighed. "OK. You can fill me in on the detail after this. Dennis, let's talk to Coutts."

CHAPTER FIFTY

HARRY COUTTS WAS WAITING in an interview room, a uniformed PC watching over him.

"Has his lawyer arrived yet?" asked Lesley.

"She's on her way," the PC said.

Coutts looked Lesley up and down, his gaze hard. He had bags under his eyes and there were lines on his face from whatever he'd been sleeping on.

"Who is the lawyer?" she asked.

The door opened behind her.

"You shouldn't be talking to my client without me here."

Lesley turned, her chest falling. "Elsa."

Elsa held out her hand.

"Elsa Short. Nevin, Cross and Short criminal lawyers. I'll be representing Mr Coutts."

Of course you will, Lesley thought.

"Very well," she said. "Do you need a moment with your client before we start?"

Elsa looked at Coutts who shook his head.

"It seems not," she said. "Shall we begin?"

Lesley swallowed. She took a seat opposite Elsa and Coutts, Dennis beside her. His body language was as tight as she felt.

She placed her elbows on the table and leaned forward, looking at Coutts. "Please state your name."

He looked at Elsa.

"My client's name is Harry Coutts," Elsa said. "My name is Elsa Short, his solicitor."

"DCI Clarke and DS Frampton," Lesley said. "OK, Harry. Can you tell us where you were on Tuesday night?"

He looked down at the table in front of him, silent.

"Harry?" she repeated.

He hunched his shoulders. Lesley sighed and looked at Elsa.

"Is your client going to speak?"

"It is his right not to."

"It doesn't exactly work in his favour."

Dennis cleared his throat. He shuffled in his chair.

Lesley looked back at Coutts. "Harry, do you know a man called Paul Watson?"

He muttered.

"I can't hear you."

He looked up. "No comment," he said.

Lesley closed her eyes for a moment.

"Once again, where were you on Tuesday night?"

"No comment."

"Does this note mean anything to you?"

She opened the file in front of her and took out a photo of the *go home* note from Paul's jacket. She pushed it across the table and Elsa took it from her.

She exchanged glances with Coutts, who shook his head.

"My client doesn't recognise it," she said, keeping her hand on the photo.

"I need *him* to answer the question," Lesley told her. "Harry, do you recognise this?"

"No comment."

Lesley leaned back in her chair.

"Are you going to say anything other than *no comment*?" she asked, her gaze level on his face.

He looked at Elsa who leaned in and muttered in his ear. He shrugged and looked at Lesley, the fire still in his eyes.

"No comment," he said.

She watched Coutts. Petra's words were in her head.

"Why did you do it?" she asked. "Was it because Paul Watson was Black?"

Coutts shrugged. "No comment."

Lesley stood up. She touched Dennis's shoulder.

"Come on," she said to him. "We're wasting our time here."

She turned back to look at Coutts, her hand on the door-knob. "You might want to be aware of this, though."

His gaze was on the table. He didn't look up.

"Speaking up is in your interest, Harry. We've got enough to charge and probably convict you. If you don't defend yourself, well..."

She turned back to the door and hesitated before opening it. But it hadn't worked. Coutts remained silent.

CHAPTER FIFTY-ONE

GERAINT EVANS TURNED to close his front door and then gave it a tug. He always liked to check it was firmly locked.

It was unlikely that his house would be broken into, what with this being Swanage, but you couldn't be too careful. He'd spent thirty-six years living in a part of Cardiff with high crime rates, and he wasn't about to ditch the habit of a lifetime just because things were a bit more peaceful in this corner of Dorset.

Satisfied that the house was secure, he walked between the flower beds of his front garden, noting that they needed weeding, and turned down the hill towards the seafront.

He checked his watch. Half past six. He was running late. Aren would be in the pub already, he liked to get there early. Geraint's friend would have been on one of his long walks in the hills beforehand. His way of earning it. Aren always felt guilty if he didn't earn his pint. Geraint didn't care; he'd long since earned all the pints he could drink.

Thirty-two years working in an accountancy firm, wearing himself out for a good enough pension to retire somewhere nice. He'd had clients down here and he'd always been jealous.

As he was halfway down the hill, a car slowed next to him. He ignored it. People were always driving up here, trying to find a footpath up to Ballard Down.

In the summer, they'd hike past his house on sunny days, heading down into the town after tackling the Purbeck Way. It was how he'd discovered this spot himself. On a work trip in 1994, he'd taken a turn down this road and fallen in love. The neat houses, the views over the sea. He'd vowed that he would live here one day. And now, he thought with a smile, he was living his dream.

The car was still next to him. It moved slowly, keeping pace with him. He could just make out two figures inside, but couldn't see their faces.

He slowed his pace, uneasy. The car slowed alongside him.

Geraint swallowed.

He stopped walking and pulled his phone out. If he pretended to be on a call, maybe they'd go on their way and ignore him.

He turned away from the car, his phone to his ear. He hadn't dialled yet, he was still pretending.

"Excuse me."

He turned. A man had got out of the car. He was young, with acne-scarred skin. He wore a hoodie: grey, nondescript. People like him always wore hoodies.

"I can't help you," Geraint said. "I'm sorry, I'm not local."

The man laughed.

"Yeah, you are," he said. "You are now, anyway."

Geraint felt his skin ripple.

Did this man know who he was? How did he know that Geraint had only recently moved to Swanage?

Don't be stupid. How could he possibly know?

It was Geraint's accent, it always gave him away.

He pushed his shoulders back, trying to look confident.

"Anyway," he said. "I'm meeting a friend."

If the man knew someone was expecting him, maybe he'd leave him alone.

Geraint picked up pace, heading down the hill.

The man followed.

The car was ahead, driving slowly, waiting. Geraint felt a chill grip his heart.

Should he turn back, head home? His house was closer than the pub.

But the man was behind him.

No, he thought, *keep going*. Once he was at the bottom, there would be shops, there would be people. He would be safe.

He picked up pace again.

The car stopped and another man got out.

Like the first, he wore a grey hoodie. He pulled it higher over his head so Geraint couldn't see his eyes.

Geraint stopped walking as the man approached.

The first man was behind him, his footsteps growing louder.

Geraint turned. He was about to step into the road when he felt the second man's hand on his shoulder.

He froze at the sound of the man's voice.

"You're not going anywhere, mate."

CHAPTER FIFTY-TWO

TINA WAS SITTING on Mike's desk when Lesley entered the office. She quickly scooted off it and returned to her own chair.

"My office, now," Lesley said.

She spotted Tina and Mike exchanging glances before they followed, Dennis frowning at them. Petra followed, her jaw tight.

"Close the door," Lesley told Dennis as he entered.

He stood against it. Mike and Tina hovered in the middle of the room, neither wanting to take a chair. They could sense Lesley's mood, and didn't know whether she was still angry at them, or if it was something else entirely.

"So," she said. "You might have guessed why we got back so quickly."

"No comment interview?" asked Mike.

"Bingo," Lesley said. "Little bastard wouldn't say a thing."

Dennis's jaw clenched. Lesley ignored it. She looked at Petra. "You would have predicted that, I suppose?"

"I'm not psychic. But it's not a surprise. Given the nature of the evidence."

"And he was represented by Elsa Short," said Dennis.

Mike's gaze went to Lesley. "Oh."

"That's irrelevant," Lesley said. "I knew that at some point I would face her across that interview room table. In fact, I'm amazed it's taken this long. So get any ideas out of your head that my relationship with Elsa has anything to do with that shitstorm of an interview we just sat through."

"Boss..." said Dennis.

Lesley ground her fist into the table. "I'm sorry, Dennis. I'm just annoyed."

"I know," he said. "I am, too."

"We still got him on film, though," Tina said. "He can't deny he was one of the ones that killed Paul Watson."

"He can," Lesley said. "All we've got is him and the other guy dragging Paul onto the Globe. A good lawyer, and believe me he's got a good lawyer, is going to make out that he didn't kill anyone. That video doesn't show Paul dying, it doesn't show his murder, you can't even tell he's already dead."

"But surely..." began Mike.

Lesley pointed at him.

"His lawyer will tell a jury that Harry's just a small-time lowlife whose mates coerced him into shifting Paul's body. A good lawyer will make out that Harry Coutts is a victim of police intimidation."

Mike paled.

"Sorry, boss," muttered Tina.

"It's not your fault. I know you're both good coppers, you did it properly. But he'll have registered the fact that we disagreed with each other, and it was clear that something was up when we were standing there in the room with him and his mum. That's going to work against us."

She fell into her chair. "Any ideas?" she asked Petra.

"There's no doubt he's your man. But the question is why."

"Which I was hoping you could help us with."

"I don't think it's racial. It might not even be personal. What was he like, in the interview? Did he show any reaction?"

"He was a blank," Lesley said.

"No emotion," Dennis added.

Petra nodded. "Whoever the other guy in your video was, I think he was the ringleader."

"We need to find him," Tina said.

"We certainly do," agreed Lesley.

"I'll call Gail," Mike said.

"You do that," Lesley told him. "And I want to follow up on all of the threads with Paul Watson's personal life. His debt, his business partner, that company."

Petra nodded.

"Have we got any more on the holding company?" Dennis asked.

"There's a link between the building contractors and one of the directors," Lesley said. "A woman called Amanda Bennett, she's the sister of Darren Mathieson. The question is, did she suggest that they hire him because of that, or because she thought he could do the job?"

"Is that relevant?" Tina asked.

"I've got no idea, Tina," Lesley said. "Anything could be relevant, nothing could be relevant. I want to clear it all up, I want to know as much about Paul as his wife did. In fact, I want to know a lot more about Paul than his wife did."

"D'you want me to go back to her, boss?" Mike asked.

"No," she replied. "We've got as much out of Sherry as we're going to. I want to follow up with Bella Phipps again, I'm sure she'll tell us more. From what you've told me about Johnny's interview, she doesn't seem exactly distraught at the whole thing. Maybe she knows what's been going on."

"Do you want me to call Johnny?" Mike asked.

"No," Lesley said. "I want to talk to her myself."

"Go to London?" Dennis asked.

Lesley nodded. "There's enough of us here now for you guys to cover what we've got going on locally. I can nip up to London tomorrow to talk to Bella Phipps. I'll go early, be back by lunchtime."

"Do you want me to come with you?" Dennis asked.

"No," she said. "I want you here. Find out everything you can about Sunrise Holdings. Talk to all the directors, find out about the links between them all."

"Even Arthur Kelvin?" Dennis said.

"You OK with that?"

"Why shouldn't I be?"

"Good," she said.

Her phone buzzed on the desk.

"I've got a visitor," she said. "I'll be back shortly."

CHAPTER FIFTY-THREE

Lesley hurried down the stairs and into the foyer of Dorset Police's HQ building. She pushed the irritation from her mind and smiled at her visitor.

"Zoe," she said. "My God, it's good to see you."

"Everything OK, boss?" Zoe replied.

Lesley put a hand on her shoulder. "I thought you'd got out of that dirty habit."

Zoe laughed. "It's just seeing you in the flesh again..."

"I'm not your boss anymore, Zoe," Lesley said. "I'm your friend."

Zoe cocked her head. "Really?"

Lesley frowned. "Well, what else am I? Of course I'm your friend. You're certainly *my* friend, using your personal time to come and help with this."

"It's the least I could do," Zoe said. "It's not like I've got anything else going on."

"How's your son getting on? First term at university, yes?"

"He's fine, having a good time. Too far away for my liking."

"Where did he go?"

"Stirling."

Lesley whistled. "That is a long way. Has he been back to visit yet? Brought his washing home?"

Zoe laughed. "Believe it or not, Nicholas used to do *my* washing."

Lesley looked her up and down. "You look like you've got used to it."

Zoe was well turned out. She wore a freshly-ironed white shirt under a blue suede jacket and her customary jeans and boots.

"This shirt's new," Zoe said. "I didn't have to iron it. Straight off the hanger."

Lesley smiled. "That's one way around the problem. Gets a bit expensive, though."

Zoe nodded. "Unless they promote me to DCI, I'll have to learn to iron."

Lesley tightened her grip on Zoe's shoulder. "Let's take a walk outside."

Zoe looked past Lesley, towards the PC at the reception desk. Nobody here knew Zoe was coming, Lesley hadn't even informed her team. She would have to tell them something.

She steered Zoe out of the building.

"Where's your car?" she asked.

Zoe pointed to a green Mini on the far side of the car park.

"Horrible drive," she said. "I got caught in traffic around Winchester."

"You always get stuck somewhere," Lesley told her. "I tend to get the train most of the time."

"Wise move," said Zoe. "I'll do that next time I come down."

"You think there will be a next time?"

"Depends how we get on with this case," Zoe told her. "So what do you need me to do?"

Lesley looked back at the building, her gaze sliding up to the window of her office. Dennis stood in it, looking out at them. He turned away as he caught her eye.

"Who's that?" Zoe asked.

"You and he spoke on the phone," Lesley told her.

"Ah, DS Frampton. That doesn't surprise me."

"You thought he'd look like that?" Lesley asked her.

Zoe shrugged. "Shouldn't make assumptions, I guess."

"No. Anyway, you can use my house in Wareham. I'll be staying in Bournemouth for the next few nights."

"You sure about that? You're not having to get a hotel room or anything?"

"Nothing of the sort." Lesley hesitated. "I've got a girl-friend. Elsa."

Zoe raised her eyebrows. "Good for you. I hope she's nice."

"She's a criminal lawyer."

"Ah. Well, not for me to judge, I guess."

Lesley laughed.

"She's got a flat in Bournemouth. I spend most of my nights there. Dorset Police rented me this pokey little cottage in Wareham. It's nice if you like that sort of thing."

She pulled her keyring out of her pocket and peeled off the key to the house.

"Thanks." Zoe pocketed it. "You're going to give me the address?"

"I'll text it to you. I'll give you a call later on, we'll meet up. I'll run you through what's been happening."

"Thanks," Zoe said.

"How long are you down here for?"

"Until Tuesday," Zoe replied.

"Only two days leave?"

Zoe shook her head. "They're counting weekends these days."

Lesley nodded. "It never gets easier, does it?"

Zoe shrugged. "It's a lot easier now Randle's gone."

Detective Superintendent Randle had been Lesley's boss. Zoe had uncovered his corruption and the man was now in witness protection.

"I'm hoping your experience with Randle will help us with our delicate matter," Lesley told her.

"Mackie," Zoe muttered.

"Don't say his name, please. Not here."

"Sorry." Zoe looked up. "Anyway, I think you need to get back to your DS."

Lesley resisted the urge to turn and look at Dennis.

"I'll see you later," she said.

CHAPTER FIFTY-FOUR

Lesley turned to see Petra standing on the stairs.

"I remember her. Zelda?"

Lesley snorted. "Zoe. DI Finch, from West Midlands Force CID."

"The one from the homophobic killings. What's she doing here?"

"She's helping with another case."

Petra cocked her head. "Your new team not good enough?"

"It's complicated. And I'd rather you didn't mention it to the others."

Petra surveyed her for a moment, then mimed zipping her lips. "You can trust me."

"It's no big deal. Just—"

"You get a West Midlands DI all the way down here, hide her from your team, and it's no big deal?"

Lesley realised she was chewing a fingernail. She dropped her hand. "It's not relevant to what you're here for."

"Like I said, my lips are sealed. Anything I can help with?"

Lesley hesitated, thinking of what she'd learned about Mackie's mental state. "No," she said finally.

"Fair enough. You know where I am, if you need me. Speaking of which..."

"Yes?'

"This crime isn't what your superintendent thought it was."

"How so?"

"It's not a complex one. No more psychological than your average murder."

"There's such a thing as an average murder?"

"You and I both know there is."

"So what are you saying?" Lesley asked.

"You don't need me. I'll go and get my things from the hotel, then I'll head back to Dundee."

"Now wait a minute—"

Petra held up a hand. "DCI Clarke. You're an efficient woman. You get to the point, and you don't waste time. I'm sure you don't want to waste mine."

Lesley felt herself deflate. Her instincts had been telling her this wasn't a hate crime, but she'd expected Petra to tell her she was wrong.

So why did she feel so disappointed the psychologist was leaving?

"I'll need to speak to Carpenter."

Petra smiled. "I'll handle that." She held out her hand. "It was good to work with you again, however briefly."

Lesley shook the hand. "Likewise," she said, not sure how sincere she was being.

CHAPTER FIFTY-FIVE

TINA HAD input a list of the Sunrise Holdings directors to the case file on HOLMES. Dennis ran through them.

Amanda Bennett the DCI had already spoken to. Arthur Kelvin... he would come later. The other two were Shahid Jain and Douglas Spencer.

Dennis hadn't heard of either of them. Their home addresses were listed on Companies House, and in the case file. Douglas Spencer lived in Scotland. Why he was interested in a company that was building properties in Swanage, Dennis had no idea. Maybe the company worked up there too.

Shahid Jain had an address in London, not far from where Paul Watson had lived. Dennis wondered whether the two were connected.

He dialled Jain's number.

"Shahid Jain speaking, can I help you?"

"Hello, Mr Jain. Detective Sergeant Frampton from Dorset Police here. I'm calling you in connection with Sunrise Holdings. I believe you're a director."

"That's correct."

"Can I ask how closely involved with the company you are?"

"Not very. I've been to three shareholder meetings, taken part in a couple of directors' meetings. That's about it, really."

"So what is it that makes you a director?"

"Money, mainly. Contacts. I manage an architectural practice here in London. I've helped Sunrise make connections with some movers and shakers in the industry."

Dennis shuddered. The very concept of movers and shakers left him cold.

"Did you know Paul Watson?" he asked.

"Tragic affair," said Jain, his voice not registering emotion. "Is that what you're calling about? You're investigating his murder?"

"We're trying to find out what we can about his business activities."

"You think somebody from his professional life killed him? I'd have thought it was Bella."

"Bella Phipps?" Dennis asked.

"Is there another Bella?"

"You know her?"

"It's a small world, this profession. Yes, I do know her."

"And you think she would be the one who killed Paul Watson?" Dennis asked.

"Just an assumption. Crime of passion and all that."

Johnny had been to see Bella. The woman had claimed that she and Paul had split up eighteen years ago, so why would Shahid Jain be expecting her to commit a crime of passion?

"How well do you know Bella?" Dennis asked.

"Not very. Professional acquaintance. I've just heard the gossip, you know how it is."

Dennis had no idea *how it was*. But he'd worked cases where gossip had led them astray. He made a policy of not listening to it.

"Mr Jain, would you happen to know anything about Phipps and Watson's financial affairs?"

"Bella and Paul's firm? None of my business," Jain said. "Haven't a clue, sorry."

"Do you know Darren Mathieson?"

"I know of him, he's the lead contractor on the Horizon development. Interesting project, should win some awards."

"So I've heard," said Dennis. "But you've never met him?"

"I was there when we approved his involvement in the project. Amanda recommended him."

"Amanda Bennett?" Dennis asked.

"She's another one of the directors."

"She's also Darren Mathieson's sister," Dennis said.

Jain winced. "She didn't tell us that."

"No?" asked Dennis.

Jain said nothing. Dennis waited.

"Anyway," Jain said. "If you want to question me formally, you'll have to get a warrant."

"That's not quite correct. But you're not a suspect, Mr Jain."

"I'm not saying I am. But if you want to question me formally, I suggest you go through the proper channels."

He hung up.

Dennis stared at his phone.

Shahid Jain would know the implications of Amanda

Bennett concealing her relationship with Darren Mathieson. She would have been expected to declare an interest.

Had Paul Watson found out the truth? Had Mathieson or Bennett perhaps wanted to shut him up?

He hung up and dialled the DCI.

CHAPTER FIFTY-SIX

As LESLEY OPENED the door to the team room, her phone rang. It was Dennis.

"I'm standing right behind you," she told him.

He turned, blushed and put his phone down.

"I thought you'd want to know about the conversation I just had with Shahid Jain," he said.

"Who's Shahid Jain?"

"Another one of the directors at Sunrise Holdings. He knows Bella Phipps, he's got a theory that she killed Paul."

"On what basis?"

"Crime of passion."

"So he knew the pair of them?"

"Only by reputation. He says there was gossip about their relationship."

"But Johnny believed what she told him. They split up years ago."

"Still," he said, "I thought you'd want to know seeing as you're off to interview her in London tomorrow."

"Thanks."

She looked at her watch: half past six.

"I'm going to head home and look through the case file. I'll be leaving for London early. You go home too."

"You're sure, boss?" he asked.

"Yes." She looked across the desks. "Tina, Mike, time for everybody to knock off for the night. We can continue with this tomorrow."

Tina and Mike exchanged smiles.

"Pub?" Mike said.

Tina smiled. "Why not?"

Dennis looked at them, as if waiting for an invitation. When none came, he shrugged.

"I can't go just yet," he said. "I haven't spoken to the other directors."

"Arthur Kelvin?" Lesley asked.

"And Douglas Spencer."

"Fine," she replied. "Try calling Spencer. If you don't get through to him, head home."

"What about Kelvin?" he asked.

"I want to speak to Carpenter first. Did Shahid Jain say anything else?" she asked.

Dennis nodded. "He didn't know that Darren Mathieson was Amanda Bennett's brother. When I told him, he cut the conversation off. Couldn't get away fast enough. I imagine you have to declare that kind of thing if you're the director of a company."

Lesley sighed. "OK. Tina, before you head off, see what you can find out about the Sunrise directors' contracts."

Tina looked at Mike. She shrugged an apology. Mike's expression drooped.

"You alright, Mike?" Lesley asked.

"Fine, boss. You need me to stay and help out?"

"You're fine. Wait till I've seen Bella tomorrow, then we'll decide what to do next."

"Fair enough." He walked to the door, glancing at Tina. "What happened to Doctor McBride?"

"She decided she couldn't be of any use to us. She's left."

"Already?" Dennis asked.

"Already." Lesley looked at him. She didn't feel like trying to explain. She wasn't sure she could. "Let me know if you find anything important, Dennis."

CHAPTER FIFTY-SEVEN

Elsa looked up at a knock on her office door: Aurelia Cross. She nodded for her colleague to enter.

"Aurelia," she said, checking the clock. "What can I do for you?"

Aurelia closed the door and sat down.

"I hear you finally had to sit in an interview with your girlfriend today."

Elsa clenched her toes inside her shoes. "It was going to happen eventually."

"Harry Coutts," Aurelia said.

"He gave a no comment interview."

"Was that on your advice?"

"To be honest, it probably would have been if I'd had the time to advise him."

"It was done in a hurry?"

"DCI Clarke and DS Frampton were already in the room when I arrived."

Aurelia looked surprised. "That's not like Frampton."

"It's also not like Lesley," Elsa told her. "She keeps telling me she's a stickler for procedure, but they were in there talking to my client. I never got a chance to brief him before the interview."

"You asked for it?"

"I did, but he refused. We went straight into it, he decided not to talk."

"And did he talk to you afterwards?"

"Not enough. I'm going to have to go and see him again tomorrow."

"Tomorrow's Saturday."

"So?"

Aurelia smiled; you didn't get to be partner in a successful law firm by worrying about weekends. "Where is he right now?"

"He's in police custody, their twenty-four hours runs out tomorrow afternoon."

"And what do you think the chances are of them charging him within those twenty-four hours?"

"High," Elsa replied. "They've got him on video at the site where Paul Watson was left. Apparently, it shows Harry dragging Paul up onto the Globe."

Aurelia winced. "Video?"

"I have a copy. I was just about to watch it."

"But the video doesn't show him killing Watson?"

"I imagine that will be the basis of our defence," Elsa told her. "If they can't produce anything else, they can't prove Harry was involved in Watson's murder."

"False imprisonment?"

"Possibly. If there's evidence the victim was alive in that video, then we're probably looking at that, and assault. And we might have to beat a conspiracy charge. If Watson was already dead..."

"Assisting an offender?"

"Perhaps. I need to watch the video. And talk to my client."

"Perverting the course of justice may come into it," Aurelia said.

Elsa nodded. "Anyone finding a body in that condition would have known they needed to alert the authorities."

"And your client didn't."

"No."

Aurelia sniffed. They were both used to dealing with men like Harry Coutts. Elsa would do her best for him, but he wasn't helping himself.

"How did he die?" Aurelia asked. "Paul Watson?"

"His throat was slit. If it had gone much deeper, he would have been decapitated."

"I presume they've been searching your client's home."

"His home address is a flat in Weymouth, he tells me he hasn't been there for over two weeks. He's been living at his mum's."

"And they're searching that?"

"CSI are there now," Elsa said. "I've spoken to Mrs Coutts, she says they won't find anything. She insists her Harry wouldn't hurt a fly."

Aurelia scoffed. "How many times have you had to act for him?"

"More than I'd like," Elsa said. "But it'll be fine. We'll come up with something."

"Even if he refuses to speak?"

"Even if he refuses to speak."

"Very well." Aurelia stood up. "And what about our other matter?"

Elsa looked up at her. "That's in hand."

"It is?"

Elsa nodded.

"You going to be more specific?" Aurelia asked.

"I'm not ready to give you full details yet, but I think the firm will be in the clear very soon."

"Good."

Aurelia tapped the back of the chair she'd vacated. "I'm counting on you for this. We'll never find another named partner while we've got this hanging over us."

"We can always promote from within," Elsa told her.

"That's worse. Whoever we promote will know we've been lying to them."

Elsa swallowed. Her partner was right.

"Deal with it, Elsa," Aurelia said.

"Yes, Aurelia."

CHAPTER FIFTY-EIGHT

THE DCI HAD SAID she wanted to speak to Carpenter before Kelvin. But she hadn't specifically told Dennis that applied to him. He knew he was grasping at straws, but he didn't want the boss wading in here without knowing the lie of the land himself first.

He pulled his shoulders back as he entered the spacious office at the back of Arthur Kelvin's house. The room had broad windows and a view across the mouth of Poole Harbour to the Isle of Purbeck. Thin autumn sunlight sparkled on the water and yachts glided past. The room itself was almost as impressive. The desk was heavy, made of smooth oak, and the carpet was the kind that absorbed every sound.

Kelvin turned in his chair as Dennis entered. The woman who'd brought him in, clad in a fawn dress and spotless white apron, nodded and closed the door as she left.

Kelvin gave him a supercilious smile. "DS Frampton. To what do I owe the pleasure?"

"I imagine you're aware that we're investigating Paul Watson's murder," Dennis told him, standing by the door.

Kelvin gestured towards the leather chair opposite his desk. "Take a seat, Sergeant. Make yourself comfortable."

He stood and walked to a cabinet near the window.

"Can I get you a drink?"

"No, thank you."

"I'm sure you won't mind if I have one."

Dennis said nothing.

Kelvin picked up a crystal whisky decanter and poured a generous measure into a heavy-bottomed glass. He lifted it to his nose, inhaled and smiled. He turned to Dennis, swirling it around the glass.

"So what brings you to my door?" he asked.

"Paul Watson was the architect on the Horizon development."

"Was he? I'm afraid all I know about the man is that he was brutally murdered and left on top of a local landmark on Tuesday night. Tragedy. His poor family."

Dennis felt his jaw clench. The thought of Arthur Kelvin feeling sympathy was beyond him.

"The Horizon development was owned by Sunrise Holdings," Dennis stated.

Kelvin looked at him. He took a swig of his whisky and peered into the glass.

"That's interesting," he said.

"And Companies House lists you as a director of Sunrise Holdings," Dennis added.

"Ah," said Kelvin. "It does, does it?"

He sat down in his chair and swung it from side to side.

"I'm sure you'll forgive me for not remembering, I have involvement in a few businesses."

Dennis pursed his lips.

Arthur Kelvin had a revolving portfolio of businesses. He would drop them as soon as they became liabilities, either financial or legal. Then he'd pick up more. Most were a front for his criminal activities. But Dennis knew how difficult that was to prove.

"So Sunrise Holdings," he said. "Is that a legitimate business?"

Kelvin smiled. "You've read the listing on Companies House. What do you think?"

"The accounts seem to be in order. The accounts that have been submitted, that is."

Kelvin raised an eyebrow. "You think the submitted accounts aren't the real accounts?"

"I wouldn't know. But that's not what I'm here to ask you about."

"Good," said Kelvin. "I had a nasty feeling I might have needed to call my lawyer. What can I help you with?"

He took another swig of the whisky.

"Was anybody in the business unhappy with Paul Watson's work?" Dennis asked.

Kelvin placed the glass down. "In what way unhappy?"

"I heard it was a complex piece of engineering. If it turned out not to be feasible, then it would be a costly and embarrassing situation."

"Do you have evidence that the construction wasn't going according to plan?" Kelvin asked.

Of course they didn't, thought Dennis. The project hadn't even reached the phase where the cantilevering would be constructed.

"Did you and Paul Watson ever meet?" he asked.

"Avoiding my question?"

"I'm here to ask the questions, Mr Kelvin. In case it's escaped your notice, this is a murder inquiry."

Kelvin nodded. "Of course, Sergeant, and I'm only too happy to help. So you want to know about the relationships within the business? Whether I had any direct dealings with Paul Watson?"

"Did you?"

"No. Very few of the directors did."

"When you say very few," Dennis said, "does that mean some of them *did* work directly with Paul?"

"I believe Amanda did. Amanda Bennett. A non-executive director, but she likes to stick her oar in."

"Her brother, Darren Mathieson," Dennis said. "Do you know him?"

Kelvin looked back at him for a moment, not speaking. He licked his lips.

"Not sure that I do," he said. "Is he another director?"

Dennis leaned forward.

"I'd expect you to know the names of the other directors."

"Until five minutes ago I'd forgotten I was even a shareholder. You'll have to forgive me."

"So you don't know him?"

"Sorry to disappoint, Sergeant."

Dennis placed his hands in his lap. "Darren Mathieson is the managing director of Swanage Building Services. Lead contractor on the site. But you don't know him?"

"Never heard of the man," Kelvin replied.

"That surprises me. I imagine you come into contact with the building trade on a regular basis."

"There are plenty of builders in this neck of the woods," Kelvin told him. "And I don't always work with local men. Now, is there anything concrete you want to ask me about, or are you just conjecturing about people involved in the Horizon development?"

"Did you ever come across Bella Phipps?" Dennis asked.

"Never heard of her."

Kelvin stood up. He downed the last of his whisky and placed the glass on the table, slightly harder than was necessary.

"Have you got anything specific to ask me? I've got a meeting."

"Do you know Laurence Smith?"

"I know his name. Swanage Council. Weaselly little man. I've met him once or twice, through friends. But no, I wouldn't say I *know* him. Is that all?"

Dennis stood up. "For now."

"Good." Kelvin gestured for him to leave.

Dennis turned towards the door.

"By the way, how's DC Chiles?" Kelvin asked.

Dennis stiffened.

"He's fine," he replied, not turning to face the man. "Transferred to the Met."

"So I heard. How's his brother?"

Breathe. "I wouldn't know."

Dennis opened the door and left the room, his heart pounding.

CHAPTER FIFTY-NINE

LESLEY'S PHONE rang as she drove towards Wareham.

"DCI Clarke."

"That's very formal."

"Sorry, Els. What's up?"

"I've just been to your house. There's a redheaded woman in there. Tells me she's a DI from your old force."

Lesley pulled in a breath. "I was going to tell you about that." Although exactly what she was going to tell Elsa, she hadn't decided.

"You and she haven't got a history, have you?" Elsa asked.

"Only a professional history, if that's what you mean."

Elsa laughed. "Don't worry, I didn't get any vibes from her."

"You know my relationship history," Lesley told her. "I married Terry when I was in my twenties, and now I'm with you."

"So why is one of your old colleagues down here?"

"She's helping me with a case."

"You're short-staffed?"

"You could say that."

"Which case is it? Paul Watson?"

This was the other downside to a relationship with a criminal lawyer.

"Yes," she lied. "The Watson case. We needed an extra brain on it."

"She's good, is she?" Elsa asked. "She seems bright."

"She is. I'm just on my way to see her. How's your day been?"

"I think you know the answer to that," Elsa said.

"Yeah."

Lesley thought about the look on Elsa's face when she'd walked in to find her and Dennis in the interview room with Harry Coutts.

"Is Harry Coutts going to say anything more than *no comment* tomorrow morning when we interview him again?"

"I don't have that in my diary," Elsa said. "You need to alert me if you're going to be talking to him again."

Lesley rolled her eyes. She turned into the road where her cottage was.

"I'm at the house now," she said. "Where are you?"

"Duke of Wellington," Elsa replied. "Told Tom I'd help him out for a couple of hours. Why don't you come in? I'll pour you a G&T."

"I'll be driving," Lesley said. "I was hoping you'd let me stay at your flat tonight."

"Of course I will, sweetie, you never have to ask."

"I just thought maybe what happened with Coutts..."

"That was professional," Elsa said. "If you and I are going to make this work, we have to keep the professional and the personal separate."

"Good." Lesley got out of the car. "I'll see you in about half an hour."

"Will do. Love you."

CHAPTER SIXTY

"Don't go just yet, Mike," Tina said. She leaned in to her screen.

Mike had his hand on the office door. "You changed your mind about the pub?"

"Not that. I might have something."

He let his hand drop. "Have something on what?"

She pointed at her screen.

"This guy, Vick McCarty. Every time Harry Coutts has been arrested, he's been with him."

Mike stood behind Tina's chair. She could smell his after-shave mixed with sweat. It had been a long day.

"Every single time?" he asked.

"Every single time," she confirmed. "Maybe we should have a chat with him."

The two of them looked at the picture on the screen. McCarty was white, slightly overweight, with brown hair and a kiss curl in the middle of his forehead. In the mug shot, he wore a tightly buttoned shirt and a blank expression.

"So he's a member of the WDL?" Mike asked.

"He was at one of their marches last year."

"I'll call the sarge."

"OK."

Tina waited while Mike dialled. After a few moments he put his phone down and nodded.

"Sarge says we should talk to him. Just a chat."

"When?" she asked.

"Tomorrow morning," he said. "You want to do it together?"

She smiled.

"It's a date."

His eyes flashed at her. "Really?"

"I'm joking, Mike."

His expression dropped.

"See you in the morning, Mike."

"See you, T."

CHAPTER SIXTY-ONE

ZOE SAT BACK on the sofa and lifted her feet, crossing her ankles on the coffee table in front of her. This room might be small, but it was warm and tidy. Her own living room in Birmingham was a tip. Her son Nicholas had been accustomed to tidying up after her, and since he'd gone to university, she'd not got into the habit of doing it herself.

She breathed in the smell of cleaning fluid and fresh air and grabbed the remote control from the arm of the sofa. She flicked on the TV. Lesley had Netflix too.

There was a knock at the door. Zoe turned the TV off and went to answer it, expecting to find a neighbour wondering who she was.

"Lesley," she said. "Why did you knock?"

Lesley smiled at her. "I didn't want to intrude."

"But it's your house, you can just let yourself in."

Lesley shook her head. "While you're staying here, this is your space."

"Thanks. I guess I'd better ask you in then."

Lesley laughed and followed Zoe into the living room.

"You making yourself at home?" she asked.

"Nice place you've got," Zoe said.

"Really?"

Zoe looked around the room. "What's wrong with it?"

"It's tiny," Lesley said. "The TV's about two metres away from your face when you sit in that sofa, and it takes three strides to get into the kitchen."

"I like it," Zoe said. "Your kitchen is bigger than mine at home." Cleaner, too, she thought.

Lesley flushed. "Sorry."

"It's OK. Your girlfriend came by earlier. She was looking for you."

"Elsa."

Zoe smiled. "Unless you've got a bunch of women on the go down here?"

"It's hard enough to manage one relationship in this job. Did she ask you about the case?"

"I made something up, if that's what you're thinking. I know she's a criminal lawyer, didn't know how much you'd..."

Lesley felt her face heat up. "Thanks." She didn't feel comfortable with Elsa getting too close to the Mackie case.

"So are you going to brief me on this case then?" Zoe asked. "DCI Mackie?"

"Let's have a coffee," Lesley said.

"You got anything decent?"

"That'll be for you to judge."

Zoe waited for Lesley to lead her into the kitchen.

Lesley had a filter machine and a tin of ground coffee in a high cupboard. It seemed to be the closest she came to food. Zoe had already looked in the fridge and found a bottle of gin and a pork pie that looked a week old.

"You don't spend much time here?" she asked.

"No," Lesley said as she filled the coffee maker. "I'm normally in Bournemouth at Elsa's."

Zoe nodded. "Her being a criminal lawyer must make for interesting conversations across the interview table."

Lesley laughed. "It certainly did today. Our first time in the interview room together."

"You've done well to avoid it so far," Zoe said. "But then I imagine you don't make as many arrests down here as back in Brum."

"Don't be so sure," Lesley told her. "When there's a murder down here, it tends to come as part of a job lot."

"Are they all linked?"

Lesley shrugged. "A couple might be, others definitely not. There was a case on Brownsea Island in the summer. Domestic, nothing sinister about that. Then the case we had before that, well..."

"What about it?" Zoe asked.

Lesley pulled out two coffees. She leaned against the worktop and looked at Zoe.

"It involved Elsa. Her business partner was killed. It turned out to be his mistress who did it, but there might be a connection to Mackie's death."

"How so?"

"Arthur Kelvin. You've been looking into him."

"Certainly have," Zoe said, sipping her coffee. "Reminds me of Trevor Hamm."

"He's small compared to Hamm, but he's of the same ilk. Elsa's his solicitor. I think Harry, her partner, was before he died. I'm still not convinced Kelvin didn't have anything to do with his murder."

"OK."

Zoe wondered if she'd need to question this Elsa woman. It could get complicated.

"This coffee isn't bad."

Lesley laughed. "I remembered you like good coffee."

"Nothing else in the fridge, though," Zoe said. "Good job I don't take milk."

"That's what comes with hardly ever being here," Lesley told her. "I should probably tell them to stop paying the rent. It feels like a bit of a commitment, especially when I'm supposed to be back in Birmingham in a couple of months."

"You're not going to settle down here, then?"

Zoe knew that Acting DCI Frank Dawson was hoping Lesley would stay in Dorset and he'd be in with a chance of getting her job on a permanent basis. How she felt about it herself, she wasn't so sure.

"I don't know yet," Lesley told her. "It might depend on Mackie. Whether Elsa's firm has got anything to do with it."

"You think they have?" Zoe asked.

"I don't know. All that I'm certain of is that Mackie didn't commit suicide. Gail, she's my CSM, she showed me the site where he was found. It just doesn't fit. The angle of his fall, the fact that he wasn't depressed. He'd bought a cruise holiday. Who buys a cruise holiday and then kills himself?"

"You'd be surprised," Zoe said.

"I can feel it in my blood," Lesley told her. "He didn't commit suicide. Somebody killed him, and I think it was because he was onto Arthur Kelvin."

"You don't think he was in cahoots with him?" Zoe asked. "Another Randle?"

Lesley shuddered. "Dear God, no."

Zoe nodded. She was hoping Mackie wouldn't turn out

to have been corrupt. But she wasn't ruling anything out just yet.

"So where do you want me to start?" she asked.

"I think with Mackie's wife. You're not connected to him in the same way the investigating team would have been. Go to see her, she might talk to you. Get some background on his mood in the days before his death. Whether he told her about anything unusual that was happening. See what you can unearth."

"What about this Sadie Dawes person?" Zoe asked. "You think she's already spoken to his wife?"

"I imagine she's tried," Lesley told her. "Let's just hope she didn't succeed."

"You think she knows something concrete?"

Lesley shrugged. She took another sip of her coffee.

"No idea. That's what I want you to find out."

CHAPTER SIXTY-TWO

DON PAUSED for breath halfway up the hill. He'd been walking the steps up to the obelisk for thirty years, but it didn't get any easier with practice.

He turned to see Mary labouring up behind him, a dozen or so steps below.

"Come on, love," he said. "Nearly halfway there."

She stopped and looked up, panting.

"I hate it when you make me come this way," she told him. "Why can't we go round the coast path?"

"Because this way, you get to walk towards the sea. Better views."

"I've done it before, Don," she said. "I do know what the views look like."

He smiled down at her. "Come on, fourteen steps and you'll be with me. We can pause, have a cup of tea."

Don always brought a flask of tea in his rucksack. He liked to open it when he reached the top of the steps, to sit on the base of the obelisk and admire the views.

From up there you could see all the way across to Poole

in the north and past Swanage to the Jurassic Coast in the south. Very few people climbed up here, and the wildlife was undisturbed. In spring, he liked to listen to the skylarks rising over the obelisk. Right now, in October, he hoped to hear linnets and wagtails.

He opened up the flask and poured her half a cup.

"Drink up," he said. "We can have a proper cup at the top."

She sighed. "You go on without me, I'll be fine here."

"No," he told her. "We'll go at your pace. It's not as if we've got anything else to do this morning."

She took a sip of the tea. "That's better."

He kissed her on the forehead and she smiled back at him.

"Come on, then," she told him, her eyes glinting. "Drag me up to the top of the hill, why don't you?"

He gave her a grin and put the flask back in his rucksack.

He shouldered it and started walking up the hill. Mary was faster this time, only having to stop twice before they reached the top.

When Don mounted the last step, his wife was twenty or more steps behind him, but going strong. She hadn't been walking these hills as long as he had. When the kids had been young, she'd preferred to stay at home. He'd brought them up here, showing them the views, insisting that they were happier here than they would be watching the television.

He made for the obelisk, pulling his rucksack off his shoulder and anticipating his first cup of tea.

Another walker was up here, leaning against it. The man was very still – probably listening for birds, Don thought.

And then he stopped.

"Mary, don't come any further," he said, without turning to face her.

Don stared at the man.

He wasn't resting.

His arms reached behind the obelisk. Don could see ropes attached to his wrists.

He swallowed down anxiety.

"Excuse me? Are you OK?"

No response. The man was very still. Don took a step forward. He recoiled. The man's fleece was dark, which was why Don had missed the blood.

He put his hand to his mouth.

"Stay where you are," he called to Mary. "Don't come any further."

"What is it, Don?" she shouted back up.

"There's a man up here," he said. "I think he's been..."

Don swallowed back a wave of nausea.

The blood was concentrated around the man's neck. His fleece was zipped up, so Don couldn't see if there was more. Something poked out of his collar. It was white, daubed in blood.

Don knew better than to touch him.

"Mary," he called down. "Have you brought your phone up?"

"Of course I did. Not sure if I'll get a signal up here, though."

He turned back towards her.

"Pass it here," he told her. "We need to call 999."

CHAPTER SIXTY-THREE

LESLEY WAS COMING off the M3 when her phone rang. She glanced at it then looked back at the road.

"Tina," she said. "I'm half an hour from Bella Phipps's office. What's up?"

"I found something last night, boss," Tina said. "I hope you don't mind me calling you now."

Lesley looked at the clock on the dashboard. It was 8am. She'd woken at five, left Elsa's flat at half past. The traffic hadn't been too bad, but she knew it was about to get worse.

"That's fine, Tina," she said. "What is it?"

"I was going through Harry Coutts's arrest records from the previous times we nicked him. He's got a mate who was always with him. Every single time."

"What's his mate's name?" Lesley asked.

"Vick McCarty."

"And what kind of offences are we talking about?"

"Assaulting a man during a WDL march last year. A couple of criminal damage arrests."

"Has this Vick McCarty had any other arrests? Anything where Coutts wasn't there?"

"None."

"OK," said Lesley. "You want me to tell you to go see him?"

"The sarge already said that Mike and I should."

"Well what are you waiting for?"

"Just thought you'd want to know."

"Thanks, Tina. Tell me if you get anything useful from him."

"Will do."

Tina hung up.

Forty minutes later, Lesley pulled up outside Bella Phipps's office. It was a smart, glass-fronted unit on Putney Bridge Road. A far cry from Paul Watson's shabby little office in Swanage.

She parked her car and spent a few moments navigating the app she was expected to pay for parking with, then walked to the office. The door was locked but there was movement inside. Lesley lifted her arms to the glass, shielding the light so she could see past the reflections.

A tall Black woman in a purple suit stood up from a desk and walked towards the window.

"Can I help you?" she called through the glass.

Lesley held up her warrant card. The woman frowned, then nodded, and opened the door.

"I've already spoken to your colleague. DC Chiles."

"Are you Bella Phipps?" Lesley asked.

"I am. You're from Dorset." She indicated Lesley's ID. "You're here about Paul."

Lesley nodded. "Are you going to let me in, then?"

Bella shrugged and stood back to let Lesley past.

Inside, the office was an open space. Four desks, only one of which was occupied.

"Nobody else in yet?" Lesley asked.

"My assistant doesn't get in until half past nine. That desk over there used to be Paul's."

"He kept a desk here after the move to Swanage?"

"It wasn't like the office was going anywhere."

"Did he often work from here?"

"Occasionally," Bella said. "He came up once a fortnight. Client meetings, business reviews. I took over most of his London clients but he still managed a couple of them remotely, in between the Horizon job."

"So you took over responsibility for the vast majority of the business while Paul focused on the one project?"

"It was a big project." Bella gestured towards a chair. "Why don't you sit down?"

The chair was one of three in a corner. Lush pot plants surrounded the chairs, and in front of them was a glass-topped coffee table with architectural magazines. Lesley chose a chair facing the office and the street beyond.

"Can I get you a coffee?" Bella asked.

"I won't be here long," Lesley told her.

"But you drove all the way up from Dorset."

"I wanted to talk to you in person."

"You could have done that over the phone."

Lesley shrugged. "Sometimes these things are better done face to face."

"Fair enough." Bella sat down. "I've already told your colleague about Paul's working habits. Surely that can't have anything to do with his death?"

Lesley looked at her. "How has it affected you, Paul

being killed? Will you have to take on responsibility for the Horizon development?"

Bella sighed. "I haven't really thought about that yet. Too busy fielding questions from clients." She tugged at a fingernail. "He'll be missed. He was the creative one. I was the one with the head for business."

"But you gave him responsibility for your most important project?"

"Paul was the best person for the job. It was him who designed the cantilevering system for those apartments. I would never have thought of it. He found a way round the planning regulations that said we couldn't build above the cliff top. The apartments will be below the line of sight of the cliffs, almost hanging off the edge of the headland. It'll be beautiful."

Lesley wasn't so sure whether a building tacked onto the end of Peveril Point would be beautiful, but she imagined she wasn't the one to judge.

"So tell me about your relationship with Paul," she said. "You used to be an item, yes?"

"Again, I told DC Chiles all this. We split up eighteen years ago. Before he met Sherry."

"And do you and Sherry get on?"

Bella pulled back in her chair. "Fine."

"You're sure about that?"

"She's a nice woman, she was good for him. She dotes on those kids."

"But you haven't seen Sherry since she moved down to Swanage?"

"I didn't have cause to." Bella's voice was clipped.

"I'm getting the impression from your reaction to my questions that you didn't like Paul's wife very much."

"I never said anything of the sort."

"Why didn't you like her?"

"I never said I didn't like her."

"Was there jealousy between the pair of you? Were you jealous of her marriage to Paul? Was she jealous of you for the time you spent with him professionally?" Lesley eyed the woman. "If you were having an affair, you should tell me."

"No, we weren't having an affair. Why does everyone assume we were? And I certainly didn't want him dead, if that's what you're thinking." Bella's voice went quiet. "I'll miss him. He was a good man."

"So I've heard. So, I still can't understand why anybody would want him dead."

Bella shrugged. "Nor can I."

"You've got no idea who might have killed him?" Lesley asked. "No professional rivalries, no clients that he pissed off?"

"Paul was the height of professionalism. If a client wasn't happy, he wanted to know about it. He would always address it, it was his mantra. An angry client can be your best client if you deal with them the right way."

"Hmm." Lesley wasn't so sure. For her, an angry client was somebody resisting arrest.

"How much did you know about Sunrise Holdings?" she asked.

"They were our biggest client. Still are." A shadow crossed Bella's face.

"But you don't like working with them?"

"The woman we've been dealing with, Amanda Bennett. She's got an edge to her. I don't think she likes me."

"No?"

"She seemed to like Paul, though. So it's not a race thing, if that's what you're thinking."

"Did DC Chiles tell you about the note that we found on Paul?"

"What note?"

Lesley watched her for a reaction. "It said *go home*."

Bella's eyes widened. "So you do think it was a racist attack?"

"Why do you think somebody might want him to *go home*?"

"I've no idea," Bella replied.

"What about Laurence Smith? You know about him?"

Bella scoffed. "If every nimby who didn't like a new building killed the architect, there wouldn't be an architect left on Earth."

Lesley smiled. The woman had a point.

"OK," she said. "So have you spoken to Sherry Watson since Paul's death?"

"I'll be speaking to her at the funeral," Bella replied. "Assuming she wants me there."

"You think she'll keep you from going?"

"She won't appreciate me being there. But she can't stop me."

Lesley nodded. If Bella and Paul weren't having an affair, why would Sherry want her to stay away from the funeral?

"Why wouldn't she want you there?"

"She won't want *anyone* there, Detective. She liked to keep Paul to herself. It was part of the reason they moved."

Lesley found this hard to believe. "Where were you on Tuesday night?" she asked.

"I've already given my alibi to your colleague," Bella said. "I was with friends."

"So you were," Lesley replied. "We checked them out."

"Good," Bella said, relief coming into her voice.

Lesley stood up. She needed to get back to Dorset. She'd learned nothing new here.

"Thank you for your time, Ms Phipps. If you do decide there's anything you want to tell us, here's my card."

Bella looked at it then placed it on the coffee table.

"I will," she said.

CHAPTER SIXTY-FOUR

MIKE PULLED up outside Vick McCarty's address. It was a narrow, semi-detached house in Broadstone outside Poole.

He looked at Tina. "What d'you think?"

She shrugged. "Looks nicer than I expected."

Tina had come in her own clothes today. She'd spoken to the sarge and got his permission not to wear uniform, and they'd taken Mike's car instead of a squad vehicle. Vick McCarty had a history of antipathy towards the police. This way, he was less likely to run before they even got in the house.

"Let's hope he's in," Mike said.

"It's eight thirty-four," said Tina as she got out of the car. "He hasn't got a job, as far as we can find. Hopefully he's still in bed."

Mike knocked on the door and waited, Tina a pace behind him. She tugged at her jacket. She wore a maroon jacket and white blouse, more figure-hugging than her uniform. It had been all Mike could do to tear his eyes away from her on the drive over.

The door opened and an elderly man holding a walking stick looked back at them.

"Whatever it is you're selling, I'm not buying it."

Mike held up his ID. "I'm DC Legg, Dorset Police. This is PC Abbott."

"She doesn't look like a PC to me."

"I'm not in uniform today." Tina got out her own ID.

The man grunted. "What d'you want?"

"Does Vick McCarty live here?" Mike asked.

The man sniffed. A noisy, textured sniff that made Mike recoil.

"Think I'm going to tell you if he is?"

"Granddad," a voice came from inside the house. "Who is it?"

"Little fucker," the man muttered. "Now you know he's here, don't you?"

If the man had been quick-witted, he might have claimed to have as many grandchildren as he wanted. But now, they knew Vick was here.

"We just want to talk to him," Mike said. "He's not under arrest."

"Good," the old man replied.

Mike took a step forward, hoping the man would respond by stepping back. He did. Mike continued walking as the man backed into the kitchen.

"Vick!" Mike called upstairs. "Vick McCarty?"

"Who wants to know?" came a voice.

"DC Legg, Dorset Police. We just want to ask you some questions."

Silence. Mike and Tina exchanged looks.

"D'you want me to go upstairs?" she asked.

He shook his head. "Best to wait down here."

"What about the windows?"

"We're not arresting him," he replied. "Why would he try and escape?"

She raised an eyebrow.

"OK," he replied. "You watch the front window."

Tina went outside and Mike hurried up the stairs. He pushed open the door to an empty bedroom. He turned into the next room. Vick McCarty sat on the bed, hunched against the wall.

Mike put his hands out to show they were empty.

"I'm not arresting you. See, I haven't got cuffs with me. I just want to ask you some questions."

"I'm not answering."

"All I need is to know where you were on Tuesday night."

"That's easy!"

Mike turned around to see the old man behind him.

"He was at church, with me."

"Church?" Mike asked.

"Yeah," the man said. "You got a problem with that?"

"Which church?"

What churches met on a Tuesday night?

"New Life Temple," the man said. "Evangelical, meets Tuesday evenings. We both signed in when we got there. You can check with the priest."

Mike looked at him. He was pretty sure that evangelical churches didn't have priests, but he wasn't about to argue.

"Give me the address," he said.

The man gave him an address in Bournemouth.

"We'll check it." Mike turned to Vick. "Have you seen your mate Harry Coutts lately?"

Vick shook his head. "I haven't seen him for a couple of weeks, not since I got a job."

"What job?"

"Got it two weeks ago. Not a crime to get a job, is it?"

"You got a job a couple of weeks ago?" Mike asked. "So why aren't you at it now?"

"It's a Saturday, isn't it? I don't work on Saturday."

"So where's the job?" Mike asked.

"Labouring job," Vick said. "Over in Swanage, working on that new development. Horizon, at Peveril Point."

CHAPTER SIXTY-FIVE

Lesley was passing the turnoff for Southampton when her phone rang. It was Superintendent Carpenter.

"Sir," she said. "Is something wrong?"

"I need you to come and see me."

"I'm on my way back from London, interviewing a witness. I can be in the office in..." she checked the satnav "... an hour."

"It's Saturday, Lesley. I'm at home."

"Very well, sir," she said. "Give me your address."

"I'll text it through to you."

She pulled over at the services and checked the address. It was in Christchurch.

Perfect, she thought, only half an hour away. She programmed it into the satnav and was there thirty-five minutes later.

Carpenter opened the door. "Come on through," he said, ushering her into a study on the right.

A TV blared somewhere and two female voices came from a door up ahead, arguing.

"Ignore them," Carpenter said. "My daughter's trying to convince my wife to let her go clubbing tonight."

Lesley shrugged. Her own daughter Sharon had no interest in clubbing, thank God.

"Take a seat," he said.

Lesley sat in one of two armchairs in the corner of his study. She smoothed her hands over her trousers: cords today, less businesslike than on weekdays.

"Is there a problem, sir?" she asked.

"DS Frampton," he said. "He was off sick last week."

"He's back now, sir. I did a return-to-work interview with him. He had the flu."

Carpenter raised an eyebrow. "He didn't have the flu, Lesley."

She frowned. "That's what he told me. I went to see him at home. He seemed—"

"He didn't have the flu."

Lesley sat straight. "With respect, sir, why am I hearing about this from you and not from him?"

"DS Frampton went to see a psychiatrist in Bournemouth while he was off."

"A psychiatrist?" Dennis was the last person Lesley could imagine visiting a shrink. "Are you sure?"

"Let's just say this shrink is a friend of mine," Carpenter said. "He's done some work for us, occasionally seen one of our people."

Lesley frowned. If Dennis had been to see a psychiatrist, the doctor would be bound by patient confidentiality.

"Why did he tell you? And surely Dennis could have seen the police psychiatrist?"

"Dr Hawes does some work for us occasionally. Sensitive

cases. And it just so happens he's transferring to us next month."

"Ah."

"He was concerned about a potential conflict."

Lesley shook her head. "Are you sure, sir? DS Frampton hasn't shown any—"

"If your DS is about to lose his marbles, I want to know. And I also don't like that he's lying to you about it."

Lesley met the super's gaze. She didn't like him interfering in her team.

She thought about how Dennis had been over the last couple of days. They'd been working alongside each other without any problems.

"I don't think he's about to *lose his marbles*, sir. I'll talk to him."

"You do that."

Carpenter stood up and walked to the door.

"And about the other matter," he said.

Lesley stiffened. He was about to mention Zoe.

"Yes," she replied.

"Let me know how you get on, won't you?"

"Of course."

Lesley waited for him to say more. Instead, he opened the front door, expecting her to leave.

The house was quiet now, no voices. As Lesley approached the car, she looked back to see a curtain moving in an upstairs window.

She sat in the driver's seat. She wasn't sure of the best route to the office from here. She needed to hurry, the team were expecting her.

Her phone rang.

"Tina," she said. *Again.*

"Boss," Tina replied. "We've had a development."

"Yes?"

"Another body."

Lesley put her hand on the steering wheel. "Where?"

"Above Swanage, the obelisk up by Ballard Down."

Lesley had no idea where she meant.

"Is it related to Paul Watson's death?"

"There's a note, boss," Tina replied. "It says *go home*."

CHAPTER SIXTY-SIX

"Do come in. I've just brewed a pot of tea, would you like some?"

Zoe grimaced. "Have you got coffee, Mrs Mackie?"

"Call me Gwen, please. I think so. Come into the kitchen."

Gwen Mackie led her into a narrow kitchen at the back of the house. She opened and closed some doors, and eventually found a jar of instant coffee.

She held it up to Zoe, smiling. "This do?"

"It's fine," Zoe said. "I'll have a glass of water, please."

"Fair enough. So you're a colleague of my late husband's?"

"Not exactly," Zoe told her. "I'm with West Midlands Police."

"So what brings West Midlands Police down here?"

"I've been asked to look into your husband's death. DCI Clarke thought an independent detective might be more appropriate."

"DCI Clarke." Gwen's hands stopped moving and she gazed out of the window. "She's his replacement, isn't she?"

"I imagine this is difficult for you."

Gwen turned to Zoe. She pulled on a sad smile. "It's fine. I understand you have questions." She picked up a mug and a glass of water and motioned for Zoe to go into the living room.

The room wasn't large, but it was light and airy. Photos adorned the mantelpiece. A wedding photo, one taken on a beach, another in this room. The fourth had Mackie in his DCI's uniform.

"Please, make yourself comfortable," Gwen said. "To tell you the truth, it's nice to have company on a Saturday. I see my daughter on weekdays, but at the weekend she's always doing her own thing. It gets lonely, you know?"

"I can imagine," Zoe said. "My son just left for university, my house feels empty sometimes."

Gwen placed the glass of water in front of Zoe. "There you are. Sorry I couldn't make you anything more interesting."

"It's fine," said Zoe. "Thank you." She took a gulp of the water.

"So," said Gwen, "how can I help you?"

"If you don't mind, I'd like to know more about the circumstances of your husband's death."

Gwen looked down at her knees. "I already told everything I know to Superintendent Carpenter."

"I understand that," said Zoe. "And I'm sorry to bring this up again for you. But like I say, I'm independent. I was hoping that without having known your husband, I might be in a better position to..."

The woman nodded. "I know what you mean. Tim went

back decades with Anthony Carpenter. Carpenter had just become sergeant when Tim started in the force, you know. He did well for himself. I always wondered why my husband didn't follow in his footsteps."

"When did your husband retire?" asked Zoe.

"Eight months ago," said Mrs Mackie. "Two months before he died."

"And how did he feel about retiring?"

"Mixed feelings. He knew he'd miss the job, his colleagues, the routine of it. But he was ready for life to slow down a bit. We were looking forward to spending more time together. We had a good relationship, Detective. We weren't one of those couples that can't stand being thrown together when one of them retires. We'd booked a cruise, the Norwegian Fjords. I was looking forward to it."

Her voice was sad.

"Like I say, I'm sorry to bring back unhappy memories," Zoe said. "But I'm puzzled. Your husband was looking forward to retirement, and you'd paid for a cruise. Did you think it was odd that he killed himself?"

Gwen's jaw tightened. "My husband didn't kill himself."

"No?" Zoe asked.

"He wasn't the sort of man who'd do that. He was too... too responsible."

She picked up her mug and held it, not drinking.

"He'd attended suicides when he was a constable. There was one time back in the eighties when he'd had to go to a train line, the level crossing up at Wool. A woman stepped onto it when a train was approaching. Ghastly it was, he couldn't sleep for a month. The driver, well these days you'd call it Post Traumatic Stress Disorder. In those days, he was given a bottle of brandy and told to get back to work the next day."

Gwen looked at Zoe, her eyes full of tears.

"You see, he wouldn't have inflicted that on his colleagues. He would have known that Dennis Frampton would have been sent to deal with it. That the DCs would have had to trawl over the evidence. My Tim would never have done that to his friends."

"So why do you think that the coroner recorded a verdict of suicide?" Zoe asked her.

"Oh, that's easy," she said. "Anthony Carpenter."

"Superintendent Carpenter?" Zoe asked. "What would he have to do with it?"

"He would have told the coroner what to say. He would have leaned on the crime scene people, wrapped up the whole affair in a matter of days. I saw it happening. I was too full of grief at the time to argue. But they all lied, and I'm sure it's because of him."

CHAPTER SIXTY-SEVEN

Dennis parked his car on the opposite side of the road, six houses along. He watched as the woman got out of her Mini and walked to the door, his eyes narrowing.

She rang the doorbell and the occupant let her in. She turned, squinting along the street before the two of them went inside. Dennis shrank down in his seat.

He watched the house, alert for signs of movement.

Nothing happened for twenty minutes until eventually, the two women emerged.

Gwen Mackie stood in the doorway, the detective talking to her from the driveway. They looked friendly, comfortable with each other. Not like two women who'd only just met, certainly not like two women who'd been discussing what they undoubtedly had been.

Why was a West Midlands detective digging into DCI Mackie's death now? Was it the DCI's idea, or had it been Carpenter? The super had acted strangely around the time Mackie had died. He'd been anxious to put it behind them, to replace him quickly.

Dennis had revered DCI Mackie. He'd followed on the man's coattails his entire career, and he'd been devastated when his former mentor had died.

But the evidence was clear. There'd been a note. No sign of a struggle at the scene.

Heaven only knew why Mackie had done it, but he had.

Maybe he couldn't face retirement. Perhaps his life was empty without the job. Dennis had an inkling of how that would feel.

The detective turned away from the house and the door closed behind her.

Dennis ducked down in his seat.

His phone rang. He grabbed it, hissing at it under his breath.

"DS Frampton," he muttered.

"Dennis, why are you whispering?" the DCI said. "Where are you?"

"Boss. What's up?" It was his day off.

"I need you to meet me at the obelisk above Swanage. D'you know it?"

"Why?"

"We've got a second victim."

Across the road, DI Finch got into her car and drove away. Dennis pursed his lips and started the car, resigned to the fact he'd have to let her continue her snooping unseen.

CHAPTER SIXTY-EIGHT

LESLEY WAS HALFWAY up the hill when she decided she needed to stop. She bent over, her fists digging into her thighs.

"Jesus," she muttered under her breath. "Surely there's a better way up here."

She looked behind her. She'd climbed at least a hundred steps, or that was what it felt like. Below her, Swanage was spread out like a toy town.

She turned to look up the hill.

"Shit." She wasn't even halfway up.

Was she in the right place?

She checked her phone. Tina had given her coordinates in the What Three Words app: *trades.unit.computers*. This was the right place.

She looked down to see a small figure at the bottom of the path, trudging up.

Dennis. She decided to wait. Any excuse to get her breath back.

As he approached, she called to him.

"Are you sure there isn't a better way up there?"

He looked up. "This is the quickest way. Certainly the quickest with parking."

"How are you doing this and not getting out of breath?"

He shrugged. "I'm used to it."

Dennis was twelve years older than she was; he should have been busting a gut. Instead, he looked like he'd barely broken a sweat.

"OK," she sighed. "Lead on."

He smiled and passed. She followed, focusing all her attention on moving her legs. She wasn't going to let Dennis get the better of her.

Twenty minutes later, they were at the top of the hill. There was a stone obelisk and a far-reaching view that Lesley couldn't care less about. Slumped against the obelisk was the body of a man. Tina, Mike and Gail were already there.

"How did you all get here so fast on a Saturday?" Lesley asked.

Gail was crouched at the base of the obelisk, taking measurements. She looked up. "I only live in Ulwell." She pointed down the hill. "I walked."

"What about your gear?"

"Gav and Brett will have to haul it up between them."

"I don't envy them," Lesley said. "You sure there isn't a way to get a vehicle up here?"

Gail squinted. "Maybe if you went round via Studland past Old Harry... You could maybe get a trolley or a bike along the path. But to be honest, Lesley, it's just not worth it. This way is quicker. They've cordoned off the road below, that means we can keep our van down there."

Lesley nodded. She'd passed the police cordon and the

squad car at the bottom of the hill. She envied the uniformed constable inside it, not having to make the climb.

"OK." Lesley took a deep breath. "What have we got?"

Gail turned towards the obelisk. The man was tied to it, his arms reaching around the back. Thick blue ropes had been used to secure him.

"Are they the same kind of ropes that were used on Paul Watson?" Lesley asked.

"Different type," Gail said. "These are a little more distinctive."

"Good," Lesley replied. "That gives us more of a chance of tracking them down."

Gail nodded. "I'll take photos and send them to you. You can try the ship's chandlers locally."

Lesley peered at the man. He was in his sixties, or maybe seventies, with thinning grey hair and a mole on his right cheek. His head was bowed and he wore a dark fleece, which all but hid the blood seeping through. The blood was heaviest around his neck. It had dried in the wind.

"His throat was slit," she said.

"Looks like it," said Gail. "I'm not touching him till Whittaker gets here."

"Whittaker? He's never going to make it up here."

Gail shrugged. "He'll have to."

"Hmm." Lesley wasn't so sure.

"So what else have we got?" she asked Gail. "Any other injuries? Any forensics left conveniently lying around for us?"

"Sorry," Gail said. "Nothing. Hardly any blood, too. He wasn't killed here."

"Like Paul Watson." Lesley wasn't surprised. "And what about this note?"

Gail gestured towards Tina who approached them with an evidence bag. Tina was wearing a maroon jacket and grey trousers, not her uniform.

"We went to see Vic McCarty, boss," Tina said. "I thought it would be best not to draw attention to myself."

"Fair enough," Lesley replied.

This was how Tina would look if she became a detective. It suited her.

"Show me this note, then."

Tina handed over a sheet of A4 paper with brown writing: dried blood. Just like Paul Watson's note. Two words: *go home.*

"Does this look like the same handwriting as the last note?" she asked. "It could be a copycat."

"We didn't release information about the note," Gail said. "No one outside the investigation would have known."

"We told some witnesses." Lesley ran through the interviews they'd done, the people they'd asked about that note.

"We'll see," she said. "Have we got an ID?"

"Not yet," Tina said. "We're working on it."

Lesley bent to get a better look at the man's face. He was a good thirty years older than Paul Watson, and he was white.

Not a racially motivated crime, she thought.

In which case, who was this man and just why did his killer want him to go home?

CHAPTER SIXTY-NINE

DENNIS HEADED down the hill towards his car, Gail behind him.

"Hang on a minute," she called out. "Wait for me."

He looked up.

"Struggling?"

She laughed. "Don't even think it. I get plenty of exercise in my job, I'm fitter than most of you lot."

Dennis raised an eyebrow. What Gail didn't know was that he and Pam liked to go hillwalking in their spare time. Dennis was the fittest fifty-eight year-old he knew.

"So what do you think?" he asked her. "Are we going to get any useful forensics?"

She sighed. "I doubt it, but we'll keep trying. If you can identify the victim, that will help us."

"That's my next call," he said. "I'll work through missing persons. Trawl the records, see if anybody matching his description has disappeared."

"Can you contact Whittaker?" she asked him. "He seems to have more time for you than he does for the rest of us."

Dennis nodded. "He's not already on his way?"

"I left him a message, but I haven't heard back. We need to get this body moved, there's a storm coming in from the east. The guys have taken a tent up, but I don't fancy its chances up there."

He nodded. "I'll give him a call on the way to the office."

"Thanks."

Gail walked towards her van which was parked beyond the squad car. Dennis breathed in the chilly air and strode to his own car.

As Dennis approached it, he spotted a green Mini up ahead of him. A redheaded woman got out and approached him.

"DI Finch," he said. "What brings you here?"

She looked at him. "Were you following me earlier?"

"I'm sorry?" He felt his heart pick up pace. "Why would I be following you?"

"You haven't answered the question. Can I talk to you about Mackie sometime?"

He felt his jaw clench.

"*DCI* Mackie was a respected colleague. I think we should leave his memory alone."

"Do you think he committed suicide?" she asked.

"That's what the coroner concluded."

"That's not what I asked you."

He gritted his teeth.

"I don't know what the DCI has you doing, but I suggest you leave well alone. Have some respect, why don't you? Poor Mrs Mackie, having to tolerate people like you trawling up the past."

"She was pleased to see me," Zoe said. "I think she's

anxious for the details of her husband's death not to be swept under the carpet."

"What details?" he sneered. "You have no idea what you're talking about."

"We'll see." She turned back to her car.

He watched as she drove away, his muscles taut. He put a hand on the roof of his car, feeling his legs weaken.

Don't, he told himself. *Hold it together.*

He slid into his car and rested his head against the steering wheel, his flesh clammy.

CHAPTER SEVENTY

LESLEY WAITED for the team to file into her office. They'd left the crime scene after the storm had hit. Gail's team were still up there, seeing what they could salvage before it was destroyed by the elements.

Whittaker hadn't arrived. He'd sent a message asking for the body to be brought to the morgue at Poole Hospital. As long as photographs were taken at the crime scene, he would be happy to examine it there.

Lesley wasn't happy about him shirking his responsibilities. It might be the weekend, and Whittaker might have recently shown signs of deteriorating health. But he could have sent a deputy.

Mike closed the door behind him. Tina was already in a chair opposite Lesley's desk, and Dennis stood beside the board. Tina had added photos of the crime scene, but they were still waiting for a decent photo of their victim. Dennis had been working through missing persons records, but there was no one fitting the man's description.

"OK," Lesley said. "The first thing we need to do is identify our body. That'll help us know if his death is linked to Paul Watson's or if it's a copycat."

"That would be unlikely," Dennis said. "There was no information about that note released to the public."

"You can't be too sure," Lesley told him. "Let's not draw any conclusions until we know who our victim is."

Her phone rang, and she glanced down to see Gail's name on the display.

"I hope you've got good news," she said, holding up her hand up for the team to be quiet.

"We've got prints," Gail replied. "Some on the note, some on the obelisk. There's some smooth stone where we were able to get a partial."

"Do you think both sets of prints are from the same person?" Lesley asked.

"Impossible to tell yet. We'll check them against the database, let you know if we find a match."

"Thanks." Lesley put down her phone.

She sighed. "We've got very little to be going with until we know who this man is."

"Should we go and speak to Laurence Smith?" Tina suggested.

"Or Bella Phipps?" added Mike.

"And then we've got Harry Coutts and his mate Vick," said Dennis.

"Harry is the only one we've got anything solid on," said Lesley. "But the problem is, he's in custody right now. So he definitely didn't kill this guy."

"Are we sure his death was recent?" Tina asked.

"Until we've got the pathology report, we can't be sure," Lesley said. "But he looked fresh."

Tina shuddered. "You think he was up there all night?"

"Who knows? He could have been dumped there minutes before he was found. Have we spoken to the couple that found him?"

"I did," said Mike. "Don and Mary Kemp. They were out for a morning walk. Don came across him first, says he didn't touch him. Mary didn't even look, her husband warned her away."

"What time did they find him?" Lesley asked.

"Seven thirty."

"OK," said Lesley. "We need to put out a call for potential witnesses, find out if anybody else was up there earlier this morning, or maybe last night. That'll help us narrow it down to a time window for him being left there."

"It looks like he was dead before he was taken up," said Dennis.

"You're right," Lesley said. "Not enough blood."

"Just like Paul Watson," Tina added.

Lesley nodded.

There were too many similarities between the two crimes. The lack of blood, the monuments, the notes. But what about Harry Coutts? What about the racial motive?

None of it made sense.

She thumped the desk.

"We need to know who this victim is. Dennis, talk to your mates at local CID. Tina, get on the phone to Uniform. Find out if there's been any sniff of someone going missing. Anybody reporting an incident, suspicious vehicles around that part of Swanage. I want to know if anything dodgy was going on last night. We need to know who our victim is, and we need to know now."

CHAPTER SEVENTY-ONE

"Hi, Tina."

"Hi, Mandy."

PC Mandy Truscott was one of Tina's old colleagues. Her beat was in Swanage.

"What can I do for you?" she asked.

"Have you heard about our body up by the obelisk?" Tina replied.

Mandy winced. "I have, sounds nasty. A second one?"

"We're not sure it's related yet," Tina told her. "But we're still trying to identify the victim."

"Your DS asked us for missing persons reports," Mandy told her. "There's nothing matching the description he gave us."

"I know," Tina said. "But I was wondering if there'd been any incidents in the area yesterday, anything that might have been an assault or an abduction?"

"Hang on a moment."

The phone went quiet. Tina drummed her fingers on the desk while she waited.

"This could be relevant," Mandy said, coming back on the line.

"Go on."

"A woman reported seeing something in her street yesterday afternoon. Two men approaching a third. The three of them got into a car and drove off. The woman who called in thought he might have been pushed into the car by the other two. One of our operators spoke to her, put it on the system, but we just thought it was three friends having an argument. You think the third man could be your victim?"

"It's worth a further look," said Tina. "Thanks, Mandy. Can you send me the case number?"

"No problem."

Tina hung up and leaned into her screen.

"Mike," she said. "I might have something."

"OK."

"We've got a report of two men pushing a third into a car yesterday in Swanage. The third man could be our victim."

"Where?" asked Mike.

"Moor Road."

"That's not far from the obelisk," Mike said.

Tina nodded. "It's the right side of Swanage."

"Hang on a moment." Mike stood up and walked to the DCI's office. The sarge was still in there. Mike knocked at the door and walked in.

The DCI stood up as Mike relayed Tina's news. She pushed past the sarge and Mike, and emerged from her office.

"Tina," she said. "Tell me more about this incident in Swanage."

"Two men pushing a third man into their car. It could have been nothing..."

"But it could be our victim," Lesley said. "Where?"

"Moor Road," said Tina.

"Do we know who the third man was?"

"No," Tina replied. "But there's a witness, she rang in."

"OK," Lesley said. "Let's get over there. You drive."

CHAPTER SEVENTY-TWO

Winifred Bailey, their witness, lived in a bungalow on a wide road above Swanage with views towards the Purbeck hills. Lesley jumped out of the squad car, dodging the rain, and left Tina to find a space. She rang on the doorbell.

The door was answered by a short woman with curly white hair and an anxious expression.

"Oh," she said. "I wasn't expecting a lady detective."

Lesley gave her a smile.

"Thank you for seeing us, Mrs Bailey. I wanted to follow up on the report that you made yesterday afternoon."

Mrs Bailey frowned. "They told me it was nothing at the time, have you changed your minds?"

"We're not sure," Lesley said. "It could be related to an investigation we're working on. Can I come in, please?"

"You and your young colleague." The woman smiled at Tina, who stood behind Lesley. "Come in."

The two of them stepped inside, shaking the rain from their jackets.

"I'm sorry. We're dripping all over your carpet, Mrs Bailey," Tina said.

"That's alright, dear. Only a bit of water. Come through to the living room."

The woman went through a door. Tina hesitated, waiting for Lesley to go first.

"Sit down, please," Mrs Bailey said.

Lesley took a bulky green armchair, while Mrs Bailey settled in a matching chair opposite. Tina perched on the sofa between them.

"Mrs Bailey," Lesley said. "You said you saw an altercation between three men?"

The woman leaned forward. She nodded, her eyes bright.

"He was walking down the road, I see him most days. I think he lives up at the end of the road, walks past here to get into Swanage."

"Who?" Lesley asked.

"I'm sorry, I don't know his name. I assume he lives along there. Either that, or he comes down from one of the paths."

Lesley nodded.

"So what did you see?"

"There was a car, it stopped next to him. I was sitting right where you are now in the window, I just happened to look around. I was about to close the curtains because the sun was getting in my eyes. Then I saw a man get out of the car and approach him. The first man walked away, but then another man got out. They cornered him, I imagine that's how you'd describe it, and it didn't look nice. I watched them for a bit and then they all got in the car."

"When you say they got in the car," Lesley asked, "did

the man you've seen before get into the car voluntarily or was he pushed in?"

"One of them had a hand on his arm," Mrs Bailey said. "But it didn't look like they were pushing him hard."

"Did he look scared?" Tina asked.

"I wouldn't know, dear. He had his back to me."

"You say you think he lives along this road," Lesley asked. "Have you seen him coming out of one of the houses?"

"Sorry, never. But he does walk past here regularly."

Lesley exchanged glances with Tina. If their victim walked along this road regularly, there was a good chance he lived here.

"Can you describe him?" she asked.

"He was wearing a fleece, same fleece he always wears. Navy or black, I think. Grey hair, thinning on top. Yesterday he was wearing a woolly hat. He doesn't always, that's how I know his hair's thinning."

Lesley swallowed. Their victim hadn't been wearing a woolly hat, but he had been wearing a dark fleece.

"How old would you say he was?"

"In his sixties maybe?"

Lesley imagined that Swanage contained thousands of men in their sixties. But not thousands who'd recently been stopped in the street.

"I don't suppose you got the registration number of the car, did you?" Tina asked.

"Not the registration number. But I did note down the colour and the model."

"Thanks."

The woman handed Tina a piece of paper. Tina passed it to Lesley.

"A red Ford." She rolled her eyes. "Can you remember

anything more specific about the car?" she asked. "What type of Ford was it?"

"I'm sorry. I don't know much about cars, I'm afraid. My son, Nigel, he does. Mad on the things, I can't be dealing with them. I'm happy getting the bus."

"Thanks for your help," said Lesley.

"My pleasure, dear. Can I get you a cup of tea?"

"It's fine." Lesley stood up. "Thank you for your time."

CHAPTER SEVENTY-THREE

Zoe had been expecting a short stroll out of Swanage to the spot where DCI Mackie had died. But it was halfway to the next village. She wondered how he had got here. Had his car been found nearby?

She surveyed the cliff edge as she walked, trying to remember from Lesley's description exactly where to stop. Lesley had provided her with photos from the case file.

Zoe reached a spot that seemed to tally with the photo on her phone. She stopped and peered over the edge. The cliff sloped away below, rough chalk leading down to rocks and the sea. Shrubs grew out from the cliff. They would have broken his fall.

She rounded the headland and came to a spot where the cliffs were steep. Ahead of her was a rock formation that rose up out of the sea. If she'd been throwing herself off, she'd have chosen this spot. The slope was almost vertical.

Two figures were walking towards her, following the coastal path. Zoe pulled the hood of her coat tighter and watched them. The rain was torrential today, and she hadn't seen anybody else out on the path. She pulled back as the two figures approached. She didn't want to draw attention to herself. Coastal walks weren't exactly something she did frequently, and she didn't relish making small talk with some local out for a hike.

She turned back towards Swanage, glancing over her shoulder from time to time. The two people walked behind, matching her pace.

They stopped at the spot where she'd been standing five minutes earlier. The spot where Mackie had died.

Zoe carried on walking.

Up ahead was a bend and a clump of hedgerow that would obscure her view back. She stopped and turned. No sign of the two people.

She walked back up a little way.

They were still at the spot where Mackie had died. Talking to each other and looking out over the cliff.

In the driving rain.

Zoe pulled back her shoulders and headed in their direction.

She would pretend she was out for a casual stroll, exchange hellos and walk past them. She wanted to know who they were.

As she approached, the shorter of the two figures turned towards her. It was a woman, blonde hair peeking from beneath the hood of her coat. She wore tight-fitting jeans and heavy walking boots. A green scarf was wrapped around her neck. As Zoe approached, she saw the woman was wearing heavy makeup. She stared at Zoe.

"Afternoon," Zoe said, not breaking stride as she passed.

"Afternoon," the woman replied.

The other person, a man, grunted. He wore a woolly hat and had a bushy beard.

Zoe didn't recognise him, but she did know who the woman was.

Lesley had shown her a video of that woman. She was the reporter from the local BBC.

Zoe picked up pace. She'd have to find a way back to Swanage via the road. Her mind was racing. What was Sadie Dawes doing up here?

CHAPTER SEVENTY-FOUR

LESLEY HURRIED out of the house.

"Call Uniform," she told Tina. "I want people knocking on every door in this street. We'll start at the far end and work our way back."

"Right, boss," Tina replied.

Lesley crossed the road. The two of them walked to the other end and started knocking on doors.

Behind every door was a person who had no idea what she was talking about. They were all puzzled and concerned.

But none of them knew the man whose description she gave them.

She was about to reach her sixth house when she saw a man walking towards her. He looked distressed, but he didn't match the description that Mrs Bailey had given. This man had dark hair and olive skin. He wore a red jacket and a blue hat.

"Excuse me," he said. "Are you police?"

"We are. Can I help you?"

"My friend Geraint, he didn't turn up at the pub yesterday, and he's not in now."

"Where does he live?" Lesley asked.

"Over there." He turned and pointed.

"Come with me."

She hurried towards the house, yanked open the gate and walked to the front door. She hammered on it and waited. No answer.

"Your friend, what's his full name?" she asked the man.

"Geraint Evans."

"And what's your name?"

"Aren Kocharyan. A-r-e-n, K-o—"

"Does he live alone?"

"Yes. Should I be worried?"

"Mr Kocharyan," she said, "do you have a photo of Mr Evans?"

"Er... Probably." He pulled his phone from his pocket. "I took a selfie in the pub three days ago. We meet every day. I like to go walking first, earn my pint."

She smiled at him. "Can you show me the photo, please?"

"Sorry."

He flicked through his phone and held it out. It showed a photo of him with another man. The man was in his sixties, with thinning grey hair, wearing a navy fleece, ripped at the elbow. He had a mole on his right cheek.

It was their victim.

CHAPTER SEVENTY-FIVE

Lesley looked at the man.

"Have you got a key to his house?"

"Sorry. Do I need one?"

She looked at Tina. "We need to get in there."

"Wait a moment." Tina turned away and made a phone call. A couple of minutes later a uniformed PC was hurrying along the street.

"You need us to break into that house, Ma'am?"

Aren looked nervous. "He might not have gone anywhere. I don't want to..."

"It's alright, sir," Lesley said. "We want to check he's OK."

"You think he might not be?"

"We just need to check on him. If you'd stand back, please."

She gestured for Mr Kocharyan to follow her. She left the house's front garden and moved to the other side of the road, putting a hand out to stop Aren moving forwards. Tina and the other constable huddled near the door. They conferred, then Tina stood back.

The PC kicked at the door. There was a crunching sound, but it didn't give. He kicked again, higher this time.

"Is everything alright?"

Lesley turned to see Mrs Bailey approaching. She was wearing her slippers and pulling a cardigan around herself.

"We think we might have found the gentleman you saw, Mrs Bailey." Lesley turned to Mr Kocharyan. "Can you show us that photograph again?"

He nodded and pulled his phone out, thrusting it in front of Mrs Bailey.

She paled. "That's him. He walks past my house most days. He's the one I saw getting into the car."

Lesley swallowed. Across the road, Tina and her colleague had disappeared inside the house.

"You stay here please, both of you," Lesley said. "Don't come any closer."

She ran across the road and went into the house.

"Tina!" she called.

"Upstairs, Ma'am," Tina called down.

The uniformed PC appeared out of a doorway. "Nobody here, Ma'am."

"It's empty," Tina called.

"Any sign of a struggle?" Lesley asked. "Any blood?"

Tina appeared at the top of the stairs. "Nothing."

"So he wasn't brought back here," Lesley said.

"It doesn't look like it, boss," replied Tina.

"Damn."

So where had Geraint Evans been taken, Lesley wondered, and who by?

CHAPTER SEVENTY-SIX

Dennis put a hand over his phone and walked to Mike's desk.

"The DCI's on the line," he said. "We've got an ID on the body."

"Who?" Mike asked.

"Geraint Evans, lives in Swanage. See if you can find him on the system."

He stood over Mike's desk as the DC opened up HOLMES.

"Nothing here, Sarge. Name draws a blank."

"Keep digging," said Dennis. "We need to find out if he's connected to Paul Watson." He picked up his phone.

"Dennis," Lesley said. "Have you got anything more on him?"

"Nothing yet," Dennis replied. "Maybe knock on his neighbours' doors, see if they know anything about his background?"

"No, Dennis," Lesley said. "I thought we'd just stand here and look at the view."

He clenched his jaw.

"It's OK," said Lesley. "I really don't need you to tell me how to do my job, but I appreciate that you're being thorough. We're talking to his friend. Aren Kocharyan. See if he's on the system, too." She spelled the name out and hung up.

Dennis returned to Mike's desk, trying to expel the tension from his body.

"They're knocking on the neighbours' doors, seeing what they find out about him. She said he's got a mate. He was the one who identified him."

"Hopefully between Tina and the DCI, they'll be able to work out what his connection to Paul Watson is."

"If any," Dennis replied. "It could be a coincidence."

"I'll search the local press," Mike said. "See if I can find his name."

"You do that."

Dennis went to his own desk. "I'll take a look at Companies House."

Mike nodded, his eyes on his screen. "Nothing locally. I've got half a dozen hits from Wales with Geraint Evans. But none of them are our guy."

"He must be on record somewhere," Dennis said.

He frowned into his screen as the Companies House website came up. He typed Geraint Evans's name into the search box, scratching his chin.

"Anything?" said Mike.

"Nothing," said Dennis. "I was hoping he might be another company director for Sunrise Holdings."

"We've got the list of all of those," Mike said.

"One of them was new. That means they replaced somebody; I was hoping it would be him."

Mike shrugged. "We need to find out when the post-mortem is taking place. Maybe they'll find something..."

"And follow up on the forensics," Dennis said. "Although with this weather..." He looked out of the window. The rain had gained force and was pelting against the glass.

"Wait," Mike said. "I've got him."

Dennis rounded the desks to look at Mike's screen. He'd done an image search. "How did you do that?"

"Plugged the photo from his mate's phone into Google images."

"What? What photo?"

"Tina sent it through. There's a match." He clicked through to the website of an accountancy firm.

"Llewellyn and Co," Dennis said. "Retired partner."

"Cardiff," Mike added. "Retired a year ago. Must have moved down here."

"So what's the connection to Paul Watson?"

Mike shrugged. He scrolled through more pages. "Got it."

Dennis leaned in. "What?"

"Llewellyn and Co. They acted for Sunrise Holdings."

CHAPTER SEVENTY-SEVEN

LESLEY SLID BACK into her car. Her jacket was soaked through, the waterproofing useless against this rain. Tina, sitting next to her, looked like she'd taken a shower in her clothes. Her hair was plastered to her face and her smart outfit was ruined.

"Are you OK?" Lesley asked her.

"Of course, boss. Why wouldn't I be?"

"You're shivering."

"I'm fine. I've dealt with a lot worse in Uniform."

"That's the point. When you're wearing a uniform, you're sensibly dressed. Look at you."

Tina looked down at herself. Even in the dim light of the car's interior lamp, Lesley could see her cream blouse sticking to her skin, and patches of damp on her jacket. She could smell it from across the car.

"It's fine, boss," Tina said. "Comes with the territory."

Lesley shrugged. "Let's get Dennis and Mike on hands-free."

They'd spent the last half hour working their way along

Moor Road, knocking on doors, seeing what they could find out about Geraint Evans, but it seemed his neighbours hadn't been as nosey as Lesley would have liked.

"Boss," said Dennis. "Mike's with me. We've got a link between Geraint Evans and Paul Watson."

"Go on," Lesley said.

"He retired a year ago from the accountancy firm that represented Sunrise Holdings. Llewellyn and Co. Based in Cardiff."

"What are a firm based in Poole doing hiring accountants from Cardiff?"

"That's the link to Paul," Mike said. "It's his wife."

Lesley looked at Tina. "Sherry Watson?"

"She works for Howards Estate Agents in Wareham. The managing director is Mark Llewellyn."

"Not a coincidence, I assume?"

"No. He's the brother of Carys Llewellyn, senior partner of the accountancy firm."

"So what's the connection?"

"I'm not sure, boss," Mike said. "But it has to be something."

"It does indeed." She scratched her cheek. "OK, we're coming back in. We can't do much more here now. And the crime scene's a quagmire."

Lesley leaned back in her seat. She felt suddenly tired. The climb up that hill and standing around in this weather had taken it out of her.

"Let's get back to the office," she said.

She looked at the clock on the dashboard. Ten past six.

"Sorry, folks. It's a Saturday and you all need to get home to your families. Let's just have a quick recap by phone and then we'll pull things back together in the morning."

"On a Sunday morning, boss?" said Dennis. "I tend to go to church."

Lesley punched her thigh. Of course he did.

"Whoever did this could strike again," she said. "We can't hang around."

Silence.

"Very well," she said. "I'll carry on seeing what I can get remotely. I don't suppose anybody's managed to get hold of Llewellyn and Co, or Howards Estate Agents?"

"I tried both of them," Mike said. "No answer. I'll try them again on Monday."

"No," Lesley said. "We can't wait that long. I'll go and see Sherry again."

"You want to head there now?" Tina asked.

"Not right away," Lesley replied. "Let's get you back to the office. I'll go and see her myself."

"I can join you," Dennis said.

"Fine," Lesley replied. "Can you meet me halfway?"

"Corfe Castle," he said. "I'll come to West Street car park."

"I'll see you there in about twenty minutes." She checked the clock again, remembering something. "*Damn.*"

"What is it, boss?" Tina asked.

"Harry Coutts. His twenty-four hours was up four hours ago."

Tina's shoulders slumped. "They'll have had to release him."

"We've been so busy with this we forgot to go back to him." Lesley leaned towards Tina's phone. "Mike, I want you to go down to the custody suite, find out if he's still there."

"Yes, boss."

"OK, Tina," Lesley said. "Drive me to Corfe Castle."

CHAPTER SEVENTY-EIGHT

MIKE RAN down the stairs and into the custody suite. PS Dillick was on duty.

"Sarge," he said. "Have you still got Harry Coutts here?"

The sergeant shook his head. "His time was up four and a quarter hours ago. I couldn't get hold of DCI Clarke. I had no choice but to let him go."

"Damn." Mike screwed up his face. "Where did he go?"

"How should I know?"

Mike grabbed his phone and dialled the DCI. "Boss, I'm sorry. Coutts was released earlier."

"I thought as much. Where did he go?"

"PS Dillick doesn't know."

"OK. Was he RUI'd?"

Mike turned to the sergeant. "Was he formally released under investigation?"

"Not formally, no. Look, I tried to—"

"I know." Mike gripped his phone. "Boss, did you hear that?"

"It doesn't matter. We can rearrest him if we have

grounds. Which we do. But I want to build a better case than just that video. We need evidence of him actually committing the murder."

"Like what?"

"I'm going to talk to Sherry. You keep trying those two firms. I want to know what the link is."

"OK."

"Can you ask Sergeant Dillick who took Coutts?" the DCI said.

Mike put a hand over the phone.

"Who took Coutts? Did he go with his mum?"

"No. It was..." The sergeant checked his computer. "He went with his solicitor."

"Who is...?"

"Elsa Short."

Mike stiffened. "Boss?"

"I heard." She hung up.

CHAPTER SEVENTY-NINE

Zoe sat staring at the walls of Lesley's house. She was going over what she'd seen on the clifftop. That had definitely been Sadie Dawes.

But who was the man?

Zoe wished she'd thought to grab a photo. But she hadn't wanted to arouse their suspicions.

Her phone rang: Lesley.

"Hi, Lesley," she said. "How's your day been?"

"Frustrating," Lesley replied. "I've lost my main suspect."

"He's disappeared down the back of the sofa?"

"Don't," Lesley replied. "His twenty-four hours expired and I was too busy following up on a second victim."

"Ouch," said Zoe. "Are you going to re-arrest him?"

"I want to get more evidence first."

Zoe nodded. "Can I help at all?"

"I don't want you getting involved in this case, we need to keep things separate. Have you got any news for me?"

"I spoke to Mrs Mackie."

"And?"

"You're not going to like this."

"I don't like much right now."

"She reckons your super hushed it all up."

"Carpenter?" Lesley's voice was hoarse. "Why?"

"She's adamant her husband wouldn't have killed himself. Thinks Carpenter had a word with the coroner."

"It doesn't work like that."

"I know," said Zoe. "At least it shouldn't..."

"Jesus," said Lesley. "This is all I need. Can I come back to Brum, have David Randle back?"

Zoe laughed. "And I went up to the spot where Mackie died."

"What did you think?" Lesley said. "Did it look suspicious to you?"

"I agree with your crime scene manager," Zoe said. "But that's not the most interesting thing."

"What is?"

"Sadie Dawes was there, with a man."

"Sadie Dawes?"

"Yes," Zoe said. "She's still sniffing around."

"Who was the man?"

"I don't know. I need to find out."

"Be careful. Don't put yourself in danger and try not to get me into trouble."

Zoe smiled. "You're not my boss anymore, Lesley."

"I know. But I worry about you. I've dragged you down here to investigate unofficially and I'm wondering if that was wise."

"I could have said no," Zoe replied. "Are you on your way back here?"

"I've got a witness to speak to. And I'll be at Elsa's tonight. There's something I need to talk to her about."

"Everything OK?" asked Zoe, then cringed. It wasn't her place to pry into Lesley's private life.

"Everything's fine." Lesley's voice was tight.

"OK," said Zoe. "I'll speak to you tomorrow, let you know if I find out any more about what Sadie's up to."

She thought about DS Frampton's behaviour. She could deal with him. Lesley had enough on her plate without this impacting on her team.

"Thanks," said Lesley.

Zoe put her phone on the sofa next to her and leaned back, lifting her face towards the ceiling. She'd been hit by the storm as she'd walked down from Ballard Down, and her clothes had been soaked. She'd had no idea just how forceful the weather could be down here.

Her phone rang again and she grabbed it. "You forget something?"

"I'm sorry?" The voice was female, but not Lesley.

"Who is this?" Zoe said.

"Why are you following me?"

"Is that Sadie Dawes?"

"You were up on Ballard Down today," Sadie said.

"It's a public footpath," Zoe replied.

Sadie scoffed. "We need to talk. I'll see you up there, same spot, four pm tomorrow." She hung up.

Zoe stared at the phone. She brought up the call record, but the number was withheld.

Was Sadie bluffing or did she really know something?

Only one way to find out.

CHAPTER EIGHTY

SHERRY HAD JUST GOT Amelia off to bed when the doorbell rang. Her limbs heavy, she heaved herself down the stairs. She'd been hoping for a quiet evening. The family liaison officer had left and she was planning to spend the next hour or two in front of the TV, attempting to distract herself. She'd been struggling to find out when she could have Paul's body back and arrange a funeral; the frustration of it was wearing her down.

She opened the door to see DCI Clarke on the doorstep, with a man Sherry didn't recognise.

The DCI smiled at her. "I'm sorry to bother you, Sherry. This is DS Frampton, my colleague. We've got a few questions we need to ask you."

"You've arrested someone?"

"Not yet. We just need to talk to you."

Sherry sighed. "It's Saturday night. Please, can it wait?"

"I'm sorry. We'll be as quick as we can."

Sherry felt her muscles slacken. "Fair enough."

"Thank you. Where d'you want us?"

"Come into the kitchen."

The kitchen was furthest away from the girls' rooms. If they heard, they'd want to know what was going on.

The girls had hated having the FLO here, they'd resented the intrusion. Sherry wondered if that was one reason they'd hidden in their rooms for the last two nights.

And now, here the police were. Intruding on her again.

She walked to the sink and filled the kettle.

"I'm making myself a cup of tea," she said. "I don't imagine you'll be here long enough to want one."

She turned to see the two detectives exchanging glances. She didn't care if they thought she was rude. She was tired.

"What is it you wanted to ask about?" she asked as she switched the kettle on.

"It's about your employers," DCI Clarke said.

"What have they got to do with anything?"

"Your manager, Mark Llewellyn. How well do you know him?"

Sherry shrugged. "Not very. I've only worked there a couple of months. I found the job after we moved down here."

"Was it easy to get employment with them?"

"What are you saying?" Sherry asked. "Has this got something to do with..."

"We were wondering if they approached you, or the other way round," said the sergeant.

Sherry looked at him. He was older than his boss, drab-looking in a tweed jacket.

She sniffed at him. "It was word of mouth. A friend told me they had a vacancy."

"Which friend?"

"Kate. I see her in Swanage sometimes, we got chatting in a café."

"I know this is out of the blue, Sherry," DCI Clarke said. "Are you aware that Mark Llewellyn's sister has connections to Sunrise Holdings?"

Sherry wrapped her fingers around her mug. She stifled a yawn. "To who?"

"Sunrise Holdings is the company that owns the Horizon development," the sergeant replied.

"I don't see why that's relevant."

"Llewellyn and Co are based in Cardiff," the DCI said. "We found one of their former employees this morning, near Ballard Down. He was killed in a similar way to Paul."

"Oh." Sherry felt suddenly light-headed. She lowered herself into a chair. "Who?"

"Geraint Evans," said the sergeant. "Do you know him?"

"Never heard of him. Are you sure?"

The DCI took the seat diagonally across from Sherry. She was staring into her face. Sherry wanted to rub her skin, bring the blood back.

"It seems like quite a coincidence," said the DCI, "for you to be working for a man whose sister is halfway across the country and represents the firm that your husband was working for. Not to mention the two deaths."

Sherry plunged her head into her hands. "I don't know anything about this. Mark's just... he's my boss. He's an estate agent. To be frank, I don't think he's bright enough to master-mind any sort of conspiracy, if that's what you're thinking."

She swallowed and looked up at them, feeling the pressure building behind her eyes.

"I just need to be left alone. I need to process Paul's..."

The DCI put her hand on the table. Sherry drew her hand away.

"I'm sorry, Sherry," she said, "How well do you know Mark Llewellyn?"

"I barely know him at all," Sherry said, tears pricking at her eyes. "Honestly, they're just an estate agent in Wareham. I needed a job, I applied, that's the one I got." She stared at the detective. "They're going to fire me now. If you go to them with this. I have two kids to bring up alone and now I'll be out of work."

The DCI reached out for her.

Sherry stood and walked to the sink. She tipped her cup of tea down it.

"Leave, please," she said. "I need to be alone with my children. I don't know anything about this Llewellyn and Co, I don't know anything about Sunrise Holdings. Please, just leave me."

CHAPTER EIGHTY-ONE

LESLEY STARED into the darkness from the passenger seat of Dennis's car. Her own car was still at the office. Dennis's expression was drawn, his knuckles pale on the steering wheel.

"What did you think?" she asked.

He shook his head. "I believed her."

"You did?" She turned to him. "Really?"

He frowned. "Why shouldn't I? It's a coincidence, that's all."

"I don't believe in coincidences."

"Maybe this time you should."

She grunted and looked ahead at the road.

She would ask Mike and Tina to do some more digging into Llewellyn and Co, and into Mark Llewellyn. But Sherry's reaction had seemed honest enough.

"Dennis," she said. "There's something I need to talk to you about."

His grip on the steering wheel tightened. "Yes?"

"When you were off sick last week."

"That." His voice had dropped an octave.

"You told me it was flu," she said.

"I did."

"Why did you say that?"

He turned briefly towards her and then back to the road.

"Because it was."

"I came to your house, Dennis," she said. "You were fine. You didn't have the flu. And besides, I'm pretty sure you've had the flu before and struggled into work."

"I'm not getting any younger," he replied. "Pam thought it was sensible for me not to spread my germs around."

She turned in her seat. "Did you go to see a psychiatrist?"

He drew in a breath. He opened his mouth, closed it again, then swallowed. "That's confidential."

"So you *did* go and see a psychiatrist?"

"It's none of your business, boss."

"If you're having mental health problems, you should talk to me about it."

"I'm fine," he said, blinking. "Clean bill of health, only one appointment."

"Can I ask why you didn't go to the police psychiatrist?"

His eye twitched. "Because I didn't want anybody in the force knowing my business."

She nodded. "Dennis, has this got anything to do with what happened with Johnny? With the Kelvins? Because I can't see any other reason..."

He frowned. "No. It's not about anything specific."

"So what is it that's been bothering you?"

"I was given a clean bill of health, I already told you."

His tone was brusque.

Lesley sighed. "I just want you to know that if you *have*

got a problem, you can talk to me. I won't judge you. Needing help isn't a sign of weakness, Dennis."

He said nothing.

Lesley turned to look out at the road ahead. They were approaching the office.

She forced her muscles to relax. She needed to focus on the case.

CHAPTER EIGHTY-TWO

An hour later, Lesley let herself into Elsa's flat.

"Hello!" she called out.

"In here," came Elsa's voice.

Lesley walked through to the living room to find Elsa on the sofa with her feet up on the coffee table, a glass of red wine in her hand. She looked up at Lesley and smiled.

"Hey, gorgeous. How are you?"

It had taken Lesley too long to get here from the office. The rain had turned biblical and a road had been closed on her way through Poole.

"I'm pissed off, is what I am," she said.

She threw herself into an armchair. Elsa placed her glass on the coffee table and put her feet on the floor. She reached out and touched Lesley's knee. Lesley flinched.

"This case not going well?" Elsa asked.

Lesley pulled her knee away. "No," she said. "And you could have warned me about taking Harry Coutts."

"Whoa." Elsa leaned back and raised her hands in supplication. "So that's what this is about?"

"We found a second body this morning. I was busy trying to find out who he was and meanwhile you go and spirit Harry Coutts out from under my nose without so much as a by your leave."

Elsa looked into her eyes. "I was doing my job, sweetie. The man had been in custody for twenty-four hours and you hadn't charged him. It was his right to go home. As his solicitor, I had to make sure he knew that."

"Oh, he knew that, alright," Lesley said. "Harry Coutts isn't exactly new to being arrested. You think he doesn't know his rights?"

"No matter how many times somebody's been arrested, they're entitled to protection under the law. You know that, Lesley."

"Of course I bloody know it." Lesley dug the nail of her thumb into her palm. "And now I've lost him."

"Really?" Elsa said. "I thought you'd have re-arrested him already."

Lesley looked at her. "I know what you'll do. You'll make out he had nothing to do with killing Paul Watson. You'll say that all he did was move the body."

Elsa sat back in the sofa and folded her arms. "I'm not about to tell you the details of the defence I plan to run for my client."

"Of course you aren't." Lesley rubbed at her neck. "And you're right. You were just doing your job. I fucked up."

"Sounds like you were busy."

"Even so. I knew full well there was a deadline. I was intending to go in and interview him again this morning." She caught Elsa's expression. "Don't worry, I would have warned you. But in all the rush to find out who our other victim was, I forgot."

"That's not like you," Elsa said.

"I don't know what *is* like me anymore," Lesley replied. "I've got Carpenter breathing down my neck, I've got Zoe investigating..." She stopped herself.

"Zoe investigating what?" Elsa asked.

"Nothing," Lesley said. "I can't talk about it."

"OK."

Elsa stood up. She picked up her glass and went into the kitchen.

"Do you want some?" Her voice was tight.

Lesley pinched the skin on the back of her hand. She'd developed red spots. When had that happened?

"Yes," she said, "Pour me a glass of wine. A large one. Let's not talk about work."

CHAPTER EIGHTY-THREE

"WHERE'S DENNIS?" Lesley snapped. "He knew to be here at nine o'clock."

"He'll be at church," Gail told her.

Gail was in Lesley's office leaning against her desk. Lesley stood beside the board. Mike and Tina were both in the outer office, but Dennis hadn't arrived yet.

"He actually went?" she said.

"Of course," Gail replied. "It's supposed to be his day off. It's supposed to be your day off."

"And yours," Lesley told her as she tapped a message into her phone.

Gail shrugged. "Tim's with his dad. I'm fine."

"You don't sound it," Lesley said.

"This case, it's frustrating. We've found prints, but I'm—"

"Let's wait until everybody's in here."

"OK."

Lesley walked to the door and pulled it open.

"Come on, you two. Let's get started," she said.

Mike and Tina left their desks and walked into her office. Lesley retook her position by the board.

"Right," she said. "Gail, you've got something."

"I have," Gail said. "We have clear prints. I've sent them through, you can check them against the database."

"Tina?" said Lesley.

"No problem." Tina wrote in her notebook.

"OK," Lesley said. "Is that all?"

"A boot print," Gail said. "In the mud a few yards away from the obelisk. It could be nothing."

"It could be any one of us," Lesley said. "The state of the ground yesterday."

"We were careful," Gail told her. "We put protective plates down, and the couple who found him, they've handed over their boots for comparison. It's neither of them."

"Was the victim wearing boots?" Mike asked.

"Trainers," Gail said. "The print wasn't from them."

"So we think the boot print is from his killer?" Tina said.

"Let's hope so," Gail replied. "They'll need running through the database, in the hope of a match for the manu-facturer."

"It'll probably turn out to be one with a million pairs out there," said Mike.

"Don't be pessimistic," Lesley said. "We've got to get a break at some point."

"This case feels like we'll never get a break," muttered Mike.

"Don't think like that," Lesley told him. "The evidence will turn up. There's the rope, as well."

"There is," said Gail. "My guys aren't in the office today, but I've sent through the photos so you can look for a match."

"No problem." Lesley looked at Mike. "Can you take that one?"

"Yes, boss."

Movement outside the office caught Lesley's eye. Dennis had arrived. She beckoned him in.

"Sorry I'm late, boss," he said. "Pam brought me straight from church."

"So I hear," Lesley replied. "Good service?"

"I didn't go in. I saw your message."

Lesley gritted her teeth. "I'm sorry, Dennis. I know church is important to you."

He shrugged, not meeting her eye. "He might strike again, we can't afford to dawdle."

"Good," she replied. "So, Tina's working on the prints: boot and fingers. Mike's got the rope that we found on our victim. You'll check out boating supply shops, that kind of thing, Mike?"

"Boating supplies. Ship's chandlers."

"Whatever that is." Lesley addressed the team. "And Dennis and I went to see Sherry Watson last night."

She caught Dennis's expression. "We're of slightly different opinions about the fact that she works for the brother of a woman who's connected to Sunrise Holdings."

"I think it's a coincidence," Dennis said. "She was distraught, and I really don't believe she's connected with her husband's murder."

"I don't think she *killed* him," Lesley pointed out. "And I don't believe she knew he was going to be attacked, but I do think there's the possibility that somebody used her to get to him."

Dennis sighed. "I suppose so."

"Right," Lesley continued. "We need to look into those

two companies further and we've still got those *go home* notes."

"We can't think it's a racist attack anymore," said Mike. "Not with Geraint Evans being white."

"No," said Lesley. "But it could be related to the fact that both victims were newcomers to the area."

"Dorset First?" Tina said.

"Who?" asked Lesley.

"There's only about five of them," replied Mike. "They're not up to this kind of thing. It could be Laurence Smith, though."

"Wessex Defence League, perhaps," added Dennis. "What's their view on grockles?"

"I thought it was all about race, for them," Lesley said. "Immigration."

"They could be insular enough for this," Dennis pointed out.

Lesley frowned. She wasn't convinced.

"I want you to follow up the Vick McCarty lead," she told him. "He's mates with Harry Coutts and he works at the Horizon development. It means he could have come into contact with Paul Watson *and* he was part of Wessex Defence League."

"But we've already established it's not racist," said Mike.

"Even if it's not racist, McCarty is suspicious. Dennis, I want you to talk to his employer. Find out how long he's had that job for, if he's caused any trouble."

"Who's his boss?" Dennis asked.

Lesley looked at the board. There was a list of employees of Sunrise Holdings and everyone working on the Horizon development. "Darren Mathieson's the lead contractor. Unpleasant piece of work, but hopefully he'll give you some background on McCarty, let you know if he ever met Paul Watson."

"Should I be looking for a link to Geraint Evans as well?" asked Dennis.

"If you can. We need to speak to Mark Llewellyn, too."

"Boss," Tina said. "I checked Llewellyn out on the system. He was arrested five years ago."

"What for?"

"Assault. A fight outside the Duke of Wellington in Wareham."

Lesley knew it well: that was where Elsa worked. "And?"

"No charges were brought."

"But it means we have his prints on file," Lesley said. "Run him against the prints Gail found. Coutts and McCarty, too."

"Yes, boss."

"OK, everybody get to work. We'll reconvene later on."

CHAPTER EIGHTY-FOUR

Lesley's phone rang as she left the office.

"DCI Clarke."

"My name is Dr Fiona Brightside," came the reply. "I work with Dr Whittaker."

"You're doing the post-mortem?"

"Dr Whittaker has been taken ill," the woman replied. "I'm deputising for him."

"Is he OK?" Lesley asked.

"I can't say. He's been taken to hospital."

"Which hospital?"

"I don't know. I got a call from his assistant."

"Are you a regular?" Lesley asked. "We haven't met."

"I normally work out of Dorchester. I can't say I'm happy about having to come over to Poole on a Sunday morning. But what with Henry being ill..."

"Thanks," Lesley said. "I'll see you at Poole hospital, how long will you be?" She would see if she could have a conversation with Mark Llewellyn after that.

"An hour," the woman replied.

"Very well," said Lesley.

An hour later, Lesley was standing in the entrance to the morgue, waiting for Dr Brightside to arrive. After five minutes or so, a woman in her thirties with short red hair and a round face entered. She had a brisk manner and brought a blast of cold air in with her.

Lesley stood up. "Dr Brightside?"

"You must be DCI Clarke." The pathologist held out a hand. "Pleased to meet you."

"Likewise."

"Give me five minutes, and we'll get this PM underway."

The woman pushed through the swing doors into the morgue. Her manner could hardly have been more different from Dr Whittaker's. Like him, there was a slight air of condescension, but unlike him, it was paired with energetic efficiency.

Lesley pushed through the doors, put on the overall and boots that an assistant handed to her and walked through to the post-mortem room. Geraint Evans was already laid out on the table. Dr Brightside stood over him, her hands on her hips.

Lesley cleared her throat and the doctor turned to her.

"Give me a moment, please," she said. "I always like to do this before I get into the detail."

"Do what?" Lesley asked.

"Pay my respects," the pathologist replied. "It feels like a violation, doesn't it? Opening them up like this, poking through their bodies. They've already been through enough trauma."

Lesley raised an eyebrow. "It's necessary, surely."

The doctor approached the body. "We still need to

remember that this man was a living, breathing human being just a couple of days ago."

"Do you have a time of death?" Lesley asked her.

The doctor laughed. "Straight to it, I see. I've heard that you're efficient."

"You have, have you?" Lesley asked. "I'm sorry, but I've never even heard your name before."

The doctor smiled. "That's fine, we haven't worked together. Your reputation precedes you."

Lesley could only hope that was a good thing.

"So that's enough of the niceties," she said. "Shall we get on with it? You just said that he'd been dead for a couple of days. Is that a scientific analysis, or a figure of speech?"

The doctor pointed at the body.

"Rigor mortis is almost gone. I'm told he was left at the base of the obelisk near Swanage."

"It's very exposed," Lesley told her. "At the top of one hell of a hill."

The pathologist nodded. "Which would have slowed down the process, what with the temperature. Rigor mortis is still just about apparent, but as I've said, it's almost gone. I put his death at" – she checked the clock above them – "Friday between around 4pm and 10pm."

Lesley nodded. "Can you confirm cause of death?"

"It's a bit premature, what with me not having gone inside yet. But there's the neck wound. The bruising in the area, combined with the loss of colour to the skin. He bled out."

"Does he have any other injuries?"

The pathologist lifted the man's arm. "There's bruising on his upper arm. And he's lost a fingernail. He struggled.

But there's nothing else that could have been responsible for his death."

Lesley looked down at the body, trying to imagine his last moments. She wondered if they'd been near where he'd been found.

"There wasn't much blood at the spot where he was dumped. Is there evidence of him being moved?"

"When was he found?" the pathologist asked.

"Early yesterday morning."

"The bruising isn't extensive enough for him to have been moved while he was alive, or even soon afterwards. I imagine he was moved a while after death." Dr Brightside looked up. "If he was killed early evening on Friday, he could have been moved in the night."

Lesley took a breath. The poor man had spent his working life dreaming of retiring down here, and when he'd finally achieved it, that dream had been torn away. She thought of his friend, Mr Kocharyan, waiting for him in the pub. What had he done that had made somebody want him dead?

"OK," she said. "So we've got a time of death on Friday evening, and the cause of death being that wound. Are there any marks that might help us identify the weapon?"

"The blade was serrated," the doctor told her. "See here, there's evidence of sawing. No practice wounds."

Lesley had seen practice wounds on plenty of victims. Marks on the victim's body where their killer had attempted to make the cut, but chickened out at the last moment. An inexperienced killer would often make a number of cuts before they finally found the courage to make the final one.

"I think your killer knew what they were doing," the

pathologist said. "I think they were confident and knew how to handle a knife."

"Thank you," Lesley said. "I need to follow up with my team, but you'll send me your full report when it's done?"

"It'll be in your inbox within two hours."

Lesley smiled. She could get used to working with this woman.

CHAPTER EIGHTY-FIVE

DENNIS TURNED into Darren Mathieson's road. The builder lived in a row of cottages in Kingston, near Corfe Castle. His looked as if it had been done up: new door, clean pointing.

Not wanting to draw attention to himself, he drove past the house and parked a little way along the road.

He was about to get out of the car when another car pulled up right behind. Dennis watched in his rearview mirror as a man got out and crossed the street.

It was Vick McCarty.

Dennis turned in his seat, his eyes on McCarty. He approached Mathieson's house and knocked on the door, peering up and down the street. Dennis hunkered down out of sight.

After a few moments, the front door opened and Mathieson emerged. The two men strode to McCarty's car.

Dennis waited, his eyes on his watch. Five minutes went by. He was considering going to investigate when McCarty's headlights suddenly came on, illuminating the inside of Dennis's car.

He froze.

The car pulled out. It drove past Dennis. The two men inside were talking. Arguing?

Dennis felt his heart rate pick up. He turned his key in the ignition and followed.

CHAPTER EIGHTY-SIX

TINA YAWNED as she waited for the system to run through the fingerprint database.

This was her seventh consecutive day on shift, and she was tired. She'd done long shifts before joining the Major Crime Investigations Team, but never at a desk. Driving a squad car, being on her feet, dealing with the public.

Sitting in front of a desk like this could be draining. But she loved it here. Solving problems, drilling down into crimes, being able to focus on something for more than a few hours. She'd applied for the detective's exam, and was waiting for a date. The thought of being a proper detective filled her with anticipation.

She rubbed her face, watching the screen.

Eventually, the system finished its trawl.

Two sets of prints.

The first was predictable: one set matched the victim, Geraint Evans.

The other set, however, had no match in the system. Not

Harry Coutts, not Vick McCarty. Not Mark Llewellyn. No one.

Tina's chest fell. Whoever had taken Evans up there had never been arrested.

CHAPTER EIGHTY-SEVEN

LESLEY LEFT Poole hospital and got into her car. As she hit the A350, she pressed the hands-free button on her phone.

Elsa picked up, her voice hazy.

"You having a lie-in?" Lesley asked.

"It's Sunday," Elsa replied. "I'm allowed to, aren't I?"

Lesley felt herself tense. Was Elsa still annoyed with her?

"I'm sorry I didn't speak to you this morning," she said. "I wanted to let you sleep."

"Thanks," Elsa yawned. "I needed it. It's been one of those weeks."

"I know. And I know I haven't helped."

Silence.

"I'm calling to apologise," Lesley said. "I was out of order last night. I know you were just doing your job, I was frustrated. I was angry with myself more than anything."

"It's OK," Elsa said. "I know what that feels like. Has there been any comeback on it for you?"

"Not yet," Lesley told her. "But it's Sunday. I'm expecting a bollocking from my boss at some point."

Elsa winced. "Well, you know you've got a shoulder to cry on here after that happens."

Lesley smiled. "I'm a big girl, Els, I can cope."

"I know you can."

Lesley's phone buzzed: Dennis was calling.

"Sorry, love. I've got to go," she said. "We're close to a breakthrough."

"Oh?"

"I can't tell you any more."

"I know. Love you."

Elsa hung up. Lesley flicked over to Dennis.

"Dennis, have you spoken to Mathieson?"

"I'm following him. He's driving towards Peveril Point with Vick McCarty."

"He's what?"

"McCarty turned up outside his house moments after I got there. Mathieson came out, the two of them got in McCarty's car, and now they're driving through Swanage."

"To the building site?"

"That's what I imagine."

"OK," Lesley said. "Keep following them, I'm on my way."

CHAPTER EIGHTY-EIGHT

Tina looked fed up.

"You alright, T?" asked Mike.

"Just drew a blank on these prints."

"It's early days, don't let it get you down."

She leaned back in her chair, raised her arms towards the ceiling and yawned loudly.

"Tired?" he asked.

"Didn't sleep well last night," she said, "Some of those crime scene photos..."

He screwed up his face. "You get used to it eventually."

"Is that a good thing?" she asked. "Surely you *shouldn't* get used to it?"

He shrugged. "If you want to stay sane in this job, you have to let it wash over you."

"I'm not sure about that." She returned to her computer screen.

Mike was working through a list of boating supply shops. He'd already spoken to three and sent them photos of the ropes that they'd found attached to Geraint Evans's wrists. None of them recognised them.

He dialled the fourth.

"Poole Harbour Supplies, can I help you?"

"My name's DC Legg," he said. "Dorset Police. We're investigating a murder and I have some ropes. We need to identify where they were bought."

"What kind of ropes?"

"Blue. Medium weight?"

"Send me a photo, mate. Better make it quick, we're closing in five minutes. We don't normally open on a Sunday."

"What's your email address?"

The man gave him an address.

"Fine. Can you stay on the line while I email it to you?"

"Sorry mate, just had a customer come in." The line went dead.

Mike gritted his teeth. He fired off the email and tapped his fingers as he waited for a reply. He dialled the number again. Engaged.

His email pinged a response.

We sell it.

Mike shifted in his chair.

"You look like you've got something," said Tina.

"An email. I'll phone them again."

He dialled: still engaged.

"I don't fucking believe it."

"What's up?" Tina asked.

"Boating supplies shop in Poole. They say they sell the rope, but I can't get hold of them."

He sent a reply to the email.

I'm trying to call you. Pick up please.

He dialled again. *Still* engaged.

"Maybe they didn't hang up after you spoke to them before?" Tina suggested. "They might still be on the line."

He pulled in a breath. "I'm heading over there now, T."

She looked up at the clock. "Sunday afternoon traffic, should take you about half an hour."

"He said he was closing up."

"Then you'd better hurry."

Mike stood up and grabbed his keys. "Let me know if they call back, yeah?"

She nodded as he ran out the office.

CHAPTER EIGHTY-NINE

TINA OPENED up HOLMES and typed in Darren Mathieson's name.

She knew she'd get nothing.

Sure enough, Mathieson had never been arrested.

Could that mean...?

But plenty of people had never been arrested.

She checked for Vick McCarty. His arrest record appeared, but there was no mention of anyone with him other than Harry Coutts.

Tina frowned.

She found the Swanage Building Services website and copied a photo of Mathieson. She'd run it through an image search.

She twirled her hair in her finger as she waited for the search to run.

She scrolled down and then stopped.

There was a picture of Mathieson, with Coutts standing behind him, at the front of a WDL march in Poole from eighteen months ago.

She stared at the photo for a moment and then remembered something.

Darren Mathieson's sister, Amanda Bennett.

Tina went back into HOLMES and did another check: Darren Bennett.

Nothing.

She tried Amanda Bennett.

"Shit," she muttered.

There she was. She'd been arrested at the same march, along with Coutts and McCarty.

CHAPTER NINETY

Vɪᴄᴋ McCᴀʀᴛʏ's car pulled up along the road leading to the Horizon development. Dennis stopped a few hundred yards behind, anxious to stay out of sight.

It was getting dark, dusk descending over the cliffs. He turned off his ignition and waited for the men to emerge from the car.

The two men got out. They looked along the road, not seeming to notice him. They ran towards the development.

Mathieson unlocked the main gate and the two of them went inside.

Dennis got out of his car and crossed the road, keeping his footsteps light.

He walked along the fencing that separated the development from the road, peering through, staying a few feet away so they wouldn't see him.

What were they doing here on a Sunday evening? Could they have a body in there?

He flinched as he heard a sound behind him, a car approaching. Headlights swept the road.

Dennis pulled in behind a tree and watched. A red Saab pulled up and a woman got out. She looked up and down the road, then hurried across to the gate in the fencing.

Dennis narrowed his eyes as he watched her.

She turned in his direction, her face caught by the streetlight.

He'd seen that face before. There was a photo of her on the board. Dennis drew in a breath.

Amanda Bennett, Mathieson's sister. The woman who'd worked with Paul Watson on the Horizon development.

So what was she doing here?

CHAPTER NINETY-ONE

TINA RUBBED her eyes and peered into her screen. The office was quiet and she longed to go home, but there was no way she was leaving now.

She flicked through Amanda Bennett's record and grabbed her phone.

"Sarge."

"Tina," came the sarge's voice. "I can't talk right now." He was whispering.

"Where are you, Sarge?"

"I'm in Swanage, Horizon development. What is it?"

"Darren Mathieson's sister. Amanda Bennett."

"She's one of the directors."

"Yes, Sarge. She was arrested eighteen months ago. At the same march with Coutts and McCarty."

"What?"

"She was there. Wessex Defence League. Mathieson was there too, but he wasn't arrested."

"You think she's connected?"

"I don't know, Sarge, but if you're planning to speak to them, please be careful."

CHAPTER NINETY-TWO

Mike hammered on the door of the ship supply shop. It was ten to four; hopefully the place would still be open. A light was on inside.

"Alright, alright," came a voice from inside. The same voice he'd heard on the phone.

Mike cupped his hands around his face to peer inside. A man was approaching. He looked pissed off.

Mike took out his warrant card and held it against the window. "Dorset Police," he called. "I phoned you before."

The man unlocked the door and stood back. "What's all the hurry?"

"I talked to you about a piece of rope, I was hoping you might know who bought it, or at least whether it was bought here."

The man looked at him, his expression wary. "Why is it so urgent on a Sunday afternoon?"

"Two people have died already, we don't want a third."

The man raised his eyebrows. "Come on, then."

He retreated inside the shop and walked behind the counter. "Let's take a gander at this photo of yours again."

Mike brought out his phone. "Where do you keep rope samples?"

"Over there."

The man pointed at a display. It was dimly lit, like the whole shop.

"We were just closing up," he said. "Not much trade, it's getting dark."

Mike approached the display, holding out the photo on his phone. The man stepped out from behind the counter and stood next to him, sniffing noisily.

"That looks like Qualtec," he said. "That one up there. We don't sell much of that. It doesn't have the best water resistance, not so popular on the water."

"So what is it used for?"

"Tying down covers, sometimes. I sold a load to a guy last week who was going to use it on a building site."

Mike caught his breath. "A building site?"

"I was glad to get rid of some of the stuff. Won't be stocking it again."

Mike grabbed his phone, almost dropping it in his haste.

"You alright?" the shopkeeper asked.

Mike thrust out a photo. "Was it this man?"

The man grabbed the phone from Mike and pulled it closer. "Could have been."

Mike found another photo. "Any more confident with this one?"

A nod. "Yeah. I'm pretty sure that's him."

CHAPTER NINETY-THREE

DENNIS WAS STILL behind the tree when his phone rang. He picked it up, his muscles taught.

"Boss," he said.

"I'm ten minutes away," she told him. "Where are you?"

"I'm at the Horizon site, I'm parked up just along from it. Mathieson's inside with McCarty and Amanda Bennett."

"Amanda Bennett?"

"She just turned up. Tina found her on HOLMES, she was arrested at a march."

"I've just had a call from Mike. Looks like it was Mathieson who bought that rope."

"The rope that Geraint Evans was tied up with?" Dennis asked.

"The very same," the DCI replied. "Watch them. I'm on my way. I'll call for backup."

"Yes, boss."

Dennis put his phone into his pocket. He sat straighter in the driver's seat and watched the building site.

It was too gloomy to see anything. The clouds were thickening overhead and rain threatened.

He put a hand on the door handle, impatient.

A light came on, beyond the gates. Dennis held his breath.

Mathieson was coming out, his sister with him. They were walking towards her car.

He couldn't let them get away.

He slid out of his car and approached them, holding up his ID. "Darren Mathieson and Amanda Bennett," he said. "Don't go any further."

"Run!" Mathieson shouted.

He grabbed his sister's arm and ran back into the building site.

"Oi!" called Dennis. He ran after them.

The gate clanged shut in his face. He threw it open and followed them in.

The building site was dim, the ground muddy. He knew it would be peppered with ditches and drains.

Dennis gritted his teeth, focusing as hard as he could on the ground as he hurried after the pair. He knew he was at a disadvantage.

But there was nowhere for them to go. The fence led down to the cliff edge.

"Mathieson!" he called. "Stop! It's a dead end."

Dusk was gathering, and the clouds were heavy over the sea. Mathieson might know his way, but did Amanda Bennett?

"Stop!" Dennis cried.

He heard a strangled cry from up ahead just as the first drops of rain fell.

In front of him was a pile of concrete blocks. Dennis

rounded them and came out on a ledge. He skidded to a halt, mud hitting his trousers.

Three feet below him was a wide step, carved into the hillside. Dennis took a deep breath and jumped down. He winced as his bad knee felt the force of his landing.

Keep going. You'll be fine.

He pulled himself up. The knee was OK.

"Where are you?" he called. "You can't go anywhere."

He should have locked the gate behind him. He should have waited for the DCI. Mathieson and Bennett might find a route back around the site.

But even if they did, there was only one road out of here. The DCI was close enough, she'd see them coming.

"Darren, stop!" A female voice, below Dennis. Towards the sea. He put out a hand, but it fell through air.

He squinted to see where the voice had come from, knowing he was heading towards the cliff edge. His heart whooshed in his ears and the sea hammered against the rocks below. He felt his shoulders tighten.

"Darren! Amanda!" he called. "Don't go any further."

Dennis held his hands out in front of him, feeling for obstacles. Suddenly a light appeared in front of him. He closed his eyes momentarily. When he opened them again, he could make out a shape. Mathieson. He was illuminated by a mobile phone.

"Stop right there!"

Dennis scanned the ledge below him.

Where was Amanda?

"Darren, no!" Her voice was coming from the same direction as Mathieson and the light. Dennis stumbled towards them, swallowing down the lump in his throat.

"Don't do anything stupid," Dennis called out.

He could see both of them now: Mathieson and Bennett. They were illuminated by the phone. Mathieson had hold of his sister. She twisted in his grip, trying to pull her arm free.

"You're both under arrest!" Dennis called out. He bent his knees, then jumped down to the next level. The sea felt so close now.

Amanda screamed. Darren pulled her back, wrenching her down next to him.

"Stop it, Darren!" she cried. "I'm not going to help you!"

"Shut the fuck up, sis!"

Dennis took a step forward, his arms up. "Stop right there, both of you."

Amanda screamed. "Let go!"

She was right on the edge, the waves almost deafening behind her. Dennis heard a shout from behind him. Vick McCarty?

"Leave us!" Mathieson yelled against the sound of the water. He grabbed his sister tighter.

CHAPTER NINETY-FOUR

ZOE HAD BEEN STANDING above the spot where Mackie had died for over an hour, waiting for Sadie Dawes.

She'd looked at her watch dozens of times, checked her phone messages. She'd called Sadie's number, no answer.

Maybe she'd misremembered. Maybe Sadie had wanted to meet somewhere else, or at a different time.

After an hour and a half, it was getting dark. Zoe decided to walk back towards Swanage.

It was starting to rain and the town was obscured by cloud. Zoe was glad that a hedge separated her from the cliff top.

She trudged along the coastal path, reaching a turning where the shrubs fell down towards the sea. She needed better light. She pulled out her phone and held it up with the torch switched on.

She continued towards Swanage, cursing herself. It had all been a smokescreen. Sadie was probably trying to distract her.

Something up ahead caught the light from her phone. An object caught in a bush. Zoe approached it.

It was to her left, partway down the cliff. Could she reach it?

She sat down on the path, lowering her centre of gravity and spreading herself out as far as possible to make herself more stable. She reached out and felt for the object.

It was green, a silk scarf. Zoe frowned. Sadie had been wearing a scarf like that when she'd seen her up here yesterday.

She stood up.

"Sadie!" she called. "Sadie, are you here?"

Nothing. All she could hear was the wind out to sea and the waves below her on the rocks.

"Sadie!"

Still nothing. Zoe peered over the edge, but it was too dark to see anything.

She was perhaps a quarter of a mile past the spot where Mackie had died, closer to Swanage.

What had happened to Sadie? Was she down there too?

CHAPTER NINETY-FIVE

LESLEY'S HEADLIGHTS shone through the rain and into Dennis's car as she approached the building site. It was empty.

"Damn."

She stopped her car, feeling it slither on the muddy ground. She jumped out and ran towards the open gate into the site.

"Dennis!" she called. "Dennis, where are you?"

Was he in here?

She hadn't realised how dark it would be up here. She stepped inside the gate. She'd called for backup but the nearest squad car was fifteen minutes away.

She could see a light up ahead, moving behind a pile of blocks. She scrambled past the blocks and approached the light.

"Dennis!" she called. "Dennis, where are you?"

"Boss!"

He was up ahead. She heard another voice.

"Darren, stop it! Let me go!"

"What's happening?" Lesley called.

"He's got Amanda, boss," Dennis replied. "Don't come any closer!"

"Yeah, he's right," came a male voice. "Don't come any closer or I'll push her off the edge."

Lesley stopped. She planted her feet in the mud.

"Why would you do that?" she called out. "She's done nothing to harm you."

"Shut up!"

"It was him!" came a female voice. "He killed them. Him and Harry."

"You bloody made me!" the man replied.

"Amanda?" Lesley called. "Show yourself."

"I can't. He's got me."

CHAPTER NINETY-SIX

GAIL WATCHED as Gavin hauled open the garage door. This building came with the lease on Paul Watson's Swanage office, but was tucked in a side road behind it. If Gav hadn't found the paperwork in a filing cabinet, they never would have known about it.

"OK," she said, pulling on gloves. "We're looking for documentary evidence, and forensics. There's a chance Watson might have been brought here before he was taken to the Globe."

Gavin stepped forward into the gloom. Gail fished in her bag and brought out a torch. She shone it ahead. The garage was mainly empty, but there was a pile of boxes in a corner at the back.

Treading carefully, her torch flicking between the walls and the floor, she approached it. She nodded for Gavin to open a box.

"Cleaning materials," he said.

Gail peered in. "Bleach. Brushes." She sniffed. "It's been used here."

She swept her torch across the floor again. "But where?"

"Over here." Brett was behind them, near the door to the garage. "Blood stains."

Gail allowed herself a fist pump. "Show me." She hurried towards him.

Brett stood up, giving her a satisfied look. "It's been scrubbed, but not well enough."

"There's more over here," Gavin called. "Shit."

"What?"

He held up a scrap of fabric. "Fleece. Looks like Geraint Evans's top."

Gail resisted plunging her gloved fist into her mouth. If this was what she thought it was...

"Get samples," she said. "We need to know whose blood that is. And bag up the fleece."

"On it." Her team grabbed their toolkits and started to work.

CHAPTER NINETY-SEVEN

LESLEY TOOK A FEW STEPS FORWARD. Dennis was in front of her, standing on a ledge beneath her feet.

"Dennis?" she hissed. He didn't respond. She repeated herself, louder this time. The waves were thunderous below them, crashing against the headland.

Lesley clenched a fist. She longed for solid ground, but the earth here was muddy and uneven.

"Vick McCarty's up there somewhere," Dennis called to her. "Be careful!"

She turned to scan the site. Her eyes were adjusting and she could see machinery and materials. No sign of McCarty.

"I can't see him. Are you sure?"

"He was up there," Dennis called. He was facing away from her, watching the brother and sister on the cliff edge. Lesley could see them now. Mathieson had Bennett in a tight grip and was shaking her.

"Amanda!" she called. "Hold as still as you can. We'll get you."

She jumped down to bring herself level with Dennis.

"No sign of McCarty," she told him. "What's going on with these two?"

"They were yelling at each other. I couldn't make it all out but I think she was stealing from the company. Paul Watson found out."

"And Geraint Evans?"

"No idea, boss."

She nodded, her gaze still on the two suspects.

"OK," she said. "I'm going down. Back me up."

"Shouldn't we wait for Uniform?"

"We might not have that long."

Lesley jumped down to the next ledge, and in the same movement reached out her arm. She grabbed Amanda Bennett's hand, the one Mathieson didn't have hold of.

She pulled the woman towards her and at the same time kicked out to hit Mathieson in the shins.

He let go of his sister and stumbled towards Lesley. "Fuck!"

Lesley allowed herself a smile. Bennett was in her arms now, her brother had lost his grip.

"Dennis!" she called.

"Right behind you, boss."

She turned to see Dennis standing on the same ledge. His hair was wet and his skin pale.

"Take her," she said. "I've got him."

"You sure?"

"Just take her."

She turned towards Mathieson as Dennis helped Bennett up to the next level. He stared back at her, his hands out in front.

"Go easy on him," Amanda called down. "It wasn't his fault."

Lesley turned to her. She still had to unpick exactly who had done what, but from what she'd heard, it sounded like the two of them were just as guilty as each other. Not to mention Vick McCarty.

Where had he got to?

She grabbed Amanda's arm. "Amanda Bennett, I'm arresting you for the murder of Paul Watson and Geraint Evans. You don't have to—"

"What? You've got nothing—"

"Ma'am?"

Lesley turned to see two uniformed constables approaching, McCarty between them. She felt the tension in her body sag.

"We found him trying to break into your car, Ma'am."

"Bloody idiot."

McCarty struggled, but he was going nowhere. Lesley looked from him to Mathieson, who was kneeling on the ground, clutching his leg.

"You too," she said. "The three of you are under arrest."

CHAPTER NINETY-EIGHT

LESLEY DROVE into the car park behind Dennis's Astra. A squad car followed in behind her, Darren Mathieson and Vick McCarty in the back. In a second squad car was Amanda Bennett. Lesley hoped that one of them would open up in interview; she still didn't know exactly who had done what.

She parked her car and walked to Dennis, who was climbing out of his own.

"You OK?" she asked him. "That can't have been easy."

He shook his head. "I'm fine, boss."

She put a hand on his shoulder. "You should have waited for backup."

"They would have got away," Dennis said. "Or he might have killed her."

Lesley said nothing. If Dennis hadn't been there, Mathieson wouldn't have run to the cliff edge.

Carpenter wasn't going to be happy.

"Go up to the office," she told Dennis. "We'll have a chat after they've been processed."

"You're going to do the interviews now?"

"I am."

"I'll do it with you."

"No, you won't," she told him. "It's a Sunday night. You need to get home to your wife. You missed church this morning because of me."

He stared back at her. "So I did."

"Take tomorrow morning off," she told him. "You need time to get your breath back. And if you need to speak to the police psychiatrist, I can refer you."

"I'll be fine."

She removed her hand. "You *will* be fine, if you get the help you need."

His body deflated. "Yes, boss." He turned and walked into the office.

CHAPTER NINETY-NINE

Tɪɴᴀ ᴀɴᴅ Mɪᴋᴇ were still in the office when Lesley finished her interview with Amanda Bennett.

"Well done, both of you," she said. "You found the evidence that linked Mathieson and Bennett to the murders."

"It was definitely them?" Tina asked.

"Yes," Lesley said. She'd just spent thirty minutes listening to Amanda Bennett, who was telling all – almost all – in the hope of getting a reduced sentence. Her brother was still waiting for a solicitor.

"Mathieson was conning Sunrise Holdings," she said. "Putting materials on receipts that didn't exist. Bennett was the one who got him the job, it was her idea."

"I've done more digging on HOLMES, boss." Tina said. "She's got shares in six other construction companies across the south of England. All different counties."

"Different counties, different forces. I'll bet we'll find she's defrauded all of those firms, with her brother's help."

"You want me to call them?"

"Tomorrow. It's late."

Tina nodded.

"So what did Paul Watson have to do with it?" Mike asked.

"He worked it out," Lesley told him. "When he needed to borrow money for his house, he looked through the financial records for the project, hoping to bury his own financial problems in the business. He worked out what Mathieson and Bennett had been doing. She says that killing him was Darren's idea, but I don't believe her. She's cleverer than him."

"But Mathieson did it."

Lesley shook her head. "It was McCarty and Coutts who killed Paul. Mathieson stepped in when it came to Geraint Evans, when we had Coutts in custody."

"Why?"

"He was a diligent accountant. He spotted the discrepancies in the books. Amanda persuaded him to retire, but it wasn't enough for her brother. Or so she says."

"You really think it was her idea, boss?" Tina asked.

"That's what my gut's telling me, although she'll deny it all. We may need to get Petra back in."

Mike raised an eyebrow. "You sure?"

Lesley laughed. "Don't worry. She can watch the video tape, tell us what she thinks. No need to fly her in."

Dennis emerged from her office.

"I told you to go home," Lesley said.

"I wanted to see if you'd charged any of them."

"Not yet. In Amanda's case, we have more questions to ask. McCarty's refusing to talk. As for Mathieson, we're waiting for a solicitor."

"Who will be...?"

"Someone from Nevin, Cross and Short." Lesley sniffed.

"I don't know who." Not Elsa, she thought. She would be too busy with Coutts.

She eyed Dennis. "You know what's happened now."

He nodded but didn't move. "But what about Geraint Evans?"

"He knew about the financial irregularities, but had been pressurised by his company to let them deal with it internally. When he retired down here, Mathieson got jumpy. Or so his sister says."

"So it wasn't about race, or outsiders, at all," Mike said.

"They certainly went to a lot of effort," Tina said. "Getting poor Geraint Evans down from the Obelisk was a major operation, can't have been easy getting him up."

Lesley nodded, remembering that climb. "That was part of the effort to make us think the crimes were symbolic. Not just a bunch of crooks trying to take out someone who might have exposed them."

"It worked," said Dennis.

"Speak for yourself," grunted Mike. He blushed and put his hand to his mouth. "Sorry, Sarge."

Dennis frowned. Mike opened his mouth to speak but was interrupted by the office door flying open.

Zoe ran in. Tina and Mike turned to stare at her.

"Zoe," Lesley said. "What's up? You look like you've seen a ghost."

Zoe shook her head. She grabbed the back of Mike's chair.

"Sorry," she muttered to him. "It's Sadie Dawes," she said to Lesley. "I was supposed to meet her earlier."

"So?" Lesley said. She caught Mike and Tina looking at each other. "Can we talk about this in my office?" she asked Zoe.

"It's not that," Zoe replied. She dragged her hand through her hair. "She didn't turn up, she's not answering her phone."

"She's a journalist," Lesley said. "Maybe she was called away to a story." She wanted to finish this conversation. She could sense Dennis's ears pricking up.

Zoe pulled a green scarf from her pocket. She waved it at Lesley.

"This is Sadie's scarf. I found it on the cliffs outside Swanage. I think someone pushed her off."

CHAPTER ONE HUNDRED

THE NEXT DAY was a clear and bright Monday, the sun shining as Lesley drove to the office from Elsa's flat. It felt good to be wearing clean, dry, clothes, even if Lesley's limbs did ache from yesterday's exertions. She marched straight up to Superintendent Carpenter's office. She knew she would be expected.

She knocked on the door and waited.

"Come in."

He was sitting on the sofa by the window. Lesley joined him without asking permission.

"I don't know whether I should congratulate you or give you a reprimand," he said.

Lesley met his gaze. "It could have been handled better. I take full responsibility for that. But ultimately, DS Frampton did his job and we were able to make the arrests. Nobody was hurt."

"More through luck than judgement, I heard," Carpenter replied.

"No," Lesley replied. "It was judgement. DS Frampton did a good job."

Carpenter grunted. "And what about Sadie Dawes?"

"What about her?" Lesley asked.

"You reported her missing last night. Apparently your friend DI Finch was supposed to meet her and she didn't show up. Something about a scarf?"

"Yes," Lesley said. "Zoe was worried that she might have fallen off the cliff."

"Fallen?"

"Or worse."

"They called out the coastguard," Carpenter told her. "It costs a lot of money to do that, you know."

Lesley didn't care about the money. "And?"

"There was nobody on those cliffs, no sign of a fall. Or worse. I think your friend was imagining things."

"The scarf wasn't imagined," Lesley said. "It's in the evidence store right now."

"You've opened a case?"

"Not formally. But if she's missing..."

"I spoke to her manager," Carpenter said. "Matt Crippins, her editor. He said she's got leave booked, she's gone to Malta."

"Malta, sir?"

"So she wasn't meeting your friend DI Finch at all. She was jetting off on her holidays."

"What about the scarf?" Lesley asked.

"It's a plain green scarf," Carpenter told her. "It could have been dropped at any time. By anyone."

Lesley gripped the fabric of the sofa. He had a point. But then, she trusted Zoe's instincts.

"Lesley," Carpenter said. "The woman's an investigative

journalist, her editor too. He rang the airport. She checked in for her flight, she's gone to Malta. You don't need to worry about her."

Lesley swallowed. She hoped that Zoe would be satisfied.

Zoe would want to know why Sadie had asked to see her when she was supposed to be leaving the country.

"So that's sorted." Carpenter stood up. "You make sure that Dennis Frampton's mental health is looked after, won't you?"

"I told him to take this morning off and I recommended that he sees the police psychiatrist."

"Good. That way we can keep an eye on him. Much better than a private shrink."

She swallowed. More confidential too, it seemed.

"Is that everything, sir?"

"Your four suspects," he said. "You've charged them all?"

"The three men, sir. They're not going anywhere."

"And Amanda Bennett?"

"We're still trying to work out exactly what her part was. Then we'll charge her."

"Hmm," said Carpenter. "Anyway, you look after your team and tell that DI she can bugger off home to the West Midlands. Oh, and I think you owe Doctor McBride an apology."

"Sir?"

"What did you do to make her leave so fast?"

Lesley shook her head. "She didn't think she could help us. She was right."

His face darkened. "Hmm. That'll be all."

"Yes, sir."

CHAPTER ONE HUNDRED ONE

Lesley hit hands-free on her phone as she got into the car. She yawned and started the car.

"Lesley. Don't tell me you're summoning me back?"

"Sorry, no."

"Don't apologise," said the psychologist. "It took me eleven fuckin' hours to get home. I've only just unpacked."

"You made the right call," Lesley said. "It wasn't racial."

"See, I do know what I'm talking about. You cracked the case, then?"

"One of the company directors and her brother, a builder, were defrauding the company. The two victims found out."

"Ah, an old fashioned 'slit their throat to shut them up' case."

"Indeed."

"Average."

"That's the word you used." Lesley knew that for Sherry Watson, none of this was average.

"Well, I hope I didn't cause you any problems with your wee team," Petra said.

"Nothing I can't handle. But that's not all I'm calling you about."

"No?"

Lesley sensed Petra's voice picking up. She turned onto the road for Bournemouth, stretching her neck as she drove.

"I'd like you to give me your professional opinion on a death that was recorded as suicide."

"Recorded as suicide."

"Yes."

"So you don't think it was suicide."

"No."

"And you'd like my view on the mental state of the deceased."

"Yes."

"Is this anything to do with your DI Finch being down there?"

"It might be."

"OK. If my input can be useful, then I'm happy to help."

Lesley smiled. She regretted being so abrupt with the psychologist. The woman was only doing her job. "Thanks. I'll send you the files."

"You do that. Now go and get some rest. You sound like you need it."

"That bad?" Lesley yawned.

"That bad. I'll be in touch, DCI Clarke."

"Thanks, Dr McBride."

CHAPTER ONE HUNDRED TWO

LESLEY LEANED back on the sofa, her arms draped over the back of it. She was contemplating an early night. She'd have a long hot bath and then put her pyjamas on and read a book. Elsa wouldn't be home from the pub for hours yet.

The doorbell rang. *Typical.* Lesley sighed and walked to the intercom. She pressed the button to see Zoe on the screen.

"Come on up," she said. She returned to the sofa and yawned.

Zoe entered the room carrying a briefcase.

"What's that?" Lesley asked.

"Case file."

"You've not taken anything from Dorset Police records?"

"This is a case I'm starting on back at home. Frank wants me on it tomorrow."

"Fair enough," Lesley replied. "It was nice to see you."

"You too." Zoe looked around the flat. "You've done well for yourself. I'm pleased for you."

Lesley smiled. "Thanks."

"So, about Sadie..." Zoe said.

Lesley folded her arms. "She's not missing, Zoe. She's gone on holiday."

"Are you sure?"

"Her boss rang the airline, she checked in for her flight to Malta."

"So why would she have arranged to meet me when she should have been in the air?"

Lesley shrugged. "Why does anyone do anything? Sadie Dawes can be erratic. She forgot, that's all."

Zoe grunted. "I still think you should keep an eye on her. Check that she gets back from Malta when she's due, and if she doesn't..."

"If she doesn't, we'll speak to Matt Crippins. We'll open a missing persons investigation if we need to." Lesley rubbed her eyes. "It won't come to that."

"OK," said Zoe. "But if it does, well, by then she would have been gone a week."

"She's not gone," replied Lesley. "She's an annoying journalist who went on holiday."

Zoe looked down at the floor. "Maybe you're right."

The door opened and Elsa entered. Lesley looked up, surprised.

"I thought you were working at the pub tonight?"

"Tom said he doesn't need me. He's got a new barmaid."

"You've been replaced?"

Elsa laughed. "I'm not an official employee, remember? Besides, the new barmaid's also his girlfriend."

"Nice," Lesley replied. "So he can spend more time with her when he's managing the pub."

"Exactly."

Elsa threw her bag onto the sofa and walked into the

kitchen, where she opened the fridge and brought out a bottle of wine.

"Zoe," she said, "you want one?"

Zoe shook her head. "I don't drink, but thanks anyway. And I'm heading back to Birmingham."

"You can stay one more evening," Lesley said. "Have a meal with us." She looked at Elsa who nodded.

"That would be lovely," Zoe told her. "But I've got this case to work on." She held up her briefcase. "I want to be in the office early tomorrow, Mo will be expecting me."

Lesley stood up and took Zoe's hand. DS Mo Uddin was Zoe's colleague and friend, a member of Lesley's old team. "Give Mo my regards, won't you?"

"I will," Zoe said. "He'll be an inspector soon."

"Good," Lesley replied.

"And let me know if Sadie turns out to have disappeared after all, won't you?" Zoe said as she made for the door.

Elsa looked across from the kitchen. "What's this, a missing persons case?"

"It's nothing," Lesley said. "A journalist who went on holiday."

"You hope so," Zoe told her, as she turned and left the flat.

I hope you enjoyed *The Monument Murders*. Do you want to know more about DCI Mackie's death? The prequel novella, *The Ballard Down Murder*, is free from my book club at rachelmclean.com/ballard. *Thanks, Rachel McLean.*

READ A FREE PREQUEL NOVELLA,
THE BALLARD DOWN MURDER

How did DCI Mackie die?

DS Dennis Frampton is getting used to life without his old boss DCI Mackie, and managing to hide how much he hates being in charge of Dorset's Major Crimes Investigation Team. Above all, he must ensure no one knows he's still seeking Mackie's advice on cases.

But then Mackie doesn't show up to a meeting, and a body is found below the cliffs a few miles away.

When Dennis discovers the body is his old friend and mentor, his world is thrown upside down. Did Mackie kill himself, or was he pushed? Is Dennis's new boss trying to hush things up? And can Dennis and the CSIs trust the evidence?

Find out by reading *The Ballard Down Murder* for FREE at rachelmclean.com/ballard.

READ THE DORSET CRIME SERIES

Buy now in ebook, paperback or audiobook

ALSO BY RACHEL MCLEAN

The DI Zoe Finch Series - Buy in ebook, paperback and audiobook

Deadly Wishes, DI Zoe Finch Book 1

Deadly Choices, DI Zoe Finch Book 2

Deadly Desires, DI Zoe Finch Book 3

Deadly Terror, DI Zoe Finch Book 4

Deadly Reprisal, DI Zoe Finch Book 5

Deadly Fallout, DI Zoe Finch Book 6

Deadly Christmas, DI Zoe Finch Book 7, coming late 2022

Deadly Origins, the FREE Zoe Finch prequel

The McBride & Tanner Series

Blood and Money, McBride & Tanner Book 1, coming Summer 2022

Printed in Great Britain
by Amazon